A Feiwel and Friends Book

An imprint of Macmillan Publishing Group, LLC

The Monster's Daughter. Copyright © 2017 by Paul Gamble. All rights reserved. Printed in the United States of America by LSC Communications, Harrisonburg, Virginia. For information, address Feiwel and Friends, 175 Fifth Avenue, New York, N.Y. 10010.

Our books may be purchased in bulk for promotional, educational, or business use. Please contact your local bookseller or the Macmillan Corporate and Premium Sales Department at (800) 221-7945 ext. 5442 or by e-mail at MacmillanSpecialMarkets@macmillan.com.

Library of Congress Cataloging-in-Publication Data is available.

ISBN 978-1-250-07683-0 (hardcover) / ISBN 978-1-250-12341-1 (ebook)

Book design by Liz Dresner

Feiwel and Friends logo designed by Filomena Tuosto

First Edition—2017

10 9 8 7 6 5 4 3 2 1

mackids.com

PAUL GAMBLE

THE MONSTER'S DAUGHTER

BOOK 2 OF THE MINISTRY OF SUITs

WITHDRAWN

FEIWEL AND FRIENDS

NEW YORK

*To Gemma, my agent and friend, who is almost always right,
but has the decency not to be overly smug about it.*

PROLOGUE

The reason you can be sure that there are monsters hiding under your bed is that there is almost no proof of them whatsoever. Generally speaking, the less proof there is of something, the more likely it is that it will exist.

Although this may seem like a strange statement and is likely to give any scientist reading this a heart attack, it is almost always true—and scientists know this themselves.

In fact, it actually forms the basis of almost all scientific thinking. For example, you may have heard of the Large Hadron Collider, or LHC. If you haven't, the LHC is an enormous scientific machine that consists of a circular tunnel twenty-seven kilometers long.[1] It is used to send "particles"

---

[1] If you want a visual image of this, think of a running track designed by the world's most sadistic gym teacher.

whizzing around and around in circles until they spectacularly crash into each other. Basically, it is the particle equivalent of the world's best Hot Wheels track.

Scientists spent nine billion dollars building the Large Hadron Collider to try and find something called the Higgs boson particle. Up until that point scientists thought that the Higgs boson might exist but didn't have any really good evidence.

Now, nine billion dollars is a lot to spend on looking for something that might not even exist. But of course the scientists knew that the Higgs boson probably existed precisely *because* there was so little evidence for it.[2]

Therefore we know that when there is very little proof for things, we can be almost certain that they exist. For example, I am almost certain that I exist—and yet there is very limited proof of that. Certainly no scientists have ever set up a nine-billion-dollar experiment to prove to me that I'm definitely here.

Therefore, by a process of logical thinking it is impossible to come to any other conclusion but that, when there is

---

[2] The same was true of Sir Isaac Newton when he discovered gravity. There was actually very little evidence for gravity. You can't see gravity, it doesn't smell like anything, and it rarely if ever turns up at family reunions talking about how it's recently gotten a new job as a truck driver. The only evidence that Newton had for gravity was that an apple had fallen on his head. An apple falling on your head doesn't really prove anything. Other than that you are probably sitting in an orchard.

little proof that something exists—it almost certainly does. Equally we can conclude that if there is a lot of evidence for something it is almost certainly made up.[3]

We can therefore be sure, once and for all, that there are monsters living under your bed. Because when you were young your parents tried to tell you that they weren't there. They lifted up the bed and showed you there was nothing there. And then they said the words that made you know they were lying. "There's no such thing as monsters.... Honestly."

<hr />

Coincidentally, this is also the reason we know that the Loch Ness Monster almost certainly *does not* exist. Because there's far too much evidence for him, videos, pictures, sonar... even an image on Apple Maps. The truth is—what's lurking in Loch Ness is much stranger than any monster....

---

[3] This is most apparent because when people are telling you the truth about something, they will generally just make a statement. However, when they are lying, they will add the word "Honestly!" at the end of their sentence.

MONSTERS
The Ones Hiding under Your Bed

Ministry operatives have found no hard evidence that monsters hide under children's beds. However, we are almost certain that they are there.

The current thinking on this matter is as follows: When you look under a child's bed, you will generally find lots of fluff, sweets, comics, and sneakers.

In the past, adults have contended that fluff just gathers under beds. But this explanation is not satisfactory, as fluff doesn't gather under sofas or fridges.

The only rational explanation is that fluff gathers under beds because something fluffy is living under there.

A further reason, if one were necessary, is that you never find money dropped under beds, whereas you always find it under sofa cushions.

This is because the monsters clearly steal any money that drops under the bed and spend it—mostly on comics, sweets, and sneakers, of which monsters are so clearly fond.

Now you may ask why monsters only hide under children's beds instead of adults' beds. As always, the reason for this is obvious. If monsters hid under adults' beds, then adults would raise this matter with the authorities to be investigated.

However, when a child tells an adult that there is a monster under the bed, the child is just ignored, laughed at, and told to stop being so silly.

Until adults really start listening to children, we are going to have to accept a world with hidden, lurking monsters.

It should also be noted that it isn't just monsters hiding under household furniture. As any seasoned Ministry operative knows, there is also something hiding underneath almost every bath in the country.

1

IF YOU DO NOT KEEP UP YOUR PAYMENTS, YOUR TEETH MAY BE AT RISK
MONDAY

It was recess and Jack Pearse sat on a wall next to his friend Trudy Emerson. Normally, Jack would have considered kicking a ball around with some of the other children or something similar. However, the previous week he had joined a secret government organization called the Ministry of SUITs, uncovered a plot to turn Northern Ireland into a floating pirate ship, and had almost been trampled to death by a group of runaway dinosaurs. All things considered, it had been a tiring week and Jack was quite enjoying having a peaceful sit-down.

Jack turned and looked at Trudy. She was sitting quietly, with her blond hair pulled back in a tight ponytail. The front few strands were dyed red and fell in front of her eyes.

Jack decided to say something. He carefully got up from the wall, took two steps, and sat back down on the left side of Trudy, which Jack had recently designated to be the "safe" side. That was the side of her that had her arm in a sling. This was the only physical evidence there was of how close to death they had come the previous week.

Jack suspected she didn't even really need the sling—she just liked how it enhanced her "bad girl" image.

It was strange to think that seven days ago Jack would have tried to avoid speaking to Trudy, as she had a reputation for punching people who said anything she considered stupid. Even now, he still was slightly wary of striking up certain conversations because he was moderately terrified of saying the wrong thing. Despite the fact that they were friends, she still seemed to undertake a fair amount of her communication through punching. Jack thought that arm punching was possibly Trudy's version of a strangely violent semaphore but with thumping instead of flags.[4]

"The weekend seemed really quiet," Jack observed.

"Quiet's nice sometimes," said Trudy. "Why did you walk around to my other side?"

Jack hesitated before speaking. If he told her the real

---

[4] When Jack was in elementary school, one of his teachers had told them that if a girl hit him, it was a secret message and probably meant that she liked him. During third grade, a girl in his class had hit him regularly; however, Jack could never figure out what the secret message was. In the end, he assumed that the lumps she was raising on his arms may have been a message in braille. Over the next few months, Jack went home and checked his arms every night using the braille article in his *World Book Encyclopedia*.

As it transpired, she had spelled out I LARVE HUGH in braille bumps. Jack suspected that maybe this meant she had loved him. She had been in the remedial spelling class after all.

reason he'd swapped sides he was fairly sure that he would get hit. Because even though Trudy had a safe side, unfortunately she also had the ability to stand up and revolve 180 degrees.[5] Luckily, at exactly the right moment, a living distraction clumsily ambled across the playground and said hello. It was David, Jack's other best friend.

David was lazily chewing on a Snickers bar he had pulled from his blazer. He spoke between mouthfuls. "Hey, Jack, there's a guy in the school office looking for you."

"Oh yeah? Who?"

"Didn't catch his name," said David. "Big man, wore a tutu, was carrying a pair of pincers."

Jack's face turned white. In all the excitement, he had forgotten about the Tooth Fairy. The small white molars, incisors, and canines that were inside Jack's head technically no longer actually belonged to him. Last week Jack had made the mistake of putting a pillow over his head. Any teeth that were put under a pillow automatically became the property of the Tooth Fairy. And the Tooth Fairy had the paperwork to prove it.[6]

---

[5] Most people have the ability to turn around. Why not try it yourself? You know the way that normally someone suggests trying something at home, but then says you should make sure you have parental supervision? This isn't one of those times. Just turn around unsupervised. It's fairly safe. Enjoy it . . . knock yourself out (but only metaphorically knock yourself out, don't literally do that—because then you would need parental supervision).

[6] For those of you who have not read *The Ministry of SUITs*, legally, the Tooth Fairy owns all teeth that are placed under a pillow at any time. It's part of the small print on your birth certificate.

Jack turned to Trudy. "It's the Tooth Fairy. Do you think he's here to . . . ?"

Trudy put a hand on Jack's shoulder and spoke quietly. "You made a deal with him, Jack. He's here for your teeth."

Jack's stomach lurched. He wasn't sure whether his stomach was fearful, or merely worried about the fact that if Jack lost his teeth, it would mainly be fed on soup for the next few months.

David cocked his head to one side quizzically. "You're saying that the big man in the pink tutu is the Tooth Fairy?"

Trudy nodded. "And he's here to take Jack's teeth. We've got to get moving."

"Okay," said David.

Most people who had just been told that the Tooth Fairy was real would have at least had one or two follow-up questions. David, however, was a little bit strange and therefore accepted the fact that the rest of the world, at the very least, had a right to be as odd as he was himself.

Jack stood up suddenly. Out of the corner of his eye he had caught sight of the Tooth Fairy approaching. Six feet and six inches of bulging muscle, packed into a tutu two sizes too small,[7] was walking across the playground. When the Tooth Fairy saw Jack, an evil grin spread across his bearded face. He began striding toward the friends.

Jack developed a sudden urge to play hide-and-seek. Although it wasn't so much the seek part of the game he was interested in as the hide part.

Trudy stood up and clenched her one good fist. "The

---

[7] Try saying that quickly six times.

Tooth Fairy isn't going to get your teeth without a fight. It's time we used The Speed."[8]

Jack wasn't sure which he should admire more—Trudy's bravery, her confidence, or her entirely misplaced sense of optimism. "Trudy, The Speed is all well and good. But you'd agree that a swallow is considerably faster than an elephant."

"Well, of course. Duh!" Trudy laughed.

"Imagine an elephant in a boxing match with a swallow. Which one do you think would win?"

"The elephant, obviously."

"And that is our elephant," Jack said, pointing at the rapidly approaching Tooth Fairy.

Trudy swallowed both nervously and appropriately. Thanks to the marvelous workings of perspective, the Tooth Fairy was looking larger and larger with every step he took. "I can see your point. Do you have an alternative plan?"

Jack smiled. "My mother always says that discretion is the better part of valor."

"Sounds reasonable."

"Yes, and I always felt that running away is the better part of discretion." And with that, Jack, Trudy, and David took to their heels and ran as fast as their feet would carry them.

[8] The Speed was a skill taught to all Ministry operatives, which allowed them to move and fight more quickly than their opponents. It was a bit like a martial art, except you didn't have to wear your pajamas in order to practice it. It worked through the observation that when you are unhappy time seems to move slowly. Therefore, if you concentrate on sad thoughts, you can miraculously make yourself move impossibly fast.

The Tooth Fairy sighed, shook his head, and strode faster.

OPTIMISM
Differing Types of Optimism

Many people insist that being optimistic is a positive and useful thing. And it is true that an optimistic attitude toward life will take you far. However, as with all things, optimism can be overdone. This fact can be demonstrated by looking at the last words of famous optimists.

General Arthur McHenderson (World War I British officer): "They'll never be able to get a shot on target from that far away...."

Simon Arteson (inventor of the world's most ineffective parachute): "Just because it didn't work with the mannequin doesn't mean that it won't work for me." (For further information please see the section **Falling from Heights: Invention of the Modern Parachute**.)

Sir Henry Chichester (naturalist and explorer): "Don't worry, I'm pretty sure that when a lion roars, it's a sign that it *isn't* hungry."

Traditionally, optimists and pessimists have been identified based on the following differentiation: those who, when they see a glass of water, think "the glass is half full" and those who think "the glass is half empty." Ministry operatives, from their experience in the field, have discovered a much wider range of attitudes to life than the two mentioned above. Current thinking in the Ministry divides these groups up as follows:

Optimist—"The glass is half full."

Realist—"The glass is half empty."

Pessimist—"I bet you someone has peed in that glass of water."

Pragmatist—"Why do I have a glass of water? Didn't I order a Banana Thickshake?"

Gourmet—"Do people really expect me to drink a glass of water? I distinctly requested the 1990 Bollinger R.D."

Some Ministry operatives have suggested that a few very special individuals sit outside these wide-ranging groups. For example, the Tooth Fairy and the interdimensional monster called Cthulhu are placed in a subset of the pessimist group. That is to say, they actually go around peeing in other people's unguarded glasses of water.[9]

9 Thus converting the pessimist into the realist.

2

STANDOFF

Trudy took off running like a young gazelle. Jack took off running like a slightly older gazelle who was beginning to suffer an occasional twinge of arthritis, but who could nevertheless put on a burst of speed when approached by a fierce lion wearing a tutu.[10]

[10] It is very important that we shouldn't condemn our heroes for running away. All too often running away is considered a sign of cowardice, which it isn't. Actually, running away is a sign of intelligence. Ninety-nine percent of heroes spend most of their lives running away. The reason this generally isn't represented in historic accounts is simple. The only people who actually live to write histories are the people who survive by judiciously running away. Generally, when they write the history they then replace the passages that should read *"then I soiled myself and ran away"* with passages reading *"then I heroically fought against incredible odds, emerging victorious thanks to my bravery."*

And in normal circumstances this would have made for an excellent escape. Unfortunately they had not reckoned with trying to run near David. It would be fair, although slightly inaccurate, to describe David as clumsy. David was more than clumsy; he was closer to being "anti-coordination." He not only couldn't get his own limbs to move in the right way, he also managed to cause other people's to move in the wrong direction as well.

As Trudy and Jack started to run, David tried to do the same. However, his limbs spontaneously managed to get tangled with Trudy's and Jack's, and they all came crashing to the ground.

Trudy tried frantically to get free but found herself ensnared in David's gangly limbs. "David, how many elbows do you actually have? I think I can count three...."

"There's another one over here, I think," muttered Jack, trying to figure out which way was up.

Unfortunately, the exact number and location of David's arm and leg joints will have to be resolved on another occasion. The fast-moving Tooth Fairy had caught up with our heroes and, reaching out one hairy-knuckled fist, pulled Jack out of the writhing mass of schoolkids.

The saying "he who fights and runs away, lives to fight another day" should be replaced with "he who fights and runs away gets editorial control over historical narratives."

If only General Custer had thought to run away at the Battle of Little Bighorn, then he wouldn't have been made to seem like a crazed egomaniac with a ridiculous blond, permed mullet in all those movies they made about him.

The Tooth Fairy lifted Jack effortlessly with one hand. As Jack was hoisted into the air, his schoolbag fell off his shoulder, spilling its contents across the playground.

The Tooth Fairy reached into a hidden pocket in the frilly recesses of his tutu and pulled out a large pair of rusty black pincers. "Righto, this is going to hurt you more than it's going to hurt me."

Jack voice came out in a nervous squeak. "Well, how about you don't do it, then?"

Trudy jumped to her feet and blurred into action using The Speed. She smashed an uppercut into the Tooth Fairy's jaw, which made a clicking sound but otherwise seemed unaffected. He smiled. "That's not going to work, love."

Jack jerked his head, looking around the playground for rescue, but no one would have dared to help them against this fiend in pink. Suddenly, out of the corner of his eye he glimpsed a marker that had fallen out of his schoolbag. He had an idea . . . if only he could reach the pen. But dangling a foot above the playground as he was, the marker was definitely out of his reach. Jack wished his arms were twice as long as they actually were.[11]

The Tooth Fairy moved the rusty pincers toward Jack's

---

[11] This is a relatively foolish thing to wish. If your arms were really that long, you'd spend your life with permanently skinned knuckles, as they'd constantly be dragging along the ground. To be fair, they'd be useful for swinging between branches on trees, but would make buying a nice shirt that actually fit you almost impossible. This is why you rarely see orangutans in evening wear.

mouth. Jack clenched his mouth tightly shut. It didn't seem to overly bother the Tooth Fairy. "Up to you, mate. I can remove your teeth, or I can remove your teeth along with a lot of your lips."

Jack thought about this and realized that the Tooth Fairy had a distinct point. Trembling, he opened his mouth, his lips stretching into a grotesque grimace. Trudy threw a punch into the Tooth Fairy's side, still with no effect. Violence was not going to defeat this most monstrous of men.

The pincers were millimeters away from Jack's incisors when David spoke. "Your careers teacher must have really hated you," he said, pointing toward the Tooth Fairy's bulging tutu.

For a brief moment Jack stopped trembling. Apparently, terror wasn't as powerful as confusion. Here he was about to have his teeth painfully ripped from his mouth, and David was talking about the Tooth Fairy's career path.

However confused Jack was, he was also very lucky indeed. Because David had also managed to confuse the Tooth Fairy.

"What are you talking about?" asked a sneering Tooth Fairy.

David shrugged as he got up from the ground and dusted himself off. "Well, you know, getting you a job as a Tooth Fairy. It isn't a great job, is it? I mean, not with you having to wear that costume and all."

The Tooth Fairy looked down at his bulging tutu and thought about David's argument. Jack felt the enormous hairy hand of the Tooth Fairy loosen slightly on his blazer.

David continued his train of thought. "I mean, what kind of qualifications do you need to be the Tooth Fairy?"

"Qualifications?" The Tooth Fairy vigorously shook his head. "I don't need qualifications. This is a family business, see? I'm the owner/operator. My dad was the Tooth Fairy, and his dad was the Tooth Fairy."

David took a step toward the Tooth Fairy and poked the bulging pink tutu. "So you got the costume from your dad, then? He was a lot thinner than you, wasn't he?"

For the first time since Jack had met him the Tooth Fairy seemed to be on the defensive. "Shut up!"

David held up his hands defensively. "Hey, don't get offended. I'm sure even Santa Claus has to get his suit let out around the waist now and then."

"Ha!" the Tooth Fairy snorted, sensing an opportunity to regain the upper hand. "That's where you're wrong. You see, Santa doesn't even wear a red suit. His business runs on a subcontractor franchise model. Other people wear the red suits. He got too fat to wear his suit years ago."

At that moment Jack figured out a way he might free himself from the Tooth Fairy's grasp—just by asking a question. "Just how fat is Santa, then?"

The Tooth Fairy cocked his head to one side as he tried to remember. "Well, it's been a while since I last saw him." He thought for a few seconds. Then he slipped the pincers back into his tutu and let go of Jack's blazer——dropping him to the ground. The Tooth Fairy blew out his cheeks and held both his arms cupped in front of him to represent a bulging belly. "But back then he was about this fat."

Trudy saw that Jack had been set free. "Quick, run!" she yelled at him.

But Jack wasn't planning on running. Instead he dodged backward and grabbed the marker that had spilled out of his schoolbag. He held it out threateningly.

Four pairs of eyes darted from one face to another, wondering who was going to speak next. In the end it was David who broke the tense silence. "Look, I know the Tooth Fairy's famous and all, but I don't think that this is the time to be asking him for an autograph. . . ."

Jack popped the top off the marker with his thumb. "This isn't for an autograph. . . ."

The Tooth Fairy laughed. "So what are you going to do, then? Try and distract me with a game of Pictionary?"

Jacked stared into the Tooth Fairy's eyes and tried to look fearless. "This is a permanent marker."

"So?" The Tooth Fairy seemed unimpressed with Jack's words.

Jack didn't move his gaze from the Tooth Fairy. "You can't rub these off if they get on hard surfaces. And if you take another step, I'm going to color my teeth bright green." Jack held the tip of the pen right in front of his central incisors. "Now if I color my teeth green, they won't be any good for making into piano keys, will they? And I'm good at coloring in; I don't even go over the lines." Jack snarled, even though it was incredibly hard to be threatening when you were talking about coloring.

"You're bluffing. You'd never do that to your own teeth," growled the Tooth Fairy.

"If the choice is between having a set of green teeth and

having a maniac in a tutu pulling them out with pliers, I know which one I'm choosing."

The Tooth Fairy lowered his pliers. "It looks like we have a standoff. But there won't always be a permanent marker here to save you." The Tooth Fairy sighed, turned, and walked away.

MINISTRY OF S.U.IT.S HANDBOOK

SANTA CLAUS®
His Business Model

Many people over the years have questioned how Santa Claus® can afford to give free toys to children across the entire world. The answer is merely a matter of economics.

The truth is relatively simple. Santa runs a franchise business model. This means he is similar to Subway or McDonald's. In the same way that not every clown you see is Ronald McDonald, not every Santa you see is the actual chief executive of the enormous panglobal Santa Corporation.

But where are the profits to be made in giving out toys for free? Well, apart from the money that local franchisees make from hiring their services to shopping malls, Santa makes a huge amount of money from merchandise. Ten percent of the profit from every Santa Claus® ornament, doll, Christmas card, or wrapping paper you see goes directly into Santa Claus's® pocket. And that's without even thinking about how much he makes from licensing his image and allowing other people to play him in films, advertisements, and heartwarming holiday specials.

The toys are only used as a good public-relations exercise to ensure that the public thinks well of him and wants to buy even more of his merchandise. If you doubt this, just wait until next Christmas when he plans to bring out his own fragrance line (CLauS...for the man who wants to smell of milk and cookies).

Considering the billions of dollars he is making, there can be little doubt why Santa is always so jolly around Christmastime.

NOTE TO HANDBOOK EDITOR: We'll need to make sure that we send Santa Claus® his royalty payments for mentioning his name. His intellectual property lawyers may only be elves, but they are absolutely ferocious.

3

YOUR DOOM IS SEALED[12]

"So why did you think the aquarium would be a good place to hide?" Jack asked. Although they had outwitted the Tooth Fairy, Trudy had suggested that it wouldn't have been wise to stay too close to the school. David had offered to stay on at the school and try to cover for their absence.

"I like the aquarium," Trudy snapped and walked on, refusing to say anything else.

"I don't have a problem with it either," Jack muttered following, "but it sounds educational. If we're going to get in trouble for missing school, I'd hate to think that we might accidentally learn something."

Trudy stopped in front of a tank in which a squid was propelling itself back and forth with its webbed tentacles. Its

---

[12] Or should that be "Your seal is doomed"?

bulbous body was dark red in color, and a pair of red eyes gleamed out of the murky water.

"Vampire squid," said Trudy, pointing at the label on the tank. "Remind you of anyone?"

Jack stared into the murky water at the shape slowly undulating through the water, and he realized what she meant. "Cthulhu![13] I mean, the skin looks a bit healthier, and the eyes should be green instead of red . . . but apart from that it's a dead ringer. Do you think they're related?"

Trudy sighed. "I don't think Cthulhu has any family."

"Everyone has family," said Jack. "I mean, even Cthulhu has to have a mother, right?"

Trudy looked so sad that Jack thought she was going to try to use The Speed. For a second he feared that she was going to hit his shoulder a hundred times in a second. Instead she just turned and walked away. Jack stood for a moment and gazed into the watery tank. The vampire squid floated all alone. Jack wondered if the squid was sad that it didn't have any friends.[14]

---

[13] For those of you who don't know, Cthulhu is an interdimensional creature of enormous power who longs to drive the world insane. He also runs the filing system at the Ministry of SUITs. His head is shaped like a squid. It's best not to think about what the rest of him might be shaped like.

[14] In many ways the vampire squid is the saddest of all the squid as it doesn't even eat live animals—just dead carcasses. Therefore, the vampire squid doesn't even get a chance to have a chat with its dinner before eating it.

It's also worthwhile to note that if you are trying to make friends, it's best not to eat them. Most cultures consider this a bit of a social faux pas.

The good thing about living underwater was that even if you were really sad, at least no one could tell if you were crying.

As Trudy wandered through the aquarium, several of the employees nodded and smiled at her. Trudy tried to smile back at them, but smiling wasn't something that Trudy frequently practiced, and the result was closer to a snarl.

Jack was confused. Even adults didn't smile at Trudy—she radiated a kind of standoffishness that made people uneasy. And on top of that, Trudy certainly never smiled back—she seemed to be on her best behavior, for some reason. So that was two things that Jack was confused about. Thinking about it, Jack was uncertain which of these was more confusing. So now he was confused about being confused. . . .

Jack turned and saw that Trudy had wandered out to an open-air sanctuary where injured seals were nursed back to health. He hurried after her, not wanting to get left behind. The sanctuary contained a range of rather sad-looking seals sitting around a pool filled with rocks and inflatable toys. Some of the seals had little bandages around their flippers. The seal sanctuary had been dug into the ground. If a seal leaned against the concrete wall, it could just about reach the bottom of a Plexiglas barrier that surrounded the concrete pit. The barrier prevented the animals from escaping into the sea, which lay just beyond a narrow breakwater made of boulders.

"Have you ever wondered what's the point of aquariums?" asked Jack. "I mean, we don't have zoos in the sea, so why do we have aquariums on the land?" Jack looked at the seals and wondered to himself why they even needed a seal sanctuary. None of the seals looked that badly injured. And even if they were, would they really need medical treatment or bandages? After all, anytime he got a cut his mother merely told him to make sure that he washed it and kept it clean. The seals lived in the sea. Therefore, wouldn't their cuts be as clean as they possibly could be?

"You know you're talking out loud, don't you?" Trudy leaned over one of the Plexiglas barriers and reached down to pet a seal that was standing on its tail and leaning against the concrete side of the pit.

It had a slick, healthy gray coat and eyes that looked like pools of oil, shining purple as the light gleamed off them.[15]

"Hello, you," Trudy said, kneeling down so she could look through the glass at the seal's face. The seal seemed to be pointing frantically toward the sea. Trudy smiled and nodded. "Yes, you want to get out and be with your family, don't you?"

Jack left Trudy and walked over to where he thought the seal had been pointing. From Jack's point of view, the seal hadn't been indicating the sea, but rather a large rock that lay at the water's edge.

When he was a foot away from the rock, he heard voices speaking. He strained to hear them over the sound of the waves.

---

[15] People often assume that cute animals are not dangerous. However, Ministry field agents should be aware that "cute" is often Mother Nature's way of luring you in for a sucker punch. One of the Ministry's most deadly agents is a cuddly teddy bear with a squeezable body and an array of sharp and pointy weapons that wouldn't look out of place in a History Channel special on the Medieval period.

"I'm sure that's her. . . . Trudy. Put the plan into action. . . . I'll return to the shop later with supplies. . . ."

Jack slowly leaned around the rock and saw an aquarium employee talking to the oldest woman he had ever seen. The old woman had jet-black hair, green eyes, and skin that was so wrinkled she resembled a bulldog that had been crossed with a walnut. She was wearing a long black robe that had been embroidered with lines of silver.

But why were they talking about Trudy? The voices had gone quiet, and Jack leaned forward to see if he could hear something more. As he did, his head collided with the aquarium employee, who was walking around the rock. "Hey you, be careful—you might fall into the water!" the employee snapped as he barged past.

Jack smiled a fake apology and then peeped around the rock. He had a feeling that the old woman was more important than the employee. But she was gone. Jack turned around and looked back. The employee had gone back inside the building—and no one else was in view apart from Trudy.

Where had the old woman gone? Jack looked up to the sky to check that she hadn't flown off. It seemed unlikely that a human being could fly, but he wanted to make sure. And he'd seen stranger things in the last week, like an enormous steam-powered dinosaur for a start.

The sky remained obstinately free of flying old women.

"Hmm," Jack mused to himself as he stared out to the sea. And that's when he saw the old woman again—walking calmly into the waves. Jack's eyes widened. She was up to her neck in the waves and didn't appear to be stopping. Surely she would

drown? Now only the top of her head was visible. And then . . .
then nothing. Jack stumbled backward to where Trudy was
kneeling down at the glass barrier, still talking to the seal.

Trudy pointed at Jack. "This is Jack," Trudy said. "He's my
friend."

The seal seemed to nod at this. Normally Jack would have
been surprised that a seal seemed to understand what a person had said, but he felt it was less odd than an old woman
who had just deliberately drowned herself.

"Trudy, there's something really strange going on here."

Trudy looked up from the seal. "What, you mean the way
that this seal keeps rapping on the glass? I thought that was
odd." The seal was using its flipper to rap on the glass wall
rhythmically. "I thought that maybe it was trying to tell us a
knock-knock joke."

Trudy turned back to the seal. "Um, who's there?" she asked.

The seal rapped on the glass three times more, slowly,
then finally three times rapidly.

"If that was a knock-knock joke, then it was the worst
that I've ever heard," said Jack. "Anyway, I've got something
more important to tell you."

Jack explained about hearing the voices mention Trudy's
name and the old woman walking into the sea. Trudy's brow
furrowed.

"What do you think?"

"Well, it isn't that odd, them knowing my name; I come
here all the time. But a woman walking to her death by drowning . . . that's definitely worth asking some questions about."

Jack nodded eagerly. Asking questions was one of his

favorite things. Trudy walked toward the main building as Jack trotted along behind her. This was turning out to be Jack's second very strange week in a row.

MINISTRY OF S.U.IT.S HANDBOOK

SEALS
TIME TRAVEL EXPERIMENTATION

A Ministry scientist at one time theorized that the reason seals swim so fast is because they have flippers. She therefore wondered what would happen if she fitted a second set of plastic flippers on top of a seal's natural flippers.

This squared the seal's swimming speed and had this been where the experiment ended then all would have been well. But the Ministry scientist added another set of artificial flippers, cubing its swimming speed. Which is basically a way of saying that if you multiply something fast by something fast it doesn't just become twice as fast, it becomes super, extra fast. And if you do it again, then it becomes impossibly fast.

Six sets of flippers later[16] and the seal swam so fast that it accidentally opened a wormhole and traveled back in time to prehistoric days. Sadly, it traveled back to a period in time before modern-day seals existed.

Without any of its own kind to start a family with, the seal ended up marrying a saber-toothed tiger. Their offspring are what we in the modern world call a walrus. (For a while people considered calling it a sea tiger but decided that would be too confusing as there already was a sea lion.)

[16] I can't actually come up with a word that describes quite how fast this is. Many of you will be aware that there is a book called a *thesaurus* that allows you to look up a word and find other words with similar meanings. Normally if I needed to find another word for *fast*, I'd just look it up in my thesaurus. However, the other night I got a bit cocky and looked up the word *thesaurus* in my thesaurus and it exploded, subsequently creating an incredibly verbose dimensional rift in the corner of my room. I shouted at it, "Please get out of my office! I'm terrified." It hesitated for a moment and then, in a calm but echoey, modulating voice, explained to me that I was also frightened, petrified, scared, alarmed, and panicked. And you know what? It was right.

Many of you will be wondering why on earth a saber-toothed tiger would ever become romantically entangled with a seal. The answer as usual is simple. A saber-toothed tiger is essentially a large cat. If there's one thing that cats love, it's the smell of fish; therefore, a seal, which only eats (and therefore smells of) fish, is basically wearing the saber-toothed tiger equivalent of Chanel No. 5.

This kind of thing happens in the Ministry all too often, and we must work to stop it. Many of you will wonder why, but the world is very unfair to the walrus. Seals think they look ridiculous with their unnecessarily large teeth and mock them mercilessly. Walruses tend to become depressed and comfort-eat, hence their large size.

The only reasons seals get away with this bullying is because they look ridiculously cute. Almost everyone in the world prefers the way seals look compared to the poor obese walrus. The only recorded example of anyone preferring the walrus is the Tooth Fairy—mainly because of the enormous tusks. The walrus is the Tooth Fairy's second-favorite aquatic animal.

4

NON-FISHY SOUNDS

Jack and Trudy were walking through the corridors of the aquarium again. Trudy's head snapped left and right as she looked for an employee to start asking questions—yet there was no one in sight.

"This is weird," Jack murmured. "This place is deserted. Maybe we should get out of here—this is getting spooky."

"Come on, Jack, we're Ministry operatives—we don't scare easily."

"Really?" Jack asked. "Because in that case I need to go on some kind of a training course. I've been terrified for about five of the last seven days. And the rest of the time the only reason I wasn't terrified was because I didn't really understand what was going on."

Trudy sighed. "Jack, if there's something going on at the aquarium, I need to know what it is."

Jack considered asking her why but decided against it when he saw her hand bunching into a fist.

"Come on, Jack—we don't run from anything."[17]

Jack thought a moment. "Well, okay, but in this case there's nothing for us to actually run from. . . ."

Trudy looked around the room and realized Jack was correct. "Oh, right. Yes."

They agreed that in the absence of anything else, they should go back to the Ministry and see if their mentor, Grey, knew anything about women walking straight into the sea.

They quickly marched through the aquarium and found themselves in the empty entrance hall. They were there just in time to see the aquarium employee from the seal exhibition locking the doors . . . from the outside.

"Monday—early closing day," the employee shouted through the glass doors.

Jack wrinkled his brow. "Um, shouldn't you be locking those doors with *us* on the outside of them? I mean, we aren't fish—so we'll get lonely in here by ourselves."

The employee just smiled. "Oh, don't worry about that—someone's coming along to keep you company." The aquarium employee smiled and backed away from the door.

---

[17] Trudy is, of course, hugely factually inaccurate in making this statement. I'm sure we can all remember that just a few chapters ago our heroes were trying to run from the Tooth Fairy.
This is exactly what I was talking about back in footnote 10, about how people who run away get to "write history" and conveniently forget facts that would otherwise be embarrassing to them. . . .

"I don't like the sound of this," Jack said as he bravely hid behind Trudy. "We're trapped in an aquarium alone. We're going to get attacked by a shark."

Trudy regarded Jack with disdain. "I think we'll be okay, Jack; one thing about sharks is that they're very easy to outrun."

"Oh, right . . . yeah," Jack agreed.

"Mind you," said Trudy, "one day they'll evolve legs and that'll mean two things."

"What?"

"Well, firstly, it'll pretty much be the end for the human race."

"And secondly?"

"Well, secondly, it'll mean that the next *Sharknado* film might actually make sense."

Jack was about to ask Trudy what she meant when they heard a clattering noise coming from the corridor where the fish tanks were.

"That doesn't sound like a fish," Jack murmured.

It wasn't.

SHARKS
Why Sharks Are So Feared

Sharks are described by marine biologists as the evil brothers of dolphins. Or at least that's how they would be described if marine biologists were a bit more fun.

People often make the mistake of thinking that sharks are considered ferocious creatures because they eat the occasional surfer in their ridiculous tie-dyed shorts. Of course this isn't true. The real reason that sharks are considered scary is that they are one of the few sentient beings on Earth that are not terrified of the ruthless businessman known as the Tooth Fairy.

Sharks aren't even slightly fazed by the Tooth Fairy because, throughout their lives, they continue to grow new sets of teeth as their old ones fall out. Therefore the sight of the Tooth Fairy approaching them with a set of pliers doesn't make them shiver in the slightest. After all, when he's finished they can just start growing a new set.

5

A SNAPPY ESCAPE

Jack and Trudy had not expected an enormous crab with a three-foot-wide shell and legs eight feet long to come barreling down the corridor toward them. Which was a shame. Because if that was what they had been expecting, they would have been ready for what happened next.

"This . . . is not what I was expecting," murmured Jack, accurately summing up the situation.

The crab's shell was bright orange with random patches of white. Each of its legs were peppered with joints that bent and twisted as it scuttled toward them. Its two claws moved rapidly and snapped at the air. Instead of an ordinary orange shell, each claw was tipped with a shining metal gauntlet.

Great, Jack thought. *Not only do we get attacked by a giant crab, we get the one who happens to own a pair of steel gloves.*

The crab was within pinching distance now and one of

its long claws whizzed toward them. Trudy ducked her head just in time and it swiped past her. The claw caught hold of the metal handle on the door and snicked it in two.

"Do you reckon you can make crabsticks out of this guy?" Jack asked Trudy.

"I can try. But he's got eight legs and two pincers. And with this"—Trudy held up the arm that was in a sling—"he's got me outnumbered ten to one."

Jack saw by Trudy's face that she was already getting ready to use The Speed. Her face dissolved into sorrow. She was clearly thinking a sad thought that would cause time to slow and allow her to move impossibly fast.

Jack started to think of a sad thought, but before anything came into his mind he noticed a metallic pincer shooting straight toward his head. He was saved at the last moment when Trudy pushed him out of the way. The pincer missed him by inches and he fell on the floor hard.

Trudy took off running across the entrance hall and the crab followed her, scuttling away from where Jack sat, wondering whether his pride hurt more than his bottom.

Like all crabs, it could only scuttle from side to side and not actually go forward. Jack found the effect disconcerting, as one moment it seemed to be lurching back to attack him before another step took it closer to Trudy. At some points, watching the lurching crab made Jack feel a bit seasick.

As the crab closed in on her, Trudy blurred into action. She leapt forward, performing an amazing single-handed cartwheel, and landed on one of the crab's spindly legs. She jumped from crab leg to crab leg as it swung its metal pincers, trying to dislodge her. With one arm in a sling, she was slightly off balance and almost fell twice.

Jack decided he should at least try to help and attacked from the other side. However, the moment he stood up one of the crab's legs ratcheted out like a rocket and crashed into his rib cage, knocking him backward across the room.

"Ommmph," Jack moaned as he went smashing into the ticket counter. Trudy looked up for the briefest second, but turned back toward the crab with a look of fierce concentration on her face. She was dancing along the crab's legs like a tightrope walker. With a final leap she landed on the crab's body and drove her one good fist squarely into its back.

"Owwww!" Trudy called out.

"That crab shell seems pretty tough," called Jack.

"No kidding," said Trudy. She was in midleap when she was caught by a randomly flailing leg that sent her sliding across the floor.

The crab shuffled in one direction and then the other trying to decide who to attack first.

"Any thoughts, Jack?" shouted Trudy, who had gotten to her feet and assumed a fighting stance.

"Working on the second part of a plan," said Jack, who had gotten to his feet and hidden himself behind the ticket counter.

Trudy's brow wrinkled. "Did I miss the first part of your plan?"

Jack popped his head up from behind the counter. "The first part of *my* plan is hiding behind this counter." Jack ducked back down and started wondering what the second part of his plan might be. What he needed was an enormous pair of crab crackers like the kind that his father used when he ate lobster.

The crab had finally made a decision about whom to attack first. It would start with Trudy, as she was clearly more dangerous and less frightened. It was a particularly intelligent crab. If it hadn't been working for the aquarium, it might possibly have ended up as a site foreman or an architect.

Trudy slowly backed away as the crab approached her. "How's part two of the plan coming along?"

"I've got it!" Jack yelled, waving something in the air.

Trudy was disappointed to see that the "it" that Jack was so happy about was a large paper poster of marine animals.

"What use is that?" Trudy grumbled as she dodged two deadly claws that zoomed at either side of her body, missing her by inches. One of them smashed into a glass tank beside her. The tank cracked open and showered Trudy in water and dozens of tiny starfish. She looked like the world's first human astronomical map.

"I'm going to use this chart to find out what we're fighting and then see if it has a weakness."

"Brilliant," said Trudy as she ran out of range from another lashing leg attack. "I'll just carry on, then. No hurry."

Jack scanned down the chart quickly until he found a picture that resembled the monstrosity that was attacking them. "It's a Japanese Spider Crab, apparently."

"Great information, Jack; now you'll be able to tell the coroner what it was that killed me." The crab had cornered Trudy and seemed to be almost playing with her, throwing out a leg lazily here and there, forcing her to jump and duck alternately.

"Okay, I'm looking for weaknesses on the chart. Unfortunately, I think this is meant to be an educational tool rather than a Pokémon card—so it isn't too big on the whole strengths/weaknesses thing."[18]

"Just keep reading. Fighting this thing is like trying to wrestle with spaghetti."

Jack kept reading. "Mmmm. It doesn't say it here, but I suspect that because it's a Japanese crab it may well know some karate."

"Don't be stupid. . . ."

An enormous crab leg stretched out across the room, and the tip of it came crashing down on the edge of the ticket counter, splitting it in two.

---

[18] It is an interesting fact that the information cards at aquariums don't tell you the weaknesses of animals. If you are wondering why this is, the truth as always is simple. They want you to try and preserve the animals. Not wrestle with them.

Conservation and environmentalism are important. It's just that they're not a whole lot of fun. If someone tells you that they are, they're almost definitely trying to sell you a membership to the World Wildlife Fund. I've got one, with the cuddly panda and everything. I'll be honest: It was a mistake. Someone came to the door and asked me if I wanted to join the WWF and I thought they meant the Wildlife Wrestling Fund. Now I've got a direct debit coming out of my account every month and I keep getting newsletters about endangered species.

I wouldn't mind so much, but they won't even let me wrestle with any of the animals. Try and tell me there's a person alive who doesn't want to put a Three-toed Sloth in a headlock.

"Okay," said Jack, "now I strongly suspect that the crab may know some karate."[19]

Trudy waved at Jack through the split in the ticket counter. "We could really, really, really do with that brilliant second part of the plan now."

Jack threw the poster to one side. "There was nothing on the chart that was helpful. It didn't tell me anything that I didn't already know about crabs. I mean, everyone knows three things about crabs. They have hard shells, two pincers, and . . ."

And then Jack remembered the third thing that everyone knew about crabs and finally had one of his ideas.

[19] Jack, of course, is right about this. All crabs know karate, not just the Japanese ones. The reason for this is that crabs are builders, and as anyone who has read the first *Ministry of SUITs* book will know, all martial arts were originally invented by builders.

AQUATIC ANIMALS
The Starfish

The starfish is quite possibly one of the most amazing creatures that exists. Any schoolchild will tell you that an entire starfish can regrow from one single arm. This is true; however, what people don't realize is that all starfish start off a completely different shape and only end up as stars after regenerating several times. They are just so smug about their ability to regenerate that the shape they choose to morph into is a star—thus giving themselves "a star for effort."

However, it is important to note that being able to regenerate is not actually as great an advantage as it seems. Theoretically, a starfish that was cut into five pieces could grow into five starfish—all of whom would really be the same person and therefore have to go home to the same wife. As you can imagine, this could potentially be confusing and harrowing.

It is interesting to note that because of the above, if you wish to go to university and study Starfish Divorce Law, you will need better grades than you would need to study Starfish Medicine.

In point of fact, one area that starfish are incredibly backward in is medicine. When you can heal from almost any injury, you don't have much need for doctors. This is why starfish are the only creatures in the world who don't particularly like the television series *Doctor Who*—because they have no conception of what a doctor actually is. Which is a shame, because they'd really identify with the doctor's ability to regenerate.

There is also something very strange about starfish. Considering that they are not very fearsome, you would expect them to be frequently attacked by sharks and other marine predators. They would then be torn into pieces, each of which would regenerate into a whole starfish—thus increasing their number exponentially. Many scientists are unsure as to why the entire seafloor isn't entirely covered with the smug little five-armed animals. Something must therefore be collecting or harvesting starfish, but to date we have been unable to establish who or what.

6

PARKING

Jack jumped up and ran to the opposite side of the entrance hall to a door marked *Supplies*. Inside he found mops, buckets, and most important, an industrial-size container of pink, gloopy soap. He quickly poured a puddle of it onto the floor.

Jack looked up and shouted to Trudy, who was still dodging the flailing orange monster. "Get the crab to come here!"

Trudy cartwheeled, using her one good arm. "Get the crab over there? How am I meant to do that? Invite him over for tea?" Trudy muttered as she jumped over a snapping pincer, "I swear if I get out of this, I'm asking for Cthulhu as a partner; at least he isn't always saying ridiculous things."

Trudy tensed her muscles and then sprang into action, running straight at the crab and jumping. The crab's two metallic pincers sliced through the air, each missing her by mere inches. She landed in a forward roll and sprinted toward where Jack was standing in front of the open storeroom.

With some difficulty, the crab scuttled itself from side to side, eventually turning around to face Trudy and Jack.

Trudy looked at the puddle of pink goo on the floor. "Jack, I know that hygiene is very important, but do you think that now was really the time to be washing the floor?"

Jack stood up. "It isn't hygiene; it's a trap." Jack paused. "Admittedly it's a particularly clean trap, but it's a trap nonetheless."

The Japanese Spider Crab was facing the two heroes. Its two metal claws rang out as it snapped them threateningly. It had clearly had enough of playing with Jack and Trudy. It slowly edged from side to side and then suddenly used its spindly legs to launch itself at them.[20] At the last second before the crab had hold of them in its claws, Jack yelled, "Jump!"

Jack and Trudy dived aside, leaving the crab to go sliding on the pink soap. Watching it lift up its pincers and legs and wave them threateningly as it spun around was somewhat[21] like watching a company of semaphorists being electrocuted.

As the crab slid, Jack pulled hard on one of its legs,

[20] Being charged by a creature who moves sideways is a very strange experience. Due to perspective the creature keeps getting nearer to you, but as it's never actually facing you, you sort of assume that it's going the other way.

[21] It's interesting to note that if you had attached flags to the crab's legs and read the "semaphore" that the crab was accidentally signaling, it would have read, "Help! I'm an enormous crab and I'm about to be

sending it spinning in a circle. The crab crashed into the storeroom, its back smashing against the rear wall.

"Jack, this isn't going to work. It'll just . . ."

And then Trudy noticed something. The crab wasn't trying to get out of the storeroom. It was completely still. And it looked to be very irritated indeed.

"What have you done, Jack?" Trudy was still slightly wary of the crab.

Jack was enjoying a feeling of overwhelming smugness; if he had been able to regenerate he would have started morphing into the shape of a star. "There are three things that everyone knows about crabs. They have hard shells, two pincers, and . . ."

". . . they walk sideways," said Trudy, completing Jack's thought.

"Precisely. So I knew if we could get the crab to slip and spin on the soap, all we'd have to do was push him backward into the storeroom. Now there's no space on either side of him. And because he can only move sideways he's . . ."

". . . trapped."

"Precisely," agreed Jack.

Jack's feeling of superiority was suddenly broken when the crab reached out one of its long spindly limbs and snapped a claw at him. He fell backward, but the crab still managed to snip his school tie neatly in two. Jack felt slightly less smug.

Trudy ran forward and pushed the storeroom door shut,

---

trapped." However, this was not intentional, but just a strange coincidence. This happens a lot more often than you would think.

forcing the crab to fold up its pincers. The crab hammered at the door with his legs, but to no avail.

"That should hold him," Trudy said while helping Jack up. "Lucky this place has all doorknobs. Even if the crab managed to turn himself around somehow, he'll never be able to work a doorknob without an opposable thumb."

Jack was looking at his tie, which had been snipped in half. "How am I going to explain this to my parents?"

"Never mind that; I'm going to call Grey and see what we should do next."

MINISTRY OF S.U.I.T.S HANDBOOK

CRABS
THEIR ABILITIES AS BUILDERS

As has previously been noted, crabs are one of the many animals used to erect buildings underwater.

It is always vitally important to get the right kind of crab builder if you are considering putting an extension on your underwater house. Hermit crabs generally refuse to build extensions. Instead they will merely suggest that you find yourself a slightly bigger shell/house and move into it when the real owner is out.

Fiddler crabs also make a bad choice for undersea construction jobs, as they have one claw much larger than the other. This means that one half of your house will be far too big, while the other side will have tiny doors that you can only get through by crawling.

However, it is useless trying to argue with fiddler crabs about this—they are normally far too angry to listen to reason. Fiddler crabs are especially grumpy about the unfairness of the world, as they can never find a pair of gloves that fit. Perhaps even worse, they struggle enormously to find a suitable controller with which to use their PlayStation 4.

7

A DAMP SQUID

After Trudy's phone call, Grey had promised he would get to the aquarium as soon as possible, and true to his word, he was there less than thirty minutes later. As always, he was dressed in an immaculately tailored suit and tie, with a crisp crease down the front of his trousers. In one hand he held a tightly furled umbrella and in the other he carried a black leather briefcase.

"Why didn't you just send a car to collect us?" Jack asked.

Grey shook his head. "Don't be ridiculous—and leave a potentially criminal crab at large? What happened if it attacked someone else? Now, where is he?"

Trudy nodded toward the storeroom where the crab had been trapped. "In there—but he's just trapped. He isn't unconscious or anything. I don't know how to get him out safely."

"Don't worry about that," Grey said as he popped open his briefcase. "I've got something here that'll do the trick."

Grey took out what looked like a sleek black plastic gun. It had a contoured handle with two switches on it. The barrel was rounded and fat, narrowing to a flatter muzzle.

Jack was impressed that the Ministry of SUITs[22] had such advanced technology. His previous experience of the Ministry had led him to believe that they were mostly "winging it" in the equipment area.

"So what is that?" Jack asked. "Some kind of Taser or stun gun?"

"And more to the point, how did you get that kind of equipment off the quartermaster? Isn't he notoriously bad about actually giving people equipment?" asked Trudy.

Grey went over to the storeroom door and opened it, holding the black plastic gun in front of him. The crab took one look at what Grey was holding and snapped its metal claws into a "hands up" position.

Grey spoke over his shoulder to Jack and Trudy. "I wouldn't use a gun. Guns are random and clumsy. This is a civilized weapon . . . for a more elegant age."[23]

"So what is it, then?"

Grey signaled with the weapon for Jack and Trudy to help pull the terrified crab from the storeroom. They obliged.

---

[22] The Ministry of Strange, Unusual, and Impossible Things. You should know this already, really. It's on the cover and everything.

[23] It should be noted Grey was badly misquoting one of the best lines, from one of the best films ever. And we should be glad that he misquoted it badly. Because otherwise we would currently be getting sued for copyright infringement.

"It's a hair dryer."

"A hair dryer?" Trudy arched her eyebrows as she looked at the weapon closer and saw the *GHD* logo on the side.

"Of course a hair dryer. Crabs can only breathe if their gills are kept wet. Which is why they're terrified of hair dryers. If I aim this at his gills for a few seconds, he'll drop to his many knees, unable to breathe."

"It's strange to think that crabs are really that frightened of hair dryers," said Jack.

Grey nodded. "It's one of the reasons why you never see a crab at the hairdressers."

"Crabs don't have hair," Jack pointed out.

"Of course they do; they just keep it clipped very short with their claws—because they spend half their life in the water and half on the land. And you know if you go outside with wet hair you'll catch a cold."

Trudy still had a different question. "Anyway, how did you get the hair dryer off the quartermaster?"

Grey shook his head. "This is my own."

Trudy laughed. "I didn't imagine you'd own a GHD hair dryer."

Grey ran a hand through his hair. "How do you think I keep my side part so perfectly sharp? Anyway, enough with the hair-care tips. Let's get this monstrosity outside. We're going to have to get him to fold up a bit if he's going to fit into the trunk of the Ministry car."

"Where are we taking him?" asked Trudy.

"The Ministry fish prison," said Grey. As if that explained anything.

Grey waved the deadly hair dryer at the crab, indicating for it to move to the aquarium doors.

⸻

Ten minutes later, the superfast Ministry car dropped the heroes outside the museum that was the entrance to the Ministry. Jack felt strangely happy. Less than a week ago he had had no idea that his local museum had been the home to the mysterious Ministry. Of course that visit had been completely different from this one. The last time he had come here he had arrived because he had been attacked by a bear. This time he was here because he had been attacked by a crab. Which was a very different thing indeed.

Grey, Trudy, and Jack ran through the entrance hall of the museum with the crab clacking over the tiled floor in front of them. Occasionally a visitor would look at the enormous crab quizzically. Grey would smile at them and explain, "Just a new exhibit—all done with animatronics."

They went up the stairs and made their way straight to the Egyptology display. Once there, Trudy pressed on the fingernails of an enormous stone sculpture of a hand. This action caused the glass case over the sarcophagus of the mummy Takabuti to open. The front of the sarcophagus case swung open on its hinges, revealing the steps down to the hidden headquarters of the Ministry.

⸻

Once inside the Ministry, Grey guided them to a large, gunmetal-gray door that was secured in place with a large circular valve. It looked like the kind of door you would have expected in an old submarine. The words *Party Room* were written on the door in stenciled white lettering.

"So what's in here?" asked Jack. "Because it sounds like it's going to be fun. And you'll understand that makes me very suspicious indeed."

Grey handed the hair dryer to Trudy to hold on the crab as he grabbed hold of the valve and with a great heave turned it several notches. He then took a deep breath and turned it again.

Jack wondered what would be inside the room. He'd seen some very odd things indeed in the Ministry. He tried to guess what it might be. "Is this room host to a interdimensonal rift that spits death?" asked Jack.

Trudy considered Jack's suggestion. "Yes, or maybe it's home to a clockwork wind-up humanoid-mannequin that was wound overly tight one day, which caused it to develop self awareness and come to life."

"Ohhh!" Jack enthused. "That's a good one, Trudy. Yeah, he came to life and the Ministry had to stop him because he was trying to kill people because he went mad."

Trudy laughed. "Yeah, he went mad from the pressure because it's very stressful when you're clockwork and you have to remember to wind yourself every two hours, otherwise..."

"...you'll die!" Jack and Trudy finished the sentence together, laughing.

Grey made a tutting noise. He was looking sternly at them. "If you've quite finished? We have important business to complete." Grey turned the valve another notch and the door made a *thock* noise.

"So what is in there, Grey?" Trudy asked.

"Well," Grey said as he slowly pulled the door open, "it isn't a death-spitting dimensional rift, because they're too dangerous to be kept in the office. And for that matter it isn't the clockwork wind-up mannequin that was overwound and came to life . . . because we keep him on the seventh floor."

Grey took the hair dryer back from Trudy and signaled for the crab to walk through the door. "Instead, you're about to meet the oldest man in the Ministry and the smartest marine biologist in the world."

MINISTRY OF S.U.IT.S HANDBOOK

MARINE BIOLOGISTS
WHY PEOPLE THINK THEY ARE SO INTELLIGENT

Generally, people tend to think that marine biologists are incredibly intelligent.

It should be noted that not all marine biologists are as clever as people generally believe them to be. People always assume that they are very wise; however, this is mainly because they spend a lot of time in water and get wrinkly. Wrinkles make people look older than they really are, and it is always assumed that with age comes wisdom. If marine biologists were really clever, they would spend a little less time in the pool and a little more time applying moisturizer.

8

THE PARTY ROOM

Jack should have been shocked when they walked into the room, but he wasn't. A normal person would have been shocked upon walking into a room that seemed to be hundreds of meters tall and wide. But Jack was used to the fact that the normal rules of time and space didn't seem to apply to the Ministry.

The room was also full of dozens of enormous glass structures randomly located. They looked like tall drinking glasses. At the top of each of the containers, long glass tubes straddled the distances between them like a series of interlinking bridges. Each glass tank held the most amazing sea life that Jack had ever seen: small fish, large sharks, enormous seahorses, squid, octopuses, giant lobsters, swarms of oversized prawns.... They all darted around the tanks, dodging between tendrils of seaweed and other vegetation.

Occasionally, a fish would swim to the top of a tank, swish its tail, and zip along one of the thin tube bridges to another tank.

Jack was feeling proud of himself that he was taking such a strange room entirely in his stride. In fact, he was almost at risk of becoming a little smug. Luckily, before that happened Jack noticed the incredibly intense smell of fish that permeated the air. The stench was so awful that it caused Jack to retch a little in his own mouth. At this point Jack stopped feeling pleased with himself. It is extremely hard to feel smug while swallowing chunks of your own vomit.

Grey was shaking hands with a man—a man whom Jack literally could not take his eyes off. He was six feet tall, with wavy black hair, piercing blue eyes, and perfect olive skin. He was wearing a pair of shorts and a T-shirt that showed off his muscular arms.

He was the most stunningly attractive man that Jack had ever seen. Jack turned to look at Trudy. She was staring even more intently than Jack, her jaw was slack, and she seemed to have stopped breathing.[24]

For a few seconds Jack felt strangely jealous. Okay, the man was very attractive, but he wasn't anything that special. . . . Jack looked at the man again and was annoyed to realize that he was something very special. He was impossibly handsome.

Grey smirked. "Jack and Trudy, meet the Professor. Professor, meet Jack and Trudy."

[24] Remember this. It becomes important later on. . . .

The Professor made a small theatrical bow and held his hand out to shake. Jack shook his hand and then nudged Trudy, who was still awestruck. "You might want to try and start breathing again before you asphyxiate," Jack muttered.

Trudy shook herself and then shook the Professor's hand. She was clearly more than a little enthralled by how stunningly beautiful the Professor was. "I thought Grey said that you were the oldest man in the Ministry—but you couldn't be more than . . . twenty or thirty or something. . . ."

The Professor looked sternly at Grey, and then they both started laughing.

Jack was confused. "Is this a joke? Or what?"

The Professor shook his head. "Not at all, but it's all very predictable. This is the same reaction that I have been getting for . . . well, for the last six hundred years, at least."

Now it was Jack's jaw's turn to go slack. "You're six hundred years old?"

The Professor thought for a moment. "More like seven hundred, I think. To be honest, after my two hundred and fiftieth birthday I stopped counting. Apart from anything else, the candles on my cake were not only a fire hazard, but I suspect they were also substantially contributing to global warming."

"So if you're seven hundred, how do you look so young?" asked Trudy.

The Professor turned and placed a hand flat against the surface of one of the enormous tanks. Jack noticed that even this small movement seemed to spook the fish inside and they rapidly swam away—it was as if they were scared of the Professor's hand. "My secret is simple." The Professor smiled. "Fish oils."

"Why don't you take them on a tour and explain?" Grey suggested. "I'll put our prisoner here in one of the tanks."

Grey motioned for the crab to move toward a large hydraulic platform fixed to the side of a large glass tank. The Professor, Jack, and Trudy walked across the room, looking at the fish swimming through the tanks and also along the narrow glass bridges above them.

"It all started when I was a fisherman in Portugal," the Professor explained. "I was dreadfully poor and couldn't afford to eat anything other than what I caught. I couldn't afford bread, milk, or eggs. Just fish and nothing but fish. In fact, I ate so much fish that I actually started smelling of fish. In the end the people in my local village refused to let me into the marketplace. So I had absolutely no choice but to continue on my fish-only diet. Of course back then we scientists hadn't discovered just how good fish are for you. No one had even heard of polyunsaturated fats, essential fatty acids, or omega-3 and omega-6."

"And they stop you from aging?"

The Professor nodded. "Yes, they're incredibly good for your heart, brain, joints, eyes . . . they prevent cancer, eye disease, and bone problems. You get all these benefits if you eat fish a few times a week. Of course the effects are much stronger if you eat fish every day, for every meal. And on top of that the kinds of fish I was eating were fish that ate fish that had eaten other fish—which multiplied the effects many times over."

"And that diet of fish is what makes you stay looking so young and being so beautiful?" Trudy blushed as she realized what she had said.

The Professor smiled. "My fish-only diet has also given me bones that literally can't be broken, a heart that never gets tired and gives me limitless energy, eyes that can see in the dark, and the IQ of a genius."

Jack was still curious. "If a fish-only diet can do all that, then why isn't everyone on one?"

The Professor's face fell slightly. "I sort of explained that already."

Jack thought hard. "Did you? I think I would have noticed."

"A fish-only diet may be brilliant for health, but unfortunately it does make you smell rather badly of fish."

"Oh. . . . Ohhhhhh."

"Yes," said the Professor, looking slightly ashamed. "That smell isn't from the tanks. I'm afraid to say that's from me. That's why the door is shut with the valve. It isn't meant to be waterproof or anything like that . . . just odorproof."

Trudy leaned forward and gave the Professor a slight sniff. She grimaced.

Jack felt awkward and stammered, trying to change the subject, "So are you the only person in the world who is on a fish-only diet?"

"No, not at all. Can you think of any groups of people who are talented, good looking, and never seem to age?"

"Hollywood actors?" Trudy suggested.

"Precisely," said the Professor. "It's obvious, really. The

idea that plastic surgery can keep you young is ridiculous. If that were the case, then plastic action figures and toy dolls would never get as grimy and tired-looking as they do."

"So all film actors are on a fish-only diet?" Jack asked. "I mean . . . all of them?"

The Professor nodded. "Of course. Why do you think they built Hollywood so close to the sea? It was in order to ensure a ready supply of fish. It's also the reason they all live in those ridiculously big mansions. They have to make sure they're far enough away from ordinary people that they won't notice the ghastly smell."

"I think I'm glad that Hollywood actors smell bad," said Jack. "It makes the world seem slightly more fair, for some reason."

"Just visit Hollywood sometime and you'll see. There's a reason that every second restaurant in that town is a sushi bar."

There was a splashing from above as Grey had made the crab jump into the top of one of the giant tanks. He was now descending on the hydraulic platform.

"So why do they call this place the party room?" Jack asked.

The Professor smiled, clearly relieved to be able to talk about something other than the way he smelled.

BEING SICK
LOCATION—YOUR OWN MOUTH

It is never fun to be sick in your own mouth. However, it is interesting to note that some animals are sick in their own mouths as a matter of course. Cows have developed the rather unpleasant habit of "chewing the cud." This is basically the process of being sick in your own mouth and swallowing it again.

This is the reason why cows rarely get invited to dinner parties and never get asked to play Spin the Bottle.

9

PRISON BREAK

"Do the enormous tanks look like anything you might have seen elsewhere?"

Jack looked at the tanks. There was really only one thing. "Well, enormous glasses. And the bridges at the top are a bit like straws sticking out of one drink and into another."

"Precisely." The Professor smiled. "You see, we couldn't afford to get an architect to design this place, so I just sketched it out from an idea I had after a Ministry Christmas party. That's why we call it the party room."

Jack laughed. "You're joking."

The Professor furrowed his brow and stroked his chin. "Don't you like my design?"

"It's not that," said Jack. "But you really mean this whole place was designed on drinking glasses from a Christmas party?"

"That's precisely what I mean. It was also at that party that I got the idea for fish food."

Jack's eyebrows raised. "Now you're claiming that you invented fish food at a Christmas party? So what did you base that on? Sausage rolls? Streamers?"

The Professor sighed. "What does fish food look like?"

Jack thought back to his (now dead) pet goldfish. "Well, little multicolored flakes."

"Would you say the flakes looked like confetti?"

Jack's eyes widened. "Exactly like confetti."

The Professor picked up a rifle with a barrel the size of a tin can, which had been leaning against one of the tanks. "You see, when I was designing the huge tanks I realized I didn't want to have to climb up and down every day just to feed the fish. And seeing the confetti at the party gave me a design idea." The Professor raised the rifle to his shoulder and pulled the trigger. There was a dull *whump* and a ball of confetti rose into the air, arched over one of the tanks, and exploded into thousands of little flakes. The flakes drifted and fluttered over the surface of the water. Fish teemed upward to nibble at them.

The Professor held up the rifle. "CO_2-powered confetti cannon. I invented it to feed fish, but I believe that they also use them at rock concerts these days."

The hydraulic platform had reached the ground and Grey jumped off to join the others. "Well, that's one crab safely caught."

Trudy stared at the tanks. "Are all these criminal fish, then?"

While Trudy was asking questions about the enormous fish prison, Jack wandered over to the tank and watched the crab with the metal claws. It looked around briefly and then scuttled over to a giant octopus. It was dark blue with ten-foot-long tentacles. The crab seemed to be trying to communicate something as it waved its pincers frantically. The steel claw ends flashed in the water.

"Don't you ever worry that the fish will try and escape?" Trudy asked.

The Professor laughed and Grey slapped him on the back. "Not a problem, Trudy," said Grey. "That's one of the most amazing parts of the Professor's design. You see, he got the tanks made from prescription glass."

"Prescription glass?"

"Yes, the kind you get in eyeglasses."

Trudy didn't understand. "And is that especially strong?"

"Not strong," the Professor explained. "But it magnifies everything. So the fish are looking through a magnifying glass at us. From their perspective we look like giants. They'd never try and escape because they're too worried that we're giants and could easily defeat them."

Trudy smiled. "That's brilliant!"

Jack was still looking at the octopus and the crab, but he had overheard the conversation. "Hey, guys . . . I don't want to worry you, but I think your plan might have a flaw in it."

The Professor wrinkled his perfect nose indignantly. "A flaw? How could it have a flaw? I don't make mistakes. Did I mention how much fish oil I eat in a week?"

Jack ignored this comment. "The crab knows we aren't all

giants—and you just put him into the tank with the other fish."

The Professor stopped being indignant for a moment. "Oh dear ... normally the fish are transported in closed boxes. But still ... what can one crab do? The glass is several feet thick. Even a sledgehammer blow wouldn't crack it."

As if to prove the Professor's point, a large hammerhead shark slammed into the side of the tank next to them. There wasn't a mark on the glass.

"You see," the Professor said, gloating, "we're all entirely safe."

Jack wasn't listening. He was thinking. Although he'd been very pleased with himself when they had captured the crab, looking back now it felt as if it had been too easy. Maybe the crab had let itself be captured. And then there were the metal pincers it wore. They wouldn't be able to cut through glass ... so what was the point of them? He tried to think of something else that was made of metal and had two prongs.

The crab had stopped signaling to the octopus, which had swum away to some other octopuses that lurked in the corner of a decorative castle on the bottom of the tank. The crab scuttled over to the side of the tank where Jack was still gazing in. Jack took a cautious step back.

The crab held up one metal claw and struck it hard against the side of the tank. The tank was unmarked, but the metal claw was vibrating, giving out a piercing, high-pitched tone. Jack clasped his hands over his ears. What was happening?

A group of octopuses had swum to the top of the tank and placed themselves around the glass edge. They reached their wet tentacles out of the water and started rubbing them around the edge of the glass, then started swimming in a circle. A squeaking noise started, like when you rub a wet finger around a glass rim. But with a dozen octopuses doing that at the same time, it was rapidly getting louder. And not only louder, but more high-pitched. It was getting closer and closer to the same pitch the crab was emitting from its tuning-fork claws.

Suddenly, Jack realized what was happening and stumbled backward. "Guys, we've got to get out of here."

"Nonsense," said the Professor, "we're quite safe."

The pitch of the octopus tentacles kept getting higher as they swam faster and faster around the rim of the tank. Grey looked at Jack. "What do you think's going to happen?"

Jack looked briefly around at the tank and then back at Grey. "Have you ever seen one of those films where an opera singer sings a really high note and shatters glass with it?"

Grey took a slow breath. "Professor, I think Jack might be right. Maybe we should think about leaving."

There was a cracking noise and a long jagged fissure snaked up the side of the tank.

The Professor took a step backward. "Yes . . . maybe we should think about . . . you must eat a lot of fish, Jack."

The heroes turned and started to run, but at that very minute the noise from the octopuses finally matched the noise from the claw-based tuning fork. There were dozens of the enormous tanks in the room, and they shattered all at once. A tidal wave of water poured, gushing and foaming, into the room.

WAYS TO HELP THOUGHT
THE STROKING OF CHINS

Many people over the years have wondered why some people stroke their chins when they think. The reason is simple. This action goes back to ancient Greece. Back then philosophers were considered the greatest thinkers. All philosophers had enormous beards. Therefore, when an ordinary Greek citizen was trying to think he would try and pull hair out of his chin to create a beard—that way even if he didn't come up with a great idea, he would at least look like an intelligent philosopher with an enormous beard.

Over the years the "pulling hair" action came to resemble the stroking of the chin.

10
THE FLOOD

Jack opened his mouth to scream to the others to watch out. It was a ridiculous thing to do, as they had also seen the enormous glass tanks break and shatter. As he opened his mouth, a wave hit him and he swallowed an enormous amount of water, a certain amount of algae, and, almost certainly, some fish poo.

One of the cracking tanks threw a long, thin, jagged shard of glass past Jack. It ripped his trousers and opened a shallow cut on his leg. As Jack was buffeted against the wall, the swirling waves threw three starfish through the air, and they thunked into the wall beside his head like ninja shuriken. A second wave crashed across the room and smashed Jack, tumbling, into the wall. His eyes blurred for a second and he felt himself slip under the water.

The water was still swirling and Jack tumbled through it, not sure which way was up. His lungs howled for air—he paddled his hands frantically, not sure that he was heading in the right direction.

Jack blinked as Trudy's face suddenly appeared in front of his. She pointed in a direction Jack assumed was up, grabbed the front of his shirt, and hauled him as she kicked her feet.

Jack surfaced, spluttering and coughing. "Thanks for that, Trudy. You saved me in the nick of time. But then again, I did warn you that the glass tanks were going to shatter, so we're probably even."

Trudy frowned at him. "I'm not sure if it counts as a warning when you only give us a second's notice."

Grey and the Professor bobbed to the surface beside them. "We need to get out of here."

Jack looked around—the water was beginning to settle, but the room was half submerged with water. If they wanted to get out, they would have to dive under the water and find the door. Jack wasn't a terribly strong swimmer. "Couldn't we just wait for a while? I'm a little bit dizzy from being smashed into the wall and I think my leg is bleeding."

The Professor had been surveying the water, but snapped his head around at the mention of blood. "You're bleeding?"

Jack dog-paddled, keeping his head above water. "Yes. I think I've also rather badly bruised my shoulder. I mean, if we're making a list of all my injuries, I think it's important we include that as well."

Trudy splashed water at Jack's face. "You idiot. This isn't about you feeling bad. Blood in the water will attract sharks."

Jack gulped. He'd been concentrating on not drowning in the water released from the shattered tanks. He hadn't really thought about the fact that the shattered tanks meant that the criminal fish would be free and swimming below them. Suddenly he expected to be pulled underwater by the giant Japanese crab any second.

Grey was looking around the walls. "If my bearings are right the door should be in that wall. Follow me." Grey took a deep breath and dived under the water. The Professor and Trudy followed.

"I only have my twenty-five-meter swimming badge," Jack grumbled to no one. "And I touched the bottom twice when I was getting that." He ducked his head under the water and kicked his way toward the door.

Jack was too panicked to look around as he swam; however, he couldn't help noticing that a number of fish and undersea animals were clustered around an overflow vent that was set in a corner of the room. Hammerhead sharks were taking turns to charge the vent. Sawfish were using their serrated noses to cut the grid that covered it, and octopuses were pulling at it. Standing beside them was the crab who had caused all this. It waved at Jack. If Jack hadn't been concentrating so hard on not drowning, he would probably have waved back.

Ahead of him, the Professor and Grey had already made their way out of the door and into the corridor. Trudy had grabbed the side of the door frame and was waving for Jack to hurry up. Jack kicked as hard as he could and thrashed his arms as his vision began to blur. He was only a few meters away from the door, and he reached out a hand, which Trudy grabbed. Jack couldn't hold his breath any longer. He swallowed a lungful of water and blacked out.

When he opened his eyes, he found himself floating on top of the water in the middle of a corridor he didn't recognize. Trudy was holding his head so that it didn't go underwater. He coughed and spluttered his lungs back to life. "Why do people enjoy water parks so much?"

If Jack was being sarcastic, Trudy knew that he was going to survive. She let go of Jack's head, which went under the water again. Jack spluttered and worried for a second that he was going to drown. But he quickly realized that the water was only two feet deep. Slightly embarrassed, he stood up and tried to act nonchalant. "So what was that about?"

The Professor kicked the wall. "That was a jailbreak. Most of the fish will have escaped through the overflow vent in the party room by now."

Grey nodded. "They knew exactly what they were doing."

"That's what I thought," Jack agreed. "Although admittedly I might have come to that realization too late. We were meant to capture that crab and bring him here, weren't we?"

"But why?" asked Trudy. "Who would want to free a bunch of criminal fish?"

"I think you'll find that a bunch of fish are called a shoal," Jack said helpfully.

"Thanks for the help," said Trudy as she punched Jack in the shoulder.

Jack was pretty sure that it was going to bruise. At least it would match the bruise he would have on his other shoulder from where the massive wave had slammed him into the wall. Jack wondered what the collective term was for a group of bruises.[25]

"I'm going to go and report what happened." The Professor stalked off, leaving Grey and the children standing knee-deep in the water.

"We've just flooded the Ministry," Trudy observed.

"Everyone's going to be mad at us, aren't they?"

Grey shrugged. "I would think so. I mean, who wants to have to work in a building that's full of water? Anyway, let's get you out of here—I don't think there's anything else you can do to help."

<hr />

Trudy took the lead as they marched down the waterlogged corridors. "Last week we were worried that we were going to be floating over the waves,[26] and this week it seems like we're sinking under them."

"What on earth is that?" Jack had become distracted from the conversation by a thick green mist that was rolling along the top of the water. "Has someone let the Loch Ness Monster out?"

[25] Collective nouns are the words we use to describe groups of things. The collective noun for a group of cows is a *herd*—"a herd of cows." There are other examples—some more collective nouns would be "a vanity of films stars" or "a confusion of politicians." The collective noun for a group of bruises is "an ouch."

[26] Blackbeard the pirate had nearly stolen Northern Ireland by using wind turbines as propellers, intending to use it as the world's biggest pirate ship. This sort of thing happens all the time.

The cloud of mist seemed to be sparking small bolts of lightning. Occasionally, smaller clouds morphed into the shape of screaming, agonized faces before dissolving again into insubstantial puffs of smoke. "Well? What is it?"

Grey laughed. "Come on, Jack. This is your second week in the Ministry; you should be able to figure out what's causing that."

Jack's brow wrinkled. "How on earth would I know what's causing that? I mean, it looks like an evil, green, interdimensional cloud of unimaginable evil power that could possibly destroy . . ." And then a thought clicked into place in Jack's head. "Cthulhu!"

From the center of the cloud, rising out of the water, appeared the gray-skinned, squid-headed, green-eyed manifestation of evil that was in charge of the Ministry's filing system.

Cthulhu gave a horrific roar, which would not only have shattered glass but would also have probably turned it all the way back into sand. Cthulhu then folded his legs in front of him and somehow managed to hover a good foot above the level of the water. It was even more impressive that he achieved the hovering effect without having to flap the large pair of dragon-like wings that were affixed to his back.

There was a strange look on Cthulhu's face. Jack thought he might be . . . but he couldn't be, could he? "Umm, is he . . .?"

Grey nodded. "Smiling? Yes, I rather think he might be."

Trudy shook her head. "But why's he so happy? I mean, aren't all his files wet?"

Grey paused to waft some of the evil green smoke away from himself. "I suspect that Cthulhu was never really that interested in the filing. He's more interested in the possibilities for evil that filing offers. And at the minute he's having a field day. Everyone will probably be trying to requisition mops and buckets and sponges, and no doubt Cthulhu will refuse to help because he doesn't accept damp paperwork."

Jack thought about this problem. "Everyone could just go to the quartermaster for supplies instead."

"Jack." Grey sighed. "What do you remember about the quartermaster?"

Jack shrugged. "He was a dapper little man. Small mustache. About two feet high."

"And how far off the ground is two feet?"

Jack thought for a second and held his hand where he thought was two feet off the ground. In doing this he had to put his hand underwater. "Ahh, I can see the quartermaster's problem."

"Yes, after I've got the two of you out of here I'm going to have to go and find the quartermaster and make sure that he's managed to find himself a pair of water wings."

Cthulhu floated past them down the corridor, making the kind of noise that you would expect if a world-class opera singer was trying to yodel through jelly. Jack thought it was one of the strangest sights he would ever see until he noticed that a tall beam of blue light seemed to be following Cthulhu.

Jack jumped nervously aside as the beam of bright blue light moved toward them. "Is that one of Cthulhu's spells or something?"

A voice seemed to come from the blue beam. "New recruit?" The question came from the light, which pulsed in time with the words.

Grey nodded and spoke to the beam. "Relatively new—we just started him last week. His name's Jack. You already know Trudy, don't you?"

Trudy smiled at the blue beam. "Good to see you, Mike."

Jack still wasn't sure what was really going on. "Mike?"

"Mike," the beam pulsed. "Very nice to meet you, Jack."

Jack had never met an intelligent, talking shaft of light before. He thought Mike looked a little like the blue lights you saw on top of police cars except he was vertical. Maybe Mike was the Ministry's policeman, which would explain why he was following Cthulhu, checking that he didn't do anything evil. "So are you a policeman?"

Mike changed to a more thoughtful shade of lilac. "A policeman? No! What would make you think that?"

Grey stepped in to explain. "Mike is the Ministry historian. He collects information that he then passes on to the editorial team of the Ministry handbook."

Mike turned blue again and pulsed in agreement. "It isn't the most interesting job in the world, to be honest, but when you're a beam of sentient light and you can't actually touch anything there are a limited number of roles you can undertake."

Jack nodded. He could see how being a beam of blue light might limit your career choices.

Mike pulsed again. "And even on my days off it's sometimes hard to have fun. I'm not allowed to go to the cinema because, being a bright beam of light, I tend to spoil it for the other patrons."

Jack thought that Mike sounded a little sad. But it also made him wonder why Mike had been following Cthulhu.

After all, if you were feeling a little down, Cthulhu was the last person that was going to cheer you up.[27] "So why are you tagging along after Cthulhu?" Jack wondered out loud.

Mike beamed slightly brighter. "Well, actually this is interesting. This is the first time anyone has seen Cthulhu this happy in the last ten millennia. So it's something of a red-letter day."

"Cthulhu's really been sad for that long?"

Mike pulsed. "Yes, thousands of years ago there was a major tragedy in his life. No one apart from the Misery[28] has been brave enough to ask him what it was."

"And what did the Misery say it was?" Jack asked.

Mike shimmered slightly. "That's the second problem—no one's been brave enough to ask the Misery what Cthulhu said."

"Anyway," said Grey, "as interesting as it is talking about Cthulhu and his moods, we need to find you two some towels and then get a Ministry car to take you home."

---

[27] This statement is slightly incorrect. Cthulhu was the second-to-last person who would cheer you up. The last person who would cheer you up would be the Misery.

[28] The Misery, for those of you who have been fortunate enough to not meet him, was a teenage boy who helped train Ministry operatives for special missions. The Misery was possibly the most unhappy being in the universe and the only person who hated the world even more than Cthulhu. Unlike Cthulhu, however, the Misery was not interested in trying to destroy the world. Rather he preferred to just ignore it as much as possible. The Misery suspected that the world was just being horrible to everyone in an attempt to get people's attention. And, frankly, the Misery wasn't going to give in to any kind of universe that was that needy.

FLOODING
SANDBAGS

One of the most effective ways to stop flooding is the use of sandbags. This is a counterintuitive method. As any child who has ever built a sandcastle near the tide will be able to tell you, sand does not stand up very well to the onslaught of water.

What many people don't realize, however, is that even inanimate objects have a memory. The water in the sea can remember having been in many different places throughout its life. It remembers being in pipes and reservoirs, and most of all it remembers being surrounded by glass. As you would expect, water hates glass. When water is put in a glass container it knows that it is about to be drunk (or about to have fish poop in it, which is nearly as bad). Water does not enjoy being drunk. Especially the part where it has to go through the intestines. And even worse, we know precisely what water has to do to escape from a body once it has been drunk. Which is frankly a fate too unpleasant to be discussed.

Water is therefore scared of glass, and this is why, when you watch raindrops on a windowpane, they are always in a hurry to scurry to the bottom and get away from the glass.

As the more educated of you will know, glass is mostly made of silica, which is sand. Therefore water is distinctly wary of sand, worrying that it may change into glass at any moment. This is also why the ocean tide will creep slowly up the beach during a day, pretending to be brave, but eventually it becomes too scared of the sand, turns, and runs back down the beach. This is the effect that scientists call "tides." It is also the reason that sandbags are so effective at keeping water out of houses. Water never wants to try and get past sand, just in case the sand is planning to sneakily turn into glass and trap the water.

Many of you will think that this is ridiculous behavior. And you are right. After all, inanimate objects may have a memory, but generally they aren't very intelligent.

11

RETAIL THERAPY

Jack and Trudy were traveling home in a Ministry car. Jack's shoulder ached from where the water had tossed him into the wall. As he sat back in his seat he groaned.

Trudy didn't say anything; she was staring out the window, lost in thought. Jack wondered what was more important than his sore shoulder. He thought about pointing out to Trudy that she could be a little bit more sympathetic about his injury. However, he knew all too well that would only result in another bruise to add to his already growing "ouch." Instead he decided to groan more loudly.

"GROAN."

Trudy looked at Jack. "What?"

"I'm groaning because my shoulder hurts."

Trudy sighed. "You didn't groan. You *said* 'groan.'"

"Well, all right. I was only acting to get your attention," Jack conceded.

Trudy snorted with contempt. "Well, you aren't very good at it. You're hardly a Hollywood actor."

"I know that—I actually smell quite nice." Jack sniffed his own shoulder and realized that wasn't entirely true. "It's just I have a very sore shoulder and could do with some sympathy."

Trudy gave Jack a look that suggested he was in the wrong car for sympathy. Then she leaned forward and tapped on the glass partition that separated them from the driver. It eased down a fraction of an inch, and Trudy muttered something to the driver. Jack thought about asking Trudy where they were going, but when he saw the look on her face he decided that perhaps he should start learning to like surprises.

"A shopping center?" asked Jack as they walked past the stores. "Hey, look, maybe we could get bandages or something at the pharmacy?"

Trudy kept walking and Jack had to rush to keep up with her.

Trudy stopped outside a shop that had a large, shiny black sign with the words *Neptune's Den* written above it in letters that were clearly meant to look as if they had been made out of seaweed. "In here."

"Really?" Jack asked. "But isn't this like a soap shop?"

As Jack walked into Neptune's Den, he was momentarily stunned by a cloud of perfume smells so dense he felt as if he'd been mugged by an enormous bunch of chrysanthemums.

The shop was full of cleansing products—moisturizers, lotions, unguents,[29] bubble bath, soap, loofahs, sponges, washcloths. Every product that could be used for cleaning the human body could be found in this shop.

Trudy picked up a jar of sparkling pink bath salts, which caught the light and glittered. "Have you ever used any of these things? They're amazing. When I hurt myself in gymnastics training, I put this stuff in the bath and it really helped the pain go away. It's almost like instant healing." Trudy looked along the shelves and also picked up some lotion and a fancy sea sponge Jack could use to apply it.

"All this stuff helps with bruising and muscular pain?" asked Jack as he rubbed his shoulder. "I could be converted, I suppose." He was shocked by how much the sponge cost—after all, who really needed sponges? Wouldn't a washcloth do the same job? Luckily Jack became less shocked when Trudy sighed and said she would pay for it.

While Trudy was paying the cashier, Jack experienced a strange feeling. He was almost certain that he recognized the cashier, but he wasn't sure where from. The cashier's black hair was pulled back in a severe ponytail, and she had eyes that were as green as the sign on the front of the shop.

He decided to talk to her and see if that jogged his memory. "Umm, sorry, but I was just wondering why this stuff is all so expensive?"

---

[29] Very few people know the difference between a lotion and an unguent. They are almost exactly the same in every way. Except that for some reason an unguent costs twice as much.

The cashier flashed a cold smile at Jack. "Well, these are natural products—one hundred percent organic. These sponges are actually picked from the bottom of the ocean. The top-quality products that we sell in these shops will help you hold back the aging process and retain your youth and good looks."[30]

Jack wondered when washing yourself had become so complicated. In the old days he was fairly sure people just dumped a bucket of water from the well over their heads. He also couldn't understand why people were always so obsessed with holding back the aging process. He couldn't wait until he was eighteen and could finally do whatever he pleased. However, the thought of aging sparked something in Jack's head. Suddenly he realized where he had seen the woman before. "Last time I saw you, you were older."

The cashier and Trudy both stared at Jack. "I/she was older?"

Jack nodded. "Yes. At the aquarium."

For the merest split second the woman's face froze. "You must be mistaken. I've never been to the aquarium."

Jack stared at the woman very hard indeed. Apart from the fact that her face was no longer wrinkled and she looked fifty years younger, Jack was almost certain that this was

---

[30] People are often obsessed with holding back the aging process so they can look good forever. This seems a tad unfair for ugly people, who may be able to hold back the aging process, but will still look "young and ugly" rather than "old and ugly." Which doesn't really seem like a good deal to me.

the same woman he had seen walking into the sea at the aquarium.

"I think you may have lost it entirely this time," Trudy said, interrupting Jack's thoughts. "People don't get younger; it's impossible."

Jack knew what Trudy was saying was true, and yet he was sure. He shook his head, pretending to clear it. "Maybe I'm wrong. Sorry, it's been a hard day."

The cashier perked up again. "Hard day? Why not try one of our relaxing bath bombs?"

"Bath bomb?" asked Jack. "That sounds like the least relaxing thing ever."

Trudy laughed. "They aren't real bombs, they just fizz up in the bath, filling it with bath salts and perfume."

Jack looked at the round, orange, powdery ball that the cashier held out to him. "How much is it?"

"You can have it for free with the bath salts, lotions, and sponges your friend bought." The strange cashier smiled, and it sent a shudder through Jack's body.

JACK AND JILL
Fetching a Bucket of Water from the Well

"Jack and Jill" is a cautionary tale to which all operatives should pay attention. Jack and Jill went up the hill to fetch a pail of water. This is stupidity personified. If there is one thing we know it is that water will always flow downhill. Therefore Jack and Jill should have waited at the bottom of the hill for the water to come to them.

This would have prevented tumbling injuries and collateral damage to crowns.

12

THE THIRD DEGREE

After the Ministry car dropped them at home, Jack used a skillful combination of pretending he was doing homework and hiding in his room to avoid getting asked any questions by his parents. However, when he came down for dinner his father was ready for him sitting patiently at the kitchen table reading a newspaper. Jack's father's mustache was looking at the horoscopes. Jack's mother had just finishing setting plates of spaghetti Bolognese out for them all.

Jack's father started the questioning. "Did you get dropped off by that Trudy girl's father?"

"Um, yeah."

"That's the second time that's happened. When are we going to meet this Trudy girl?" Jack's father asked. His mustache agreed that it was a good question.

"How about never, Dad?"

"Well, if she's your girlfriend . . ."

Jack said nothing but slumped into a chair and took a mouthful of the spaghetti Bolognese. His parents had always told him not to speak with his mouth full; maybe this was a good way to avoid questions. However, it merely gave his mother a chance to start asking questions of her own. "Jack, I was just upstairs hanging up your uniform. Why has the end been cut off your tie?"

"Yes, umm, perhaps that was in some way related to . . ."

"And your trousers were very damp with a hole in the leg."

"It's like this. . . . ," said Jack, stalling desperately for time. "Ummm . . . one of the teachers asked me to help carry a refill bottle to the water cooler in the teacher's lounge."

"That doesn't explain anything," said his mother, becoming more impatient and suspicious.

"Ah, no, well . . . I got David to help me."

"David!" both his parents said at once.

"Well, that explains it," said his father.

"I'm surprised you made it back from school alive." His mother shuddered. "Look, we don't mind you hanging around with David; he's a nice boy. But you have to avoid trying to do anything with him that involves the possibility of falling over, being crushed, or anything like that."

Jack smiled. Sometimes it was good to have a friend who was almost legendary for his clumsiness. Jack bolted down the last mouthful of his spaghetti and stood up.

"Do you mind if I have a bath tonight? I've had a hard day and I need to relax."

"A relaxing bath?" Jack's mother raised an eyebrow.

"Yes, I've got myself a bath bomb."

"You got yourself a bath bomb?" Jack's father raised an eyebrow.

"Well, a friend got me a bath bomb."

"A friend got you a bath bomb?" Jack's mother raised her other eyebrow.

"What's with the questions? Trudy bought me a bath bomb."

"Trudy bought you a bath bomb?" Jack's father raised his other eyebrow.

Jack sighed. At least now that all his parents' eyebrows were raised they couldn't make fun of him anymore.

"Yes, Trudy is my friend and she bought me a bath bomb. But we're just friends."

"Just friends?" said Jack's father and raised his mustache.

Jack sighed so deeply that he almost passed out. "If either of you want me, I shall be upstairs in the bath pretending I am a shipwrecked orphan."

MINISTRY OF S.U.IT.S HANDBOOK

HOROSCOPES
WHY HOROSCOPES ARE 100% ACCURATE

Many people feel that horoscopes are antiscientific nonsense. After all, how can there only be twelve different types of people in the world? But actually horoscopes are 100 percent accurate. It's just that originally they weren't meant for people.

The clue is there in the names of the various astrological signs. People aren't fish or lions or goats. Star signs were originally not meant to be used depending on what time of the year someone was born—but rather on what kind of creature they were or what job they did. Therefore, the forecasts made by horoscopes used to be incredibly accurate.

A typical horoscope for Cancer the Crab would normally have read, *Today you will mainly wander around a rock pool. You might nip someone with one of your claws at some stage.* If you were Gemini the Twins, your horoscope would normally read, *The chance of your bumping into someone who looks a lot like you is fairly high today.*

The most boring horoscopes were always those for Libra the Scales, which generally read, *Unless someone wants to do a chemistry experiment, it looks like another day staring at the inside of the Science Room cupboard for you.*

Generally the most enigmatic of all the horoscopes is that of Taurus the Bull. Back when horoscopes were proper horoscopes this would almost always read, *Stay away from mad scientists; that would end badly. Also, try not to get lost in any mazes.*

Today's horoscopes are pale imitations of those of the classical era.

13

THE WORLD'S MOST BIZARRE
GAME OF CHARADES

Jack changed into his dressing gown and turned the tap to start the bath running. The water pipes made a clanking noise, which was something that Jack always thought was slightly odd. His parents said that the water pipes made that noise because they were old, but that didn't seem to make any sense. Why would water make a clanking and banging noise just because you had put it in a pipe? Water didn't make a clanking noise if you put it in a glass—even if you left it on your bedside cabinet overnight.

While the bath was running Jack read the instructions on the bath bomb.

Run bath. Hold bath bomb a few inches above the water and drop it in. Enjoy your relaxing bath!

Seems easy enough, Jack thought.

The bath was almost full and Jack leaned over to turn off the hot tap. He tested the water to make sure it was piping hot as he liked it. Now to add the bath bomb . . .

Jack's hand hovered above the water for a second. There was a thought in the back of his mind.

Why was it called a bath bomb? I mean, weren't bombs generally considered bad things? Didn't they hurt people? He'd never once heard a story on the news announcing "*A bomb went off today, making six people smell nice and causing dozens in the surrounding area to feel very relaxed indeed.*"

So to call something pleasant a "bath bomb" was very strange indeed. Unless it was a kind of cruel joke? Two weeks ago, before he joined the Ministry of SUITs, Jack would never have been quite this suspicious. But now . . . well, it was better to be safe than sorry. He walked over to the shower cubicle and got behind the folding Plexiglas screen. Then after crouching down as low as he could he lobbed the bath bomb toward the water.

For a second the orange powdery ball seemed to hang in the air before splashing into the water. There was a loud fizzing followed by an enormous bang and crash. A jet of water shaped like a mushroom cloud spouted out of the bath. The bath shattered and small pieces of it flew across the room. One piece hit and cracked the shower screen Jack was crouched behind. Jack threw himself back against the tiled wall in surprise. The surprise faded quickly, however, as this kind of thing seemed to be happening a lot in his life recently.

After checking that he hadn't been injured, Jack stood up and stepped out of the shower. He had briefly thought that the strangest thing he was going to see that day was an exploding bath bomb destroying his parents' bathroom. As usual he was quite badly wrong. Lying amongst the wreckage of the bath was an enormous black spider that looked slightly stunned. As if the bath bomb had not been enough, Jack now had to cope with the reality that a giant spider had been trapped in the cavity beneath his bathtub. How long had it been there? Luckily, the spider was mostly unharmed, as most of the blast had been absorbed by the ceramic bath. But then again, was that lucky?

The spider's body was almost the size of an exercise ball and its legs were at least four feet long. The spider gazed up at Jack with two sets of three eyes grouped closely together.

The sight of a strange creature in an unusual place with so many legs sent a shudder through Jack as he remembered the crab. He wondered if the spider was going to attack him. The bathroom was far too small to be able to use The Speed effectively. Jack backed into the shower cubicle again, drawing the screen in front of him. He really hoped this was as strange as things were going to get today. Then a thought hit him. How was he going to explain a demolished bath and a giant spider to his parents? He wasn't even sure he could have explained it to himself.

The spider started banging its legs frantically on the floor. It rapped and knocked at a prodigious speed.

"Why does everyone seem to be trying to tell knock-knock jokes today?" Jack muttered.

The spider stopped and seemed to be thinking for a moment. Then it held up two of its legs and joined them together. It seemed as if it was shaking hands with itself. Jack slowly leaned out from behind the screen and held out a hand. The spider extended a leg for Jack to grab hold of, and they slowly shook appendages.

"Okay, so you're friendly. But what are you doing here? You'll understand that I'm suspicious. Because you're a giant spider who was hiding under my bath."[31]

From outside the room Jack heard his parents running up the stairs.

"That'll be my parents coming up to see what the explosion was. If they find you here, they'll think . . . Well, I don't know what they'll think, because I'm not really sure what I think. Who or what are you? Apart from a giant spider that was hiding beneath the bath—because that much is obvious."

The spider stroked his chin with four legs for a moment and then held a leg up in front of himself. Using his limbs in a most amazing way, the spider contorted himself into a series of letters that spelled out a single word—

S. . . . . U. . . . . I. . . . . T. . . . . S

---

[31] Jack had used all the words in that sentence before in his life. However, he had never used them in precisely that order. Jack wondered if, when he had completed his time in the Ministry, he would have used all the words ever thought up, in every conceivable order.

"The Ministry? . . . You're an operative. . . . Or you just know . . . ?"

Before Jack could finish his sentence he could hear his parents knocking at the locked door. "Jack, there was an explosion!" It was his mother's voice.

"There's water coming through the ceiling downstairs," shouted his father.

"Yes, but we're mainly worried that you're okay."

"Oh, um, yes, that too . . ." said his father sheepishly. "Are you okay?"

Jack looked at the door and then at the spider. The spider pointed one long hairy leg at the window over the sink. Jack ran over and opened it. Before Jack could even offer to give it a leg up the spider had jumped onto the sink, clambered up the wall, and squeezed out the window. The last Jack saw of him was one hairy, beclawed leg waving through the window.

That was not the relaxing bath I was hoping for, Jack thought as he opened the door to his parents.

"What happened?" his father asked, surveying the wreckage with a look of horror.

Jack sucked his teeth. "I think it must have been a faulty bath bomb. Or maybe there was something wrong with the plumbing." The pipes under the bath were broken and twisted and still leaking water. "You know the way the pipes are always making a clanking sound? Maybe there was something more wrong than we thought." Jack steeled himself to be shouted at.

His mother hugged him. "As long as you're safe." That was the thing about mothers. They were brilliant.

SPIDERS
WHY THEY ARE SO GOOD AT CLIMBING

Scientists over the years have claimed that spiders are so good at climbing because they have sticky feet that adhere to walls. This is of course ridiculous. Things that stick are not good at climbing. They are good at sticking. That is what sticking means. It means that you have an ability to stay in the same place that you are put. If sticky things were good at climbing, that would mean that the next time you need the glue you wouldn't need to look through the drawer that you keep old hooks, dud batteries, Scotch tape, and small candles in. Instead the conversation in your house would go something more like this:

"Hey, Mum, can you bring me up a broom handle? The glue stick's escaped and climbed onto the ceiling again."

This hardly ever happens.

The real reason that spiders are good at climbing is because they have eight legs. If you ever have to climb something particularly difficult, the easiest thing to do is to ask a friend to give you a "leg up."

Spiders having eight legs can continually *give themselves a leg up* by forming a cradle of two of their other legs under a third. This makes them the world's greatest climbers.

Some physicists have said that this is ridiculous and have said that it would be similar to saying that you could pull yourself up by your own hair. Something they claim is patently impossible. However, it isn't impossible at all; you just have to *try really hard*. The reason that most physicists can't do this is because they spend all their time in the lab rather than the gym. No wonder they can't pull themselves up by their own hair when most of them couldn't even do a chin-up.

Some scientists have even suggested that spiders use little tiny hooks on their feet to climb, like you find on Velcro. Anyone who has ever had experience with Velcro knows that this is ridiculous. Spiders are silent creatures who scurry across the wall without your even noticing them. Velcro is incredibly noisy and makes a huge ripping sound when you pull it away. If spiders actually had Velcro on their feet, you would constantly be interrupted while watching television by a spider in the corner doing what would essentially be the world's noisiest tap dance.

14

BREAKFAST IN BED
TUESDAY

Jack was surprised at how easily he managed to go to sleep. Although danger was stimulating, it was also tiring. Which was good, because otherwise his life as a Ministry agent would have meant he was continually plagued by insomnia.

When Jack opened his eyes in the morning, the first thing he saw was a tray filled with bacon, sausages, and two poached eggs sitting on his bedside cabinet. His mother was also sitting on the side of the bed. Jack's keen investigative abilities told him that it was highly likely that these two things were somehow connected.

"How are you this morning?"

"Fine," said Jack. He was suspicious that his mother was up to something.

"I've brought you some breakfast."

Jack looked at the breakfast. If it had been called a

breakfast bomb,[32] he might have been reluctant to try it, but as it wasn't he tucked in immediately.

"What's all this about?"

"I just wanted to give you breakfast in bed as a bit of a treat. You got a big shock last night."

"Mmmm, that's right, I did," said Jack between mouthfuls of bacon. "Just to be crystal clear on that—you aren't holding me in any way responsible for the bathroom being blown up?"

Jack's mother smiled and shook her head. "Of course not. It must have been a faulty chemical in the bath bomb or the plumbing, like you said. You're only twelve, Jack. You're hardly capable of blowing things up."

"Yes," agreed Jack as he shoveled a yolky bit of sausage into his mouth. "That's true." He was incredibly glad that his mother didn't know anything about his adventure the previous week when he had been instrumental in blowing up a steam-powered dinosaur.

"Anyway, your dad and I were thinking. Maybe you should take today off school."

"What?" Jack had only half been listening as he was wondering if there was an age at which it was all right to start blowing things up.[33] "No, Mum, I really want to go to school."

---

[32] If Jack had really been thinking, he would have been more suspicious. After all, sausages are called bangers sometimes. However, on this occasion we can forgive his lack of suspicion, as the sausages were supplied by his mother and it was the first thing in the morning, before Jack has even kick-started his thinking with a shower.

[33] There is. It's sixteen. When you're sixteen you're allowed to blow

"Really?" Jack's mother put her hand to his forehead to test his temperature. "I offer you a day off school and you say you actually want to go? Maybe you were concussed in that blast."

"I'm fine, Mum!" said Jack as he wolfed down the last piece of egg. "I just want to go to school and see my friends."

Jack bolted out of his room and jumped into the shower. For some reason he always thought better after a shower. He couldn't help wondering why that was.

<hr>

When Jack got on the school bus, he made straight for the seat beside David. A kind person would have said that David had saved the seat for Jack. A more realistic person would have observed that David didn't really need to save the seat, as no one wanted to sit beside David. It wasn't that David was disliked, it was more that he was so clumsy that no one ever noticed if he got a tan as his base skin color was ninety percent bruise. His thatch of dirty-blond hair and angular limbs made him look like a trigonometry diagram of a scarecrow. Sadly, few people sought out his company, although it never really bothered him. David was as odd as a thousand right socks.

"Hey, Jack, I covered for you in yesterday's classes."

"You'll never guess what happened to me last night."

"Was it something unusual?" asked David.

"Yes."

"Mmmm," replied David. "Then you're right, I'd never guess. If it was something normal, I'd probably stand a chance at guessing. But not if it's something unusual."

<hr>

things up, but you're still not allowed to vote, for some reason.

Jack would have assumed that anyone else was pulling his leg, but he knew that David was being both bizarrely and deadly serious. David carried on with his whimsical train of thought. "I mean, I might have been able to guess if you'd just been watching TV, or playing a video game or having a bath. But I'd never guess if it was something unusual. I mean, it's hard to guess things when they're unusual. That's kind of what the word 'unusual' means."

"Actually, I was having a bath. . . ."

David turned and looked at Jack. "Jack, that isn't unusual."

David and Jack both simultaneously sighed at each other.

When Jack and David got to school, poor Trudy was waiting for them. Jack could tell that she was itching to tell them something and so quickly got in with his conversation first.

"You nearly got me killed last night! Never take me to a soap and sponge shop again!"

Trudy's eyes widened in surprise. "What happened?"

Jack explained about the bath bomb and the massive spider that had been hidden in his bathroom.

David tutted. "You didn't mention any of that earlier. That would have been quite unusual."

"There's something going on here," Trudy said. "The criminal fish escaping from the Ministry, exploding cleansing products, spiders under baths, women walking into the sea, giant crabs. It's all water based."

Jack nodded.

"You two and your conspiracy theories." David laughed. Jack was amazed that David could be so incredulous despite the fact that the previous week he had been kidnapped and almost surgically altered to be a pirate. David's world didn't seem to follow any kind of normal or sensible rules.

"I think we need to go back to Neptune's Den and see what's happening there." Jack wanted to know why the woman in the shop had tried to kill him. Although he was more than a little scared of the soap shop in case, alongside the bath bombs, there were exploding washcloths or poisonous toothbrushes.

"We can maybe go there later, but we've got something else we need to do first," said Trudy. "There's something you need to see, Jack. I've been waiting. Something very odd happened at the school yesterday."

Jack thought it was going to have to be very odd indeed to beat exploding bath bombs and giant spiders.

MINISTRY OF S.U.I.T.S HANDBOOK

INSOMNIA
How to Get to Sleep

If you ever find yourself wide awake due to having an overstimulating day, one of the easiest ways to fall asleep is simply to count sheep. Traditionally, people think that counting sheep is a monotonous task and thus aids sleep. This is not even remotely true. Counting large amounts of anything is boring, but if merely adding things up made people fall asleep, then accountants and quantity surveyors would need four-poster beds instead of ergonomic office chairs.

The real reason that sheep make people drowsy is because they look so much like fluffy clouds. If you are continually looking at or imagining sheep, a switch in your brain starts to assume that you must be lying down on your back staring at the sky. Because the switch assumes you are lying down it also assumes that you want to go to sleep and releases a chemical that makes you instantly tired.

Naturally the effect of sheep makes New Zealand, which has seven sheep for every one person, a very dangerous place to visit. If you aren't careful you may accidentally start counting sheep, and before you know it you'll have slipped into a coma.

Many of you may wonder how shepherds manage to deal with such large numbers of sheep without being perpetually drowsy. If you wish to know the answer, please refer to the handbook section **Whistling: Sheepdogs**.

15

A-MAZE-D

Trudy led Jack and David through the school, heading for the back entrance and the playing fields. As they pushed past some of the other pupils, Jack could hear someone quietly singing to himself something about a "sparkling night." Jack looked to see where the song was coming from—it seemed to be Edwyn.

Edwyn had always been a strange kid. And he had become even more strange since the "hero" Static had saved him from a group of bullies last week. Static himself was a bit of an oddball—a kid who believed that the ability to build up a static charge of electricity by shuffling his feet had turned him into a superhero.

Jack thought that maybe he ought to stop and speak to Edwyn and offer to arrange some kind of counseling. However, Trudy was striding ahead and he had to rush to keep up.

They arrived at the edge of the playing fields but were

stopped from going any farther by an enormous sign reading *KEEP OUT—DANGER—FRACKING*[34] *IN PROGRESS by Order of Poseidon International Drilling Company.*

Jack was confused. "What is all this?"

Trudy handed Jack a sheet of paper. "Apparently these notices went up all around the school yesterday." Jack read the note, which explained that it was suspected that there were enormous gas reserves hidden underneath Northern Ireland and that drilling was taking place to establish the value of this important fuel.

Jack handed the note back to Trudy. "But this doesn't make any sense—we know that there isn't gas underneath the playing fields—all that's under there is a gigantic hole that the pirates dug when they were trying to turn the country into an enormous galleon."

"Exactly," agreed Trudy. "So what are they up to?"

The three friends watched as groups of construction workers went about their business on the playing fields. As of yet there wasn't actually any drilling taking place, but dozens of trucks were churning up grass carrying massive steel girders back and forth.

---

[34] For those of you who don't know, *fracking* is the name for a process called "hydraulic fracturing." This is a way of drilling into the ground, then pumping in water to try and crack rocks to release natural gas. The natural gas can then be used to heat water and houses. Many of you will think that this sounds like a ridiculous explanation. And of course it is. The real and more sinister reason for fracking will only become apparent in Chapter Forty-seven of this book.

In the center of the playing fields, three cranes were helping to erect an enormous platform. In the middle of the platform a large drill was being placed.

"This looks bad," said Jack.

David shrugged. "I don't know. At least if there's one less soccer field, we might not have to do P.E. this week."

Jack looked at David incredulously. "Last time something like this happened, you got kidnapped and nearly had an arm and leg amputated."[35]

"If it means that we don't ever have to do P.E. again, that's a risk I'm willing to take."

Trudy nudged Jack and pointed. "Look what they're doing now."

Dozens of trucks had arrived carrying large panels of corrugated iron. Workers were slowly putting them up around the platform, walling it off from sight.

"There's something that they don't want us to see."

"Yeah," Trudy agreed, "which makes me want to see it even more."

---

[35] David is almost literally saying that he would give his right arm not to have to play football again. It should be noted that this saying means you really want something more than almost anything else. In the spider world the same expression merely means that you'd quite like something—after all, you have a good deal more limbs than you really need. It is difficult to definitively state how many legs are the perfect number. (Some people have suggested that three is good; if you do not believe this, please discuss with your nearest stool.) In the snake world it is a phrase that is never used except sarcastically.

The bell rang and Trudy, Jack, and David reluctantly went to class.

<hr />

"Aren't you going to get the bus home?" David asked at the end of the day.

Jack shook his head. "We're going to stay here and see what's happening with the fracking. We'll sneak in after the builders leave."

"Okay, well, I'm going home. There's going to be a documentary about newspaper shops on TV tonight. I really want to see that."

As much as he was his best friend, Jack never really understood what motivated David. "Are you sure you don't want to come with us, David? I mean, there are bound to be secrets and weird stuff and adventure."

David just stared at Jack. "Sometimes I wonder if you listen to anything I say, Jack. A documentary—about newspaper shops." David stressed every syllable of the phrase *newspaper shops*. In fact, Jack suspected he had actually thrown in a couple of extra syllables just to make his point.

"Sorry," said Jack, "I wasn't thinking—a documentary about newspaper shops. Of course you want to go home."

David wandered off toward the bus and Jack turned back to where Trudy was standing. "Do you think David's getting weirder?"

Trudy considered this. "Well, I've only actually known him for a week, but I'm going to go out on a limb and say yes."

Jack and Trudy were crouching at the side of the playing fields, watching the last few construction workers packing up before heading home for the night. The construction site had changed enormously since they had left it that afternoon. Dozens of sheets of corrugated iron had been put up, making walls around the drilling platform, which could still be seen towering into the sky at the center of all the construction.

"What did you tell your parents?"

"I phoned and told them I was studying at your house. They said they'd like to meet you sometime."

Trudy looked quizzically at Jack. "Why?"

"You're my friend. Parents care about who their children spend time with. Don't your parents want to meet me?"

Trudy looked at Jack sadly. "Shut up, Jack." Jack wasn't sure why, but he knew better than to ask any questions.

A few moments later and all the workers had finally left. Jack was slightly disgusted at the mess that they had created throughout the day. Clearly, none of the builders had thought to bring a packed lunch with them, and the playing fields were scattered with burger wrappers from fast-food restaurants. Jack started gathering them up and taking them over to a bin that was half filled with building debris. Jack stopped when he noticed Trudy staring at him.

"What?" he said defensively. "I want to save the world, but I also want it to be tidy."

Trudy grabbed Jack by the arm and hauled him over to the enormous wall of corrugated iron in the center of which was a single wire mesh gate. A sign on the gate read *PRIVATE*

PROPERTY—Poseidon International Drilling Company—KEEP OUT by Order of Chief Executive Ms. Regina Maris.

"This gate looks as good an entrance as anywhere else to me," said Trudy.

An enormous green padlock held a thick black bolt in place to stop the gate from opening. "No way we're going to break our way through this. Looks like we're climbing." Trudy stuck the fingers of her one good arm through the mesh gate and clambered over it in a matter of seconds. Even with two arms it took Jack considerably longer and several tries. He secretly wished to himself that he had an extra leg so he could have given himself a leg up.

"We have a problem," Trudy said. They had both expected that once inside the fence they would have been able to stride straight over to the drilling platform. But in front of the gate they had climbed over was another long wall of corrugated iron. They couldn't move forward—only to their left or right.

"What is this?"

"This," sighed Trudy, "is a maze."

"Why would anyone build a maze around a drilling platform?"

"Because they don't want us to see what they're doing. And we've just shown that people can climb over gates. Locks can be picked. Guards can be fooled. But a maze is something a lot more difficult indeed. There isn't any way to fool a maze. We'll just have to try and solve it."

Jack laughed. "Mazes are easy. Follow me." He strode confidently down the right path.

Half an hour later, Trudy and Jack stood at the center of a crossroads. Jack was stroking his chin to help himself think. It was largely ineffective.

"So mazes are easy?" questioned Trudy.

"I may have revised my opinion in relation to that," Jack admitted. "You see, I was thinking of the mazes they put on place mats and wrappers at burger joints. You know the ones you trace a path through with a pencil. But as it turns out those are only easy because you're looking at them from above, with a pencil. Mazes are much harder when you're actually in them."

"So what you're saying is that this would be easier if we had an enormous pencil and a helicopter?"

Jack considered. "Yes, yes it would. I don't suppose you have either?"

Trudy pretended to check her pockets. "I think if I'd worn my other jacket . . . but in this one, no."

Jack sat down on the grass and slumped back against a corrugated iron wall. "Then we are very lost indeed."

Trudy poked at Jack with the toe of her shoe. "Don't give up."

Jack looked up at her. "Oh, I'm not giving up. I'm just tired. I'm going to sit here and get a little rest. Then when I've gotten my energy back. Then . . . that's when I'm going to give up."

Trudy tutted, but the noise was almost entirely drowned out by a bellowing sound from somewhere deep within the maze. It sounded like the howl of a creature in great anguish. An *enormous* creature in great anguish. Jack didn't mind the anguished sound. It was the *size* of the anguished sound that concerned him most.

Trudy shivered a little. "Maybe it's time we should give up."

Jack shook his head. "No, *now* I'm too scared to give up. I'll let you know when my emotional state returns to a normal enough level to actually do anything constructive."

Trudy put out a hand and hauled Jack back onto his feet.

"Which way?" Jack asked.

Trudy looked and pointed. "There's a corner down that way, let's head for it."

When Jack and Trudy turned the corner they bumped into something. Something that shocked them.

MINISTRY OF S.U.IT.S HANDBOOK

HANSEL AND GRETEL
THEIR ORIGINAL PLAN TO AVOID GETTING LOST IN THE FOREST

Many fairy tales have been mistold over the years. One example of this is "Hansel and Gretel." People will tell you that Hansel and Gretel left a trail of bread on their way into the forest, which was then eaten by birds. This is clearly ridiculous. If you are going into a hostile environment, the last thing you want to be doing is throwing your only available rations about the place.

The truth, of course, is that their evil stepmother wanted to make doubly sure that Hansel and Gretel would die. So in addition to getting their father to leave them in the middle of the forest she also gave them a poisoned loaf.

Gretel spotted this immediately and told Hansel not to eat the bread but rather to drop pieces of it on the ground. Their plan was never to follow a trail of bread out of the forest but rather follow a trail of bread-poisoned crow corpses. Sadly Hansel and Gretel got distracted by the gingerbread house and the rest is culinary.

In the event that you ever do get caught in a forest or jungle, never use your only food supply to lay a trail. For that matter, don't use it for shelter or makeshift clothing either. Any decent survivalist knows this. It is also the reason you never see Bear Grylls wearing a porkpie for a hat.

16

THE SPARK KNIGHT

"Owwww!"

Jack was in pain, but was more stunned to hear Trudy cry out as well. Could anything hurt Trudy? What were they up against? It must be something horrific, something deadly, something . . . something that was wearing a white shirt tied around its neck and a school tie with two holes cut in it for a mask.

"Dawkins! What are you doing here?" Jack shouted, relieved but angry at the same time. After all, Dawkins wasn't really dangerous. He was just a slightly deluded classmate who thought that the fact that he could generate small charges of static electricity had turned him into the world's worst-costumed superhero.

Dawkins sighed. "Can't you at least call me Static? I've been working on the costume."

Jack looked at Static. The costume had been considerably

improved. The white shirt had the arms cut off and now actually looked a lot more like a cape. He also had added little bits of color to the rest of the costume by adding cut-up school ties to it. And he had a pair of rubber gloves tucked into his belt. Having said that, he still didn't look much like a superhero.

Trudy was rubbing her arm where she had touched Static. "You shocked me."

"Of course I did! I'm Static, also known as the Spark Knight. I noticed there was something strange going on out here and so I decided to investigate after school. That's what heroes do. Y'know . . . investigate stuff . . ."

"But there's no carpet[36] out here, so how did you . . . ?"

Static pointed back, presumably toward the school. "I built up a huge charge in the school before coming out here so I could be ready if anyone attacked me." Static lifted the rubber gloves out from his belt. "That's what these are for. I put them on once I'm charged up so I can touch things without losing my shocking powers. But when I heard your voices I thought it might be enemies, so I got ready for action."

Trudy sighed. "Jack, you know the way you asked if I thought David was getting stranger?"

---

[36] Static's awesome power was based on building up electricity charges by rubbing his feet on polyester carpet. His was the second-worst origin story for a superhero ever. If you are interested, the worst superhero origin story ever is that of Tea-Towel Boy. Sadly they no longer publish Tea-Towel Boy comics, as he was eventually killed by his archnemesis the Dishwashing-Machine Avenger.

"Yeah."

"He's not the only one."

"What are you guys doing out here anyway?" Static asked.

Jack and Trudy exchanged knowing glances. They had to tell Static something ... but they didn't want him to know everything about the Ministry.

"Same as you really. We just wanted to find out what was going on."

"Great, we can form a super team. Except—well, you guys don't have any superpowers, do you?"

Jack and Trudy both laughed.

"Stop laughing!" Static stamped his foot. "I do SO have superpowers. And people have started singing songs about me. And calling me the Spark Knight."

Jack thought back to earlier in the school day. He remembered Edwyn walking past him, humming and mumbling something about a sparkling knight. "Dawki ... sorry ... Static, that's just Edwyn. And I think he isn't really singing songs. He's more kind of mumbling insanely to himself."

Static's mouth contorted in an angry frown. Jack tried to appease him. "Look Static, why don't you just go back the way you came and ..."

Trudy caught Jack by the arm. "Let him come with us."

"What? But ..."

"There's something bellowing in this maze. And it might be in front of us and it might be behind. But either way we'll be safer if we all stick together."

Static had folded his arms and was pouting. "Well, maybe we don't want to go with you."

Jack was about to shout at Static and then he realized that there was something strange in what Static had said. "Stat . . . wait a minute. We? Oh, please don't tell me that you brought Edwyn, your biggest superfan, with you."

Static spluttered. "Ridiculous! You think I would endanger a civilian in what is clearly superhero business? Do you think I would put the kindly but innocent Edwyn in harm's way? That I would violate the superhero code so egregiously?"[37] Static threw his head back and stood with his hands on his hips, trying to look like a hero. Jack thought he didn't really look much like a hero. He looked a lot more like a bit of an idiot playing a game of "I'm a little teapot, short and stout" who hadn't yet decided which arm he wanted to use as his spout.

Jack wasn't entirely sure why, but Static's speech had actually made him feel a bit ashamed of himself. "Well, when you put it like that, of course you wouldn't. . . . I'm sorry that . . ."

"Anyway"—Static removed his hands from his hips—"when I asked him if he wanted to tag along he said he was going to be too busy building the Static Signal tonight."

"Uh . . . huh . . . what?" Jack was confused again. Trudy was intelligently staying out of this conversation.

"The Static Signal. It's a big light that shines the *Danger—Electricity* sign in the air. That way the city can use it to summon me when they are most in need."

---

[37] For those of you who are impressed by the fact that Static used the word *egregiously* in the correct way, it is important to know that he had a Superhero Word of the Day Calendar. Today's word had been *egregious* and he had been trying to crowbar it into a sentence since he'd gotten up.

Jack started to say something three or four times. Each time he stopped and shut his mouth without uttering a word. After a while he realized that there were some sentences that were so stupid the only reasonable way to respond to them was with a stunned silence.

Jack gathered his thoughts for a few moments before he eventually spoke. "Okay, so if the 'we' you were referring to wasn't Edwyn, who exactly have you brought with you?"

"Every hero needs a sidekick. . . . Let me introduce you to . . . VOLTY."

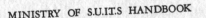

MINISTRY OF S.U.IT.S HANDBOOK

CONTACTING SUPERHEROES
THE USE OF SPOTLIGHTS

At one time, shining enormous spotlights in the sky to summon superheroes was commonplace. However, recently this practice has been discouraged by Ministry Directive 554/45K. A Ministry statistician did some research and discovered that in a period where a superhero spotlight had been used sixteen times, three people had been saved, five cats had been rescued from trees, and three bank robberies had been stopped. Unfortunately, eight pilots flying jet airplanes had been temporarily blinded, causing a series of crashes and over three thousand deaths. This is not a good tradeoff.

The other problem with using enormous spotlights to summon superheroes was that they were only effective at night. Evil geniuses quickly realized this and, following a quick trip down to the local electrical retailer to buy themselves alarm clocks, started planning for the destruction of the planet to take place during the hours of daylight.

Smoke signals were suggested as an alternative for a while; however, this was discouraged when three tenement buildings accidentally burned down. These days law enforcement officers generally find it easier to ask superheroes for their mobile phone numbers or write on their Facebook walls.

17

VOLTY

"Hi guys, I'm Volty. Static's faithful sidekick. Ain't he a swell guy?"

Jack was glad to see that Trudy was as stunned as he was. "I thought it couldn't get any more ridiculous—and yet look how wrong I am."

When Static introduced Volty, Jack and Trudy expected a sidekick to jump around the corner of one of the corrugated iron walls. What they had not expected was for Static to pull a handmade glove-puppet out of his pocket.

"You know, if we ever want David to look normal, we could just get him to stand beside Static," suggested Trudy.

Static pouted again. "You both say some very hurtful things sometimes."

"Do you want me to get them, boss, huh? You want me to give them the Volty shock?"

Jack cocked his head to one side. "Static, when you talk

through the glove puppet, you know we can still see your lips move, right?"

"Shut up," said Static. "I'm only starting out. I can't expect to become the world's best hero/ventriloquist overnight. Technically, this is still my origin story."

"You want me to lay the hurt on them, boss? You just say the word. Evildoers beware!"

Jack knew that they should have been concentrating on trying to get to the drilling platform, but there was something fascinating about how odd Static was becoming. Jack couldn't help himself from talking to the puppet. "So do you mind if I ask you, Volty—you seem to be speaking with an American accent. I take it you aren't from around here?"

"That's right, Chief, I'm Volty. I was a young newspaper boy in New York City, always ready with a smart answer and a cheeky reply. Then one day I sneaked away from my newspaper stand early to go and see a big baseball game. The New York Yankees were playing. One of the players hit a long ball and I caught it. Little did I know that the bat he was using was made of a part of King Arthur's Round Table. And the ball was an experimental ball made out of leather taken from a cow that had been genetically modified by a group of alien scientists. And just before I caught the ball it got struck by lightning. And that's what gave me my superpowers!"

Jack scratched his head. "Static, tell me again how *you* got your superpowers."

"What?" asked Static. "You know this. I rubbed my feet on the carpet and it gave me the power to give people shocks."

"Right, right," Jack said slowly, "and doesn't it worry you that your hand puppet has a better origin story than you do?"

Static looked at Jack quizzically for a second before realization dawned across his face. Static turned to look at Volty. *"Gee whiz, boss, they're right! Maybe I should be the superhero and you should be the sidekick."*

There was another bellowing noise from deep inside the maze.

"Guys"—Trudy clapped her hands to get their attention—"as much fun as it is to watch Static get outwitted by his own hand, we've got to get moving. At this rate we could still be here tomorrow morning."

"Great idea! She's a swell broad, that one."

Static fixed Volty with a stern stare. "That's enough of that. Look, you'd better get back to the Static Cave and check that everything's all right in there."

"Aww, boss, do I have to? I want to be here for the action. Vanquishing villains and maybe afterward we can all go for hot d—" Volty was abruptly cut off as Static crammed him into his trouser pocket.

Trudy started walking down one of the branches of the maze. Jack followed.

"Guys!" Static called after them. "Don't you want to go to the center of the maze and find the drill?"

"Well, of course we do."

"Then why are you going that way? This is the fastest route." He pointed down a branch of the maze going in the opposite direction.

Trudy walked back toward Static. "How do you know that?"

"Didn't you notice earlier that there were dozens of builders, but no architects or designers? No one in a suit with a plan."

Jack and Trudy thought back. When they had watched the site earlier they hadn't seen anyone who had looked like an architect.

"So what?" asked Jack.

"Well, if you're going to build a maze, you need a plan. And those guys didn't have a plan. What they did have was a lot of fast food. So before I came in here I picked up one of the wrappers. It had a design for a maze on it—you know, like one of those games for kids to play." Static took a piece of crumpled paper out of the trouser pocket that wasn't currently serving as the Static Cave. "I reckon this is what they used to design the maze—it's been right so far."

Trudy and Jack looked at each other rather shamefacedly. The second-most embarrassing thing in life was to be outthought by your own hand. The *most* embarrassing thing in life was to be outthought by a guy who had just been outthought by his own hand.

SUPERHEROES AND ORIGIN STORIES
INSECT BITES

You may occasionally wonder why there aren't more superheroes in the world. After all, many people are turned into superheroes by something as simple as an insect bite from a radioactive or genetically modified insect. People are getting bitten by insects all the time, so shouldn't the world be literally and metaphorically crawling with superheroes?

The answer, of course, is simple. Although doctors have found a cure for things like malaria, they haven't yet found a cure for radioactive, genetically altered malaria. Sadly, therefore, many potential superheroes die before they even get to use their powers.

For more information on this please see section **Superheroes: Animal Powers.**

18
TRUE HEROISM

By following the burger-wrapper map the small group of heroes made swift progress.

"You know, if someone had said to me last Friday that we'd find ourselves wandering around a maze with a wannabe superhero and his puppet sidekick, following a burger wrapper trying to find a fracking platform...I wouldn't have been at all surprised." Jack was talking to himself. "And that, in a nutshell, just shows you how badly my life has gone off the rails."

"Are you okay?" Trudy asked.

"What? Oh. Yes. Just thinking that if my life is this odd at twelve, what's it going to be like when I hit fifteen? I suppose the one positive is that at least today can't get any weirder."

Trudy punched Jack very hard in the arm.

"What was that for?"

"You know very well what that was for."

And Jack did know very well what it was for. Anytime that anyone said something like that, it was a sure and certain sign that something incredibly weird indeed was about to happen.

Static was leading the way ahead, navigating by using the burger wrapper with the map drawn on it. "Okay, guys, I think we head this way—although I'm not a hundred percent sure—there's a smudge of ketchup on the map here. Just round this corner and . . . oh . . . that's strange." Static froze as he turned around the corner.

If you have any sense whatsoever, you will know that when a man who wears a tie as a mask, believes he has superpowers, and loses arguments with his own hand says that he has seen something strange, then you should prepare yourself for something very, very, very strange indeed.

Jack and Trudy froze. They wanted to make sure they knew what they were dealing with before they took any action.

"What are you looking at, Static? Can you describe it?" Trudy asked.

Static stayed very still indeed. "I wish I hadn't lost my static charge when I bumped into you guys earlier. I can't possibly fight this. But maybe I can hold him off for a while. I mean, you know, while he's eating me, you guys could get away."

Jack's jaw dropped. Whatever was around the corner couldn't possibly shock Jack more than Static's words had. Maybe Static wasn't a superhero, but at the very least he was a garden-variety hero. No matter how deluded Static was, he was just an average boy and yet he was willing to sacrifice his life for theirs.

Trudy was a little bit more skeptical than Jack. "Static. What is it?"

"It's a Minotaur."

Jack gasped. Trudy had sufficient presence of mind to check that Static actually knew what he was talking about. "A Minotaur? As in a creature that's half man and half bull?"

"That's it exactly. But Static isn't afraid of mythical creatures. Static stands for justice and truth." Static pulled the limp Volty puppet out of his pocket and tossed it to Jack. "Jack, take care of Volty for me. Take him to go and live with his grandparents."

Trudy was still skeptical as to how much danger they were in. "Take the puppet to live with his grandparents? What are they? A pair of socks with Ping-Pong balls for eyes?"

"Trudy!" Jack yelped at her. "The guy's trying to be a hero. Don't be so mean."

"Jack, he's been trying to be a hero for a while now. Very badly. I've got a gut feeling that we aren't in as much danger as you might think."

Static bunched his fists and tightened every muscle in his body.

"STATIC AWAY!" Static launched himself at the hidden creature.

Jack leapt forward to try and stop him, but was seconds too late.

MYTHICAL CREATURES
Reasons Not to Be Scared

Many people in the Ministry have asked if they should be scared of mythical creatures. And of course the answer is a simple no. Mythical creatures are mythical. Mythical means that they don't exist. And being scared of something that doesn't exist is very foolish indeed.

However, creatures such as Minotaurs, Dragons, Chimeras, Basilisks, and Wyverns all exist. Therefore they are not mythical creatures. And any sensible person would be very scared of them indeed.

A corollary of this is that it's also a very bad idea to call a Minotaur or Dragon mythical in front of them. As you can imagine, it's very insulting to be told that you don't exist to your face. In these cases, the Minotaur or Dragon will probably try and convince you that they do exist, both by reasoning with you on a philosophical level and also by eating you.

19

ALWAYS GIVE CLEAR INSTRUCTIONS

Jack had been too slow to stop Static. Even as Static ran around the corner Jack could hear the noise of a thump and then two voices going "Ouch." Trudy sauntered behind Jack at a much slower pace.

Static was lying on the ground with a large figure standing over him. Jack should have been shocked and surprised by what he saw, but his overwhelming feeling was one of annoyance. The danger wasn't quite as Static had described it.

"I thought you said Minotaur?"

Static nodded. "I did." He pointed at the figure that had knocked him down. "It is."

The Minotaur nodded in agreement.

"See," said Static. "The Minotaur agrees with me."

Jack turned to the Minotaur. "Do you mind? I'll get to you

in a minute." Jack turned his focus back to Static. "Yes, I appreciate that it's a Minotaur; I understand—half man, half bull. But I think you could have been a bit more clear about just how dangerous this Minotaur is."

"My name is Alan. Umm, your friend seems a little bit odd."

Trudy raised an eyebrow. "He is, but you get used to it in time."

Alan was indeed a Minotaur—half man and half bull. However, he had the body of a bull and the head of a man—a mix that was considerably less frightening than the traditional Minotaur combination.

Jack was considerably more surprised than Trudy. "You can speak!"

Upon later reflection, Jack realized that it was foolish to be surprised by the Minotaur speaking. After all, it had the head of a man with an ordinary mouth, nose, and eyes. The head looked to be relatively young, although it was largely bald with only a few tufts of hair over the ears.

"Of course I can speak. Now, perhaps you'd care to introduce yourselves?"

"Sorry, we didn't mean to be rude," said Trudy. "Alan, this is Static...."

"The Spark Knight!" Static gave a flourish, standing up and putting his hands on his hips again.

"Calm down, Static. This is Jack and I'm Trudy."

Alan held up a hoof and they each shook it in turn.

"Incidentally . . . Static, is it? Just to say I'm sorry for butting you in the chest. The problem with having the body of a bull is that you have an overwhelming urge to run around charging things and butting them with your head."

Jack was wondering if it was rude to ask the Minotaur how he had become a Minotaur. While Jack was considering this, Trudy rushed in.

"So were you always . . . ?"

"A Minotaur?" Alan sighed. "No, not at all. I used to be an ordinary human. But then I tried to make some extra money by signing up for scientific clinical trials—I needed the money for my gym fees. But I hadn't read the flyer properly. I signed up for *mad* scientific clinical trials."

"Which was a bad idea?" Jack guessed.

"Very bad idea." Alan nodded as far as his bull-neck would let him. "Turned out that the mad scientist was doing a bit of work for some Queen Something-or-other. She'd asked for a Minotaur to guard her drilling platform. Unfortunately, the queen hadn't specified that she'd wanted one of those Minotaurs with the head of a bull and the body of a man. And so . . . here I am."[38]

"Who was the queen?" asked Trudy. Jack leaned forward too. Perhaps they were going to get somewhere now.

Alan tried to shrug his shoulders but couldn't. "Sorry, no

---

[38] The lesson to be learned from this story is that, if you absolutely must work with mad scientists, it is imperative that you give them very clear instructions indeed.

This is why if you leave a mad scientist to put together your IKEA furniture you're highly likely to come back and find your TV and DVD set up nestling nicely in the midst of a sideboard/Deathray.

idea. At the time I was more concerned about the fact that I had woken up with a bull's body and wasn't paying that close attention."

"That must be awful," said Jack.

Alan wrinkled his nose. "Actually it's not as bad as you'd imagine. You can get used to anything, given enough time."

There didn't seem to be an answer to that.

"Anyway, Alan, it's been nice talking to you. But we want to go and have a look at the drilling platform so..." said Trudy.

"By all means, go on. Technically I'm meant to be guarding it. But to be honest I tend to leave that to the other fella."

"Other fella?" asked Static.

"Yeah, well, apparently after they made me the queen complained to the mad scientist—so he used the other bits to make..."

A bellowing noise echoed across the maze.

Alan nodded to himself. "That'll be him. He's got my body and the bull's head."

"And this is when it starts to go wrong." Jack sighed.

HYBRID CREATURES
WHEN HYBRID CREATURES GO WRONG

There are a range of hybrid creatures that combine the parts of two different creatures. However, it is vital to ensure that you get the right part of each to achieve the desired effect. Many sailors have been amazed by the beauty of mermaids with the tail of the fish and the upper half of a gorgeous young woman. What few realize is that there is another type of mermaid altogether, with the legs of a human and the upper half of a fish. Sadly there are very few of these creatures left. Legs are of limited use when swimming, so they tend to wander ashore, panic, and then die as their fish heads drown in the fresh air.

Despite the beneficial effects of fish oil, having a fish brain generally means you aren't going to be desperately bright.

20

DRILL PRACTICE

The sounds of a bellowing Minotaur had reminded the heroes that it was time to continue on their way.

"Look, we'd love to hang around and meet your . . . other half," said Jack, feeling fairly sure that this wasn't the right phrase to use, "but we've got to find that drilling platform."

"I'll take you there; I haven't got much else to do here." Alan trotted ahead of them. Jack, Static, and Trudy looked at one another, shrugged, and followed.

"This is all getting very strange," observed Static.

"We'll explain it all to you later," said Jack, despite being fairly certain that they wouldn't. "Here—just in case it gets any stranger, you ought to have this back." Jack handed Volty back to Static, who instantly shoved him into the Static Cave.

Alan quickly led them to the drilling platform. "Here you

are," said Alan before wandering off to scratch his left flank against some of the corrugated iron.

"What a nice Minotaur," Trudy observed.

The drilling platform looked almost exactly as they had expected. An enormous drill shaft rose up from the ground, surrounded by platforms, scaffolding, and joists.

"It looks like a fracking drill to me," Jack said.

"Do you really have any idea what a fracking drill would actually look like?" Trudy asked.

"Okay, it looks like what I imagine a fracking drill would look like," Jack corrected himself. "But there is something odd about it. If they were drilling for gas, I'd have expected some kind of tanks—somewhere to store the gas. The only thing this drill looks like it could do is make a hole in the ground. But that . . . that doesn't make any sense."

Static had turned to Jack and Trudy. "Hey guys, I'm going to ask Volty what he thinks we should do." Thankfully Static didn't get a chance to remove Volty from his pocket/the Static Cave as he froze in fear.

Jack and Trudy were looking at Static. "Do you think we're going to see the other Minotaur when we turn around?" asked Jack.

"Pretty much."

Jack and Trudy spun on their heels and were confronted by an enormous hulking brute of a Minotaur. Including the twisted yellow horns on top of its angry bull face, it stood eight feet tall. A gold ring was threaded through its nostrils and long trails of saliva fell from the corner of its mouth. The human part of the body was also quite scary. It was huge and muscular—the kind of body you normally saw in movies about crazy barbarians. Like a crazy barbarian, it was bare-chested with a pair of leather trousers that had metal studs up the sides. "I think we might be in trouble," said Jack.

Alan trotted over. "Yup, that's my body all right."

"I take it you used to work out?" Trudy asked.

"All the time," confirmed Alan.

"I really wish you'd had some other hobby, like flower arranging."

"That's annoying," said Alan.

"That the bull's going to kill us?" suggested Jack.

"Not that, it's just that the Minotaur is wearing my wig." Alan gestured with a hoof.

Jack hadn't noticed it at first, but Alan was right. Between its two enormous horns the Minotaur had a wig on that was the same color as the tufts of hair behind Alan's ears.

"It's even more annoying because he doesn't even have it on straight," complained Alan.

During this conversation, Static had made the decision that perhaps he wasn't quite set on being a hero after all. He had quietly crawled into a small space between the metal girders that supported the drilling platform.

"Um, Alan, I don't suppose you could talk to the other part of yourself and persuade him to not attack us?" asked Jack.

"We're really not that close anymore. He never calls or anything. Look, guys, I don't want to have to pick a side here. So . . . y'know . . . good luck." And with those final words Alan galloped off into the maze once more.

"Any ideas, Jack?"

Jack tried to think of everything he knew about bulls. Then he had an idea. "Static, throw me the fast-food wrapper."

Static crumpled the fast-food wrapper and threw it to Jack. Jack remembered that last week he had scared a bear with a chair. Bears were scared of chairs because they thought that anyone who could make a chair could kill a tree and trees were the only thing in the forest larger than a bear.

Maybe a Minotaur would be scared of a fast-food wrapper because it would think that anyone who could turn a cow into hamburger would have to be pretty powerful.

Jack took a step toward the Minotaur and held up the wrapper in front of himself, yelling, "YAH!" Jack hoped there was enough smell of hamburger left on the wrapper to scare the Minotaur.

The Minotaur sniffed the air a few times, and then a crazy look came over its eyes. It snorted, tossed its head, and charged at Jack and Trudy, trying to gore them with its horns. Jack and Trudy dived aside in the nick of time as the Minotaur's head clattered into the metal beams of the drilling platform. "Nice work, Jack; you basically just taunted him with the fact that people have been eating his family."

"Mmmm," agreed Jack, "I might not have thought that one through enough."

"Time for The Speed?" suggested Trudy. Jack agreed that this was a brilliant idea. As usual, Trudy conjured up a sad thought much more rapidly than Jack. Jack racked his brains and then remembered the year that his parents had gotten him a Transformer for Christmas. He had spent three hours trying to turn it from a car into a robot before he realized that it wasn't a Transformer. It had just been a toy car. And now it was a broken toy car. He remembered an incredibly sad Boxing Day watching his father failing to glue a remote-control Porsche 911 back together. As he remembered, he slowly felt The Speed seep through his bones.

Trudy had already run back toward the Minotaur. It charged at her again but she leapt and somersaulted in the air. With her one good hand she grabbed hold of the Minotaur's right horn and pulled with all her might. Any other creature would have tumbled backward, but the Minotaur, with its enormous neck and powerful shoulders, barely noticed. It jerked back a step but then steadied itself. The wig fell off its head, which was at least a minor victory.

Trudy landed badly. With one arm still in a sling, she struggled to get her balance, tripped, and fell. The Minotaur turned, snorted in amusement, and lifted its head. It was going to drive itself headlong into the ground, skewering Trudy before she could get to her feet again.

Jack began running toward them, but even with The Speed he was too far away—he'd never get there in time. He could see the muscles in the Minotaur's neck tensing, ready for the strike. Jack's body sagged as he felt completely helpless . . . but at the last minute the Minotaur was distracted by something off to the side.

As the Minotaur glanced away, Trudy scrambled to her

feet and, using The Speed, sprinted across the grass to where Jack was.

They both gazed in amazement. The Minotaur had stopped to pick up the wig and was carefully placing it back onto its head.

"What happened there? I thought I was dead for sure."

MINISTRY OF S.U.I.T.S HANDBOOK

MALE VANITY
WHY MEN WEAR WIGS

Many men feel the need to wear wigs to show how manly they are. Of course, this frequently makes them seem sillier than they would have been otherwise. Interestingly enough, some of the silliest wigs of all time are worn by the guardsmen who stand outside Buckingham Palace. Tourists often mistake their two-foot-tall wigs for hats. However, if you get close enough you will realize that they are in fact wigs and are covered in hair gel.

This is why the British public refer to the guardsmen's enormous wigs as "bearskins"— because under the wig there is literally "bare skin."

Some of you may wonder why so many of Buckingham Palace's guardsmen are bald. The reason is simple: Guarding the queen is a very important job that makes the guards worry a lot. Almost all of the guardsmen have lost their hair due to the stress of their positions.

This is why if you ever visit Buckingham Palace you should not make the bald guards feel self-conscious but should try to raise their self-esteem. This is most easily done by shouting "Hey, dude, great hair!" at the guardsmen.

21

TYPICAL MINOTAUR

Jack's mind was buzzing with a dozen different thoughts at once. "I think I've figured out how we can defeat the Minotaur. But I'm going to need you to buy me some time."

"Great," said Trudy, "because that's worked so well up until now."

Jack ignored Trudy's sarcasm and started looking for what he needed to defeat the Minotaur. Unfortunately, he couldn't see a box anywhere with "Minotaur-defeating equipment" written on it. He was going to have to improvise.

The Minotaur had finally gotten the wig fixed back onto the top of its head. It turned toward Jack, but Trudy started shouting at it. "Hey, Mr. Minotaur! Over here, you big idiot." Trudy picked a rock up and threw it across the field. The rock was thrown with such accuracy that Jack rightly suspected that Trudy may well have done a lot of rock throwing in her life before she joined the Ministry. The rock smacked the Minotaur right on one of its big, floppy ears. It whinnied in pain and then turned to face Trudy with angry, bloodshot eyes. With one enormous foot the Minotaur pawed at the ground, getting ready to charge.

"You owe me for this, Jack; you owe me a lot."

"Just give me five minutes." Jack bolted up a ladder that led to the upper level of the drilling platform. He looked around the platform frantically. There were tools, pipes, sections of metal, and everything you would need if you were a construction worker. But there wasn't the one thing that Jack really wanted. Jack clenched his fists and wished to himself that construction workers wore lipstick.[39]

"Hurry up, Jack; avoiding a Minotaur with one arm in a sling[40] isn't as easy as it looks." The Minotaur charged at Trudy. Trudy stood up straight, looking as if she was about to try a somersault. The Minotaur continued to charge but raised its head, ready to try and catch Trudy with its horns if

---

[39] Jack is the first and will probably be the only person ever to wish this. When most people think about how construction workers look their first thought is that they generally wish the workers wore belts so that you couldn't see quite as much of their buttocks.

[40] Here Trudy means that avoiding a Minotaur while she had one arm in a sling is difficult. She isn't implying that the Minotaur had one arm in a sling. Because it didn't. On this occasion we can forgive her the terminological inexactitude of this statement as she is under a certain amount of pressure. *Because she is trying to avoid a Minotaur with one arm in a sling.*

she flipped in the air. At the last possible moment, Trudy ducked down and dived through the Minotaur's legs. She spun on her good hand and kicked the back of the Minotaur's knee. The Minotaur howled and fell awkwardly, embedding one of its horns in the soil.

Amongst all the building materials Jack had found what he had been looking for. It was a square of shiny metal about three feet along each edge. He spat on it.

Trudy was watching him from the ground. "What on earth are you doing?"

"Just a few more minutes." The metal was grimy from lying unattended. Jack used The Speed and the cuff of his school shirt to polish it at a frantic rate.

The Minotaur had worked its horn free from the ground. Its face was now covered in saliva, grass, and dirt. The wig was stuck to the left horn with a big clod of mud.

Jack dropped the square of metal off the side of the platform and clambered down the ladder after it. The Minotaur charged toward Trudy. She steeled herself to try one last dodge. Jack tapped her on the shoulder, having clambered down beside her.

"Jack! Get out of here. It'll be a lot easier if I try and dodge it by myself."

"We aren't trying to dodge. Here, help me with this."

Jack hoisted the shiny square of metal in front of them. Trudy looked at the metal and realized that Jack's plan was hopeless. The metal was far too thin to deflect the Minotaur's deadly horns. Looking up, she could see that it was too late to dodge. The Minotaur was almost on top of them.

POLISHING
Military Uses

Many people have said that the training soldiers undergo in the army seems pointless. For example, we have all seen films and television programs where soldiers in training are told to polish shoes, belt buckles, and buttons until the Sergeant Major *"can see my face in them."*

Admittedly this seems pointless, as battles are generally dirty and dusty things. However, Sergeant Majors are clever and cunning men. Their plan is simple—when shiny soldiers charge the enemy, the enemy soldiers are dazzled and see buttons, belts, and shoes all reflecting their faces back at them. The enemy then counts the faces and assumes that the opposing side has many more troops than first suspected and undertakes some tactical running away—or retreating, as the army like to call it.

The army is very clever in this way.

22

THE NARROWEST OF MARGINS

At the last moment the Minotaur caught sight of its reflection in the shiny square of metal and came skidding to a stop. Trudy and Jack were both holding their breath. For a few seconds the Minotaur breathed heavily and looked at its reflection. Then it started turning its head one way then another before starting to straighten the wig that still sat askew on its head.

"What's happening?" whispered Trudy out of the side of her mouth.

"Put the mirror down very slowly," Jack said in the same hushed tones. "Once we've moved to a safe distance, I'll tell you."

Very slowly and very gingerly Jack and Trudy lowered the metal square to the ground. As they did so the Minotaur slowly lowered its head, following the sight of its own reflection. When the metal square was on the ground, Trudy carefully leaned it against the side of the drilling platform so it still stood upright. By now the Minotaur was sitting cross-legged on the grass and picking pieces of mud out of its shaggy mane.

Jack and Trudy backed away and slowly moved to a safe distance.

"So what was that about, then?" asked Trudy. "Did you hypnotize the Minotaur with its own reflection?"

Jack shook his head. "No, it's a lot simpler than that. I just thought about what I knew about bulls. Look, you know the way all bulls have a ring through their nose?"

"So? Bulls have nose rings. Big deal."

"Well, don't you think that's unusual? There aren't any other animals that wear jewelry. You never see an octopus with diamond bracelets[41] or a goat wearing a tiara."

Trudy thought about this for a moment. "Actually, I'd quite like to see a goat wearing a tiara—but I'm not sure what you're getting at. Explain!"

"Bulls wear jewelry—so clearly they care about their appearance. They're vain. And I knew this one was particularly vain because instead of skewering you he stopped to pick up the wig. That's why I used the piece of metal for a mirror. I thought that he'd be concerned with his appearance. He saw he was a mess and forgot about killing us to try and tidy himself up a bit."

"You risked our lives on that?"

Jack shrugged. "It worked. Anyway, even if the bull part of the Minotaur hadn't been vain enough to be attracted by a

---

[41] Jack's suggestion here is quite clearly ridiculous. Of course you never see an octopus with bracelets. The cost would be prohibitive. If you're buying jewelry for an octopus, the sensible thing is clearly to go for a necklace.

mirror, the rest of him was made up from one of those guys who spend all their time flexing their muscles in gyms. And you know those guys can't resist a mirror."

Static had emerged from beneath the platform and stood up dusting himself off. "I imagine that's why the Minotaur attacked us. He was probably jealous of how awesome my cape looked."

"I'm pretty sure that wasn't the reason," said Trudy.

"Look, I don't know how long the Minotaur's going to be looking in the mirror. We ought to . . ."

"Get out of here?" Static offered.

Trudy stared at Static. "You may need some practice on the hero thing."

"We ought to check out the drilling platform first and find out what's so important about it that it needed a Minotaur to guard it," Jack suggested.

Jack, Trudy, and Static clambered up the ladder to the platform itself. There was little to see other than the giant drill and massive engine.

Jack kicked part of the engine. A metallic echo rang out. "I think we should try and sabotage this drill somehow. I don't know what it's for, but it's bound to be something bad."

"Really?" asked Static. "Sabotage sounds an awful lot like vandalism, and we really wouldn't want to get in trouble."

Trudy was looking at a small metal hut near the edge of the platform. "Look, most of this thing is made of solid metal. We can't possibly destroy it. But maybe there's some kind of control console inside that hut. We could smash that up." Trudy walked over and reached to open the door of the hut, but at the last second Static grabbed her hand and stopped her.

Jack froze, sure that Static was about to be punched. Trudy's eyes widened in anger, but before she could do anything Static spoke. "Wait! Can't you hear that?"

There was a noise—quiet, almost imperceptible—but definitely there. "It's like a buzzing noise," said Jack.

"Where's it coming from?" asked Trudy.

Static cocked his head to one side and listened intently. Then, turning his head upward, he pointed to the top of the metal hut. "Up there."

Standing close to the hut it was hard to notice, but taking a few steps back Jack could see that there was a small glass tank sitting on top of the hut. They watched it for a few seconds before they realized that inside the tank were perhaps half a dozen sleek shapes slipping through the water.

"Eels?" asked Jack.

Static nodded. "Electric eels. That's what the buzzing sound is."

Trudy frowned, annoyed that Static had turned out to be useful again. "Okay, maybe they're electric eels. So what?" Jack couldn't help wondering if maybe they'd been eels that had escaped from the Ministry's party room.

Static bent down, picked up a screw, and threw it against the door. There was a crack, a small blue lightning bolt, and a strange smell.

Static stared at Trudy. "They're using the eels to electrify the hut."

"He just saved you from getting zapped, Trudy." Jack thought that this would make Trudy better disposed to Static. Of course it didn't. It merely antagonized Trudy more.

"Okay, you little know-it-all. If you know so much about electricity, how do we get inside?" Trudy pushed Static backward a step.

Static rubbed his hands together and his forehead wrinkled with concentration. "Look, since the amazing events that gave me my magical powers . . ."

"Amazing events? Rubbing your feet on a piece of carpet is not an amazing event." Trudy spat the words out.

Static refused to be dissuaded and merely carried on talking in a louder voice.

". . . the AMAZING EVENTS that gave me my magical powers, I've developed the power to channel electricity. Stand back, mortals!"

Trudy turned to Jack in indignation. "Is he calling us mortals?"

Jack nodded. "Well, yeah, but we are mortals, Trudy."

Trudy paused for the briefest of seconds. "I know that. I just don't like *him* saying it."

"TEN FINGERS OF POWER, DO YOUR STUFF!"

Static stretched his fingers out and lunged forward, putting them on the door of the metal hut. There was a crack, a brief blue flash engulfed Static, and then he whimpered and fell backward onto the steel platform.

Jack was frozen to the spot. "Is he . . . is he . . ."

Trudy looked closely. "No—he's still breathing."

Jack let out a long, slow breath. Static may have been an idiot, but Jack felt that he was *their* idiot. "Right, let's get out of here. We clearly can't get into the hut—and the Minotaur isn't going to be distracted forever."

"And do we just leave Static here?"

Jack laughed. "Nice try, but you know you don't really mean that."

Trudy sighed. "I used to be Moody Trudy through and through. Now you've got me caring about people." Trudy grabbed hold of Static's arms. "You take the legs."

The hardest part of moving Static was getting him down the platform's ladder. However, with some effort they managed to lower him down, only dropping him the last five feet or so. They half dragged, half carried him through the maze until they came to the gate again.

"We'll never get him over the gate."

Trudy thought for a minute. Static started making moaning noises.

Quick as a flash Trudy grabbed the rubber gloves from Static's belt and put them back on his hands. Then she climbed over the gate. Even with one arm in a sling it only took her a matter of seconds. "Quick, Jack, get over here."

Jack didn't understand what was going on, but it was clear that Trudy had a plan. He awkwardly clambered and hoisted himself over the top of the gate, dropping heavily to his feet. He managed to straighten up just in time to see Static pull himself into a sitting position. "Uggghhh. What happened to me?"

Trudy spoke to him through the mesh gate. "We were on the other side of the playing fields and saw you fall as you were climbing over the top of the gates."

"Really?" Static seemed slightly unsure.

Trudy nodded. "Really. You hit your head on the gate as

you fell. We've been shouting at you, but you were unconscious for some time."

Static shook his head. "That can't be right. We were in the maze, there was a drilling platform, and electric eels and a Minotaur called Alan. . . ."

"A Minotaur called Alan? Does that sound realistic?"[42]

Static thought. "Well . . . now that you mention it, not really. I . . . I suppose it must have been a dream."

"Come on, Static, you've had a bad fall. Trudy's going to call her dad and get him to send a car. We'll drop you off at home."

Static stood and managed to climb over the mesh gate after three attempts.

Trudy used a pay phone to call for a Ministry car, which arrived after only a few minutes. Static was still more than a little confused and didn't even comment on how disheveled and smelly the interior of the Ministry car was. When they had reached his home Static got out, but before he ran up the driveway he turned and looked at Trudy and Jack. "It was all a dream, right?"

"Yes, we just found you lying there."

"Okay." Static seemed to be thinking. "In that case I've got to introduce you guys to my sidekick sometime. I think you're going to love him."

Static slammed the car door and ran off. Jack found himself gripped with panic. "Trudy, Static's going to realize that it wasn't all a dream. Volty will tell him that he was actually in the maze."

---

[42] A Minotaur called Alan is entirely realistic. Minotaurs exist. They have to be called something. Some of them will be called Alan.

Trudy looked at Jack sternly. "Sometimes you really should say a sentence in your head and think about it before you say it out loud."

Jack repeated the sentence he had just said, but this time in his head. Realization dawned on him. "Oh, right, yeah. That's not going to be a problem."

Trudy smiled. "I wouldn't have thought so."

MINISTRY OF S.U.I.T.S HANDBOOK

BULLS
WHY IT IS NECESSARY TO ALWAYS FLATTER THEM

It is apparent to everyone that bulls are the most vain animals that exist. After all, no other animal wears jewelry.

However, many people don't realize just how vain bulls are. The reason that they attack matadors is that matadors are always dressed up in fancy gold clothing. The bull gets jealous of the clothing and decides to charge. Bulls also think the capes that matadors have are pretty cool.

Capes are pretty cool. After all, that's why superheroes wear them.

23

TOO MANY CLUES

After they had dropped off Static, Jack and Trudy headed to the Ministry headquarters in the museum. They were sure that a lot of what had happened to them had been connected, but they just weren't sure how. They hoped that Grey could help them piece it together.

When they arrived at Ministry headquarters in the museum, it was in much better shape than it had been the last time. There were still puddles of water lying here and there, but the corridors were no longer completely flooded. They were told that Grey was waiting for them in the Passage room.

As they were walking down the corridor where they had been told the Passage room was, they found their way blocked by a very animated and annoyed Cthulhu. He was screeching at the top of his lungs.[43] His mood had definitely worsened since Monday.

"Um, can we . . . get past?" Jack asked nervously.

Cthulhu kept screaming and pointing at his feet. Jack and Trudy looked at the floor. Someone had marked a large hopscotch grid on the ground; however, whoever[44] had drawn it had made the home square in the shape of a star. Cthulhu was standing in the center of the star.

Grey wandered up behind Jack and Trudy. "Were you looking for me?"

Trudy nodded. "Yeah, but what's happened to Cthulhu?"

"Well, he was floating along on his little cloud of green mist when we got the drainage system working again. The water went down and he found himself dropped into the center of the chalk star."

"Who was playing hopscotch anyway?" Jack asked.

"That was Bigfoot. Unsurprisingly, he's the Ministry champion."[45]

---

[43] If indeed there were actually lungs inside his gray, decaying, squid-like body. The world is actually a lot neater than people realize. For example, we all have our organs on the inside of our bodies. It would be frightfully messy if they hung on the outside. However, this is exactly the kind of thing that would amuse Cthulhu.

[44] Have you ever noticed that *however* is an anagram of *whoever*? I just did. Not that I have anything very interesting to say about it. Just thought I'd mention it.

[45] You may notice that Grey called Bigfoot "Bigfoot" instead of referring

Trudy was still confused. "So why's Cthulhu so annoyed about being put in the middle of a chalk star?"

From the center of a slightly smudged chalk star the furious Cthulhu had started spitting green energy blasts from his mouth; however, when they reached the edge of the chalk star they fizzed into nothingness.

"We aren't a hundred percent sure, but we suspect that the race of evil interdimensional beings that Cthulhu is descended from can be trapped inside a star shape for some reason. It's either that or he really hates hopscotch. Or maybe he's just superallergic to chalk."

"He would really have to be absolutely superallergic to chalk, though, wouldn't he?" said Jack.

Grey shrugged. "Well, yes, but haven't you noticed that everyone seems to be allergic to something these days? I've often wondered if maybe someone shouldn't be looking into that."[46]

"Shouldn't we, umm, let him out or something?" asked Jack despite his best judgment.

A sinister smile appeared on Grey's face. "Don't worry about that; we've requisitioned a chalk duster to let him out. Although it seems that it's harder to get one than we thought. Someone made the requisition system supercomplicated for

---

to him by the term Sizularly Challenged Bipedal Simian. Grey didn't much care for political correctness.

[46] Someone should. And they would. But not until Ministry of SUITs 3.

their own evil purposes." Grey turned and nodded at Cthulhu. "Isn't that right, Cthulhu?"

Cthulhu gave Grey a look that would have melted a P.E. teacher's heart and then threw back his head in a howl of anguish.

Grey took pity on him and took a small, sealed plastic bag out of his pocket. "Snacks—your favorite, Cthulhu—seared eel cutlets; they should keep you going until the chalk duster arrives." Grey threw the bag through the air and Cthulhu caught it. The dread creature nodded his thanks to Grey before starting to howl again.

Grey turned to Jack and Trudy. "Let's go to the Passage room and continue our chat. It's a lot quieter there."

The Passage room was a large room with enormous bookcases around the edge of it and a few tables and chairs in the middle. Jack looked around. "Why is this place called the Passage room, then? It looks more like a library."

Grey smiled to himself. "Why don't you both try and look at one of the books?"

Trudy noticed Grey's sly smile, shook her head, and sat down. Thankfully Trudy didn't suffer from the same kind of burning curiosity that drove Jack's fevered imagination. Jack knew by Grey's smile that something bizarre would happen if he looked at one of the books. But he had to know exactly what that bizarre thing would be. Cautiously, he put his finger on one of of the books and started to pull it from the case. There was a click and suddenly a whole section of the bookcase swung inward, revealing a secret passage. Jack felt himself being sucked into it.

He was tumbling through what felt like an infinite blackness, not sure what was up or down. Then ahead of him there was a flash of light. For a brief second he was back in the Passage room. He seemed to have fallen out of a door in the ceiling and was hurtling toward the floor. He braced himself for a bone-crunching crash. But then at the last moment another door opened in the floor, and Jack was tumbling through even more darkness. His body was spinning and he was slightly sick in his own mouth again. Finally, he came tumbling back into the Passage room through another door that had swung open in a bookcase on the farthest wall.

"What on earth was that?!?" asked Jack as he stumbled to his feet, with his head still spinning.

"That was why this room is called the Passage room." Grey laughed. "You'd expect a place like the Ministry to have a lot of secret passages, wouldn't you?"

Trudy and Jack agreed that they would.

"Well, the problem with secret passages is that often they're so well hidden that people forget where they are. Which makes them useless. However, the clever designers of the Ministry got around that problem by building one room that had all the secret passages in it."

"Wait a minute," said Trudy. "You mean that all the secret passages in this room lead back into this room?"

Grey sucked his teeth. "Umm. Yes. I know that's a bit of a design flaw, but let's be honest—if we removed all the design flaws from the Ministry, then the whole building would fall apart overnight. Anyway, the room is rather useful precisely because it's useless—it's always nice and quiet—so it's an excellent place to meet and talk."

Jack dizzily wove his way over to the table where Grey and Trudy were sitting. "Enough about secret passages.[47] I never want to hear about secret passages again! We're here to try and figure out what's going on."

Trudy and Jack explained to Grey what had happened to them.

"And everything seems to relate to water," said Trudy. "The seals, the woman walking underwater at the aquarium, the crab, this place being flooded, and the fish escaping."

Jack agreed. "The deadly bath bomb, the giant spider under my bath . . . The only thing that doesn't seem to fit the pattern is the fracking. I mean, I know they inject water into the ground, but . . . it just seems to be different. But we looked at the drill on the playing fields. There was nowhere to store anything—so they definitely aren't drilling for gas."

Grey considered what they had told him. "Well, maybe the fracking's just a red herring. Maybe it's something

---

[47] Many of you will know that the word *passage* not only means a corridor, but can also refer to a short section of a book. The reason this happened is that in the old days secret passages in stately homes were always accessed by pulling a book out of a bookcase in a library. Therefore, eventually people started using the word *passage* in connection with books themselves. This is 100 percent true. Or at least it will be in about ten minutes after I've finished editing the right section in Wikipedia.

different. But there's definitely at least one other red herring in your story."

"What?" Trudy and Jack asked simultaneously.

"Come on! You're Ministry operatives—think! What part of the story doesn't seem sinister?"

Trudy and Jack sat in silence as they reviewed the story in their heads. Trudy exhaled after a while. "It all seems pretty weird to me."

Jack stared into space as a thought popped into his head from nowhere. "The spider . . . It's the spider, isn't it?"

Grey laughed and clapped Jack on the shoulder. "I always said that you were the cleverest of boys, Jack. But let's see just how clever you are. How did you figure that out?"

"Well"—Jack spoke slowly, thinking his way through every word—"I can't believe that I'm saying this out loud. . . . but I'm beginning to suspect that all bathtubs have giant spiders hiding under them."

Grey's smile widened. "And how do you know that?"

"Yeah," said Trudy, irritated that she hadn't figured it out. "How do you know that?"

"Well, think about how often you find little spiders in the bath. That's because they're baby spiders that have been pushed out the bath drain by a mother or father spider who's hiding under the bathtub."

Trudy snorted with derision. "That's crazy. When you find a spider in the bath, it's there because it's fallen down the slippery sides and can't climb out again."

Grey was about to correct Trudy, but Jack got in ahead of him. "Trudy, can you walk on the ceiling?"

"Well . . . not without using The Speed . . . no."

"Right, and can you climb out of a bath?"

"Of course I can."

"And yet you're saying that a spider who can climb a wall and walk on a ceiling can't climb out of a bathtub? How do you think it got in there in the first place? Slipped on the soap, maybe?"

Trudy looked as though she wanted to hit Jack on the shoulder. Jack was too excited with his train of thought to even notice.

"I'm right, Grey, aren't I?"

"Perfectly. And is there anything else about bath design that makes them suitable for spiders to live under?"

Jack racked his brain back to the enormous spider he had seen on Monday. Its six eyes staring at him . . .

"The eyes!"

Grey nodded, encouraging Jack to go on. "The spider from the other day had six eyes on the front of its body all closely grouped together. And the plug hole in our bath is split into six little segments."

"Exactly, plug holes are designed so that a spider can put its eye up against them and look out without anyone even realizing that they're there. Spiders' eyes are pitch black, so they just look like a hole. Different-shaped plug holes are designed to suit different types of spiders with different eye configurations."

Trudy shuddered. "I'm not sure that I like the thought that there's a giant spider living underneath my bath. Why do they live there anyway?"

"Well, actually that has to do with the Ministry," said Grey.

"That's a surprise," said Trudy sarcastically.

"A long time ago there were no mobile phones. In fact, there were no phones at all. But that didn't stop Ministry operatives from needing to get messages across the country quickly."

"Are you going to tell us that you used carrier spiders instead of carrier pigeons?"

"No—that's the point, Jack—any kind of creature traveling across the ground could have been easily captured by enemies. Which is why the Ministry invented plumbing."

"I thought the Romans invented plumbing," Trudy interrupted.

"They did," agreed Grey. "Roman members of the Ministry. Anyway, plumbing was just a clever way to get piping into people's houses. The plumbing was used by Ministry operatives to send messages in Morse code to each other. They would hammer on the pipes and the sound would carry along the length of the pipe to someone listening miles away. Have you ever really listened closely to plumbing? Pipes and radiators make banging and rattling noises occasionally. Which is just crazy if they were only filled with water. Water never makes a banging noise."

Jack thought that it did if you dropped an explosive bath bomb into it, but he didn't want to interrupt.

"The banging noise is just a spider sending a Morse code message."

"But if the pipes are just about sending Morse code, then why fill them with water at all?"

Grey smiled. "Well, that was the genius of the plumbing idea. The Ministry would never have had a large enough budget to install a network of pipes across the country. So instead they convinced the world that it was a great idea to have water piped into your house. That way the rest of the world paid for our communications system."

Jack still wanted to know more. "But why spiders?"

"Primarily because they work cheaply," Grey said. "But as well as that, they're quite happy living under baths. Spiders like dark, cramped areas. They get plenty of water and skin flakes to eat. And if you get a small child getting nits washed out of their hair—well that's like an all-you-can-eat buffet to a spider. . . ."

"Ugh . . . gross," complained Trudy.

"And the best thing about a spider is that it can bang Morse code out on a pipe like nobody's business. By using all eight legs working individually they put the best human Morse code operators to shame."

Jack smiled. "You really do learn something new every day in this job, don't you."

Trudy brought both Jack and Grey back down to earth with a bump. "Yes, you do, although a lot of it isn't useful. So the spider was just a useless coincidence?"

"That still leaves a lot of clues," said Jack. "Which should we focus on?"

Grey considered for a moment before speaking. "Clues don't actually ever do anything. Clues don't commit crimes, come up with plans, or attack people. So what you need to do is figure out who is behind the clues."

"We've only come across a few people so far," Trudy said. "Jack saw the strange old woman at the aquarium who walked into the sea. She seemed to know my name."

Jack nodded. "And then there was the woman who gave me the exploding bath bomb. She looked like a much younger version of that older woman."

Trudy looked at Jack. "Could they have been mother and daughter?"

Jack considered. "Maybe. . . . They did look almost identical apart from the difference in age."

Grey nodded. "Then I suggest you find those women. If they were behind the crab at the museum and the exploding bath bomb, they may well hold the key to all the mysteries. Including the fish jailbreak."

"Did they recapture any of the fish?" asked Trudy.

"Some of them—but most of the fish swam out of the overflow vent before we could get them. We lost almost all of the hammerhead sharks and sawfish."

Jack considered what kind of sea creature would be smart enough to plot mankind's demise. "Maybe it's something to do with a plot by dolphins. I mean, dolphins live in the sea and they're pretty intelligent."

Trudy shook her head. "Evil dolphins? I wouldn't have thought so—I mean, they're always so nice to humans. They've even rescued people from shipwrecks and things. Anyway, not everything has been about the sea—what about the Minotaur and the maze?"

"Well, we know that the Minotaur was from a mad scientist—although I'm not sure that helps us, really."

"Maybe it helps us a little," Trudy disagreed. "Look, the Minotaur is meant to be out of Greek mythology. So maybe we're looking for someone else who could be found in Greek mythology. They'd hardly pick a minotaur at random, would they?"

Jack agreed it was a good point. "And as for the name of the shop—Neptune was a Greek god of the sea or something, wasn't he? And so was Poseidon—the name of the drilling company. Greek or Roman or something..." Jack said, trying to remember his mythology. "So two names that have stuff to do with water. They have to all be working together."

Trudy couldn't figure it out either. "We need to find out more about the woman who gave you the exploding bath bomb. If she wants to kill you, then we should probably try and stop her."

Jack smiled. It was the nicest thing she'd said in a while. Which was disturbing in its own way.

Grey smiled. "It seems like you're beginning to put it all together. Anyway, it's getting late and if you don't go home, your parents will become suspicious. I suggest you sleep on the problem and think about it again tomorrow with a clear head."

SPIDERS
The Reason They Have Eight Legs

Having eight legs is generally a bad thing. You might think it would help you run faster, jump higher, or walk for longer, but it would do none of these things. In fact, it would make it harder to run, jump, or walk. If you've ever tripped over your own feet, you'll know that even having two feet can make life complicated enough. This is why people in three-legged races are generally considerably slower than those adopting a two-legged approach.

(There have, of course, been humans in the past who have had eight legs, such as the Yiptah tribe, who live in some of the deepest forests of Indonesia. However, we shall not consider their tragic fate at this time.)

Clearly, having eight legs makes getting around in life difficult, so why would spiders have so many? If you ever find yourself face-to-face with a spider, the reason will become immediately apparent to you. Spiders, like snakes, have no ears.

Therefore spiders mainly communicate by sign language. (Obviously spiders can lip-read what humans are saying, but this doesn't work with other spiders, as spiders don't actually have lips.)

The very first spiders had only three legs. The problem with this was that every time a spider had to sign a word that required two legs it fell over. This happened so often that in the original spider sign language the signs for OUCH and FULL STOP are exactly the same.

In order to be able to have more interesting conversations and still remain vertical, over the years spiders developed more legs until they arrived at the current allotment of eight. This means they can hold three or four conversations at the same time. If you want to imagine what that is like, try watching a DVD with the director's commentary and the soundtrack turned up at the same time. (Spiders manage to have these conversations by having not only many legs but also many eyes.)

24

THE GREAT
SOAP-MAKING DISASTER
WEDNESDAY

Jack's first three periods on a Wednesday were single geography followed by double science. Geography was interesting enough, Jack would admit, but he really looked forward to science with his somewhat eccentric teacher, Dr. Holmes.

Dr. Holmes walked in front of the class, his eyes twinkling and his blond hair waving from side to side as he moved excitedly. "I have great news for you! Today we have a special guest."

David leaned over to whisper to Jack, "I hope it's Katy Perry."

Jack almost laughed out loud. He whispered back, "Do you think it's *likely* to be Katy Perry?"

David thought about this for a few minutes. "Well, I think it's more likely to be Katy Perry than it is to be Albert Einstein or Rudyard Kipling."

"And your reasoning behind that is?"

"Well. They're both dead, aren't they? I mean, a teacher's unlikely to bring corpses into a classroom."

"That would be unusual," Jack conceded.

"So," said David, clearly warming to his subject, "out of Albert Einstein, Rudyard Kipling, and Katy Perry, it's most likely to be Katy Perry. Which means by my calculation we have a *better* than one-in-three chance of it being Katy Perry."

Jack just gazed at David. You couldn't deny that David had his very own brand of completely flawed and incorrect—but fabulously compelling—logic. This was the reason that other people found David irritating. It was also the same reason that Jack thought he was wonderful.

Jack thought of David's mind as being like a sausage. Jack had no idea what went on inside David's mind in the same way he had no idea what exactly went into a sausage. In many ways he didn't want to know what went on inside either. He just enjoyed the effects of both of them.

"You, David, are as wonderful as a sausage."

David squinted at Jack. "You say strange things sometimes."

Because of their chattering David and Jack had largely missed Dr. Holmes introducing their "special guest." When Jack looked up he shuddered. It was the woman from Neptune's Den. Her hair was still pulled back in a severe ponytail, but over the top of her business suit she was wearing a lab coat.

She was already speaking. "So, as your teacher has said, my name is Ms. Regina Maris."

Jack's jaw dropped. Regina Maris had been the name on the sign warning people to stay away from the fracking operation. Not only had this woman given him an explosive bath bomb, she was also the chief executive of the drilling company.

Ms. Maris continued. "Now, I own a lot of different businesses, but the one that Dr. Holmes asked me along to talk about is my chain of shops that sells cosmetics, natural sponges, moisturizers, and perfumes."

"Neptune's Den," Jack said. He had meant to say it quietly to himself, but accidentally said it out loud. Unfortunately, loud enough for Ms. Maris to hear.

She confidently strode from the front of the class to the back and spoke right into Jack's face. "What was that?"

Jack gulped. Ms. Maris was stunningly beautiful, with perfectly smooth skin and angular cheekbones. She didn't seem to blink as she stared at him; it was quite unnerving. The most striking thing about her, however, was the smell of her perfume. It was so strong as to be almost overpowering. It clouded the air, and Jack felt that he wasn't so much breathing as swallowing the fragrant air.

"Umm, I said that the name of the chain you own is 'Neptune's Den.' I've used some of your products—they're very . . . surprising."

Ms. Maris's nostrils flared as she spoke. "Sometimes I think they're not surprising enough, sadly." Ms. Maris turned away and walked back to the front of the class. "Your classmate is indeed right. And in Neptune's Den we sell every kind of soap known to humankind. So today I'm going to teach you the science of making soap."

Ms. Maris pulled a large white sheet off the teacher's workbench, which had been covering a range of chemicals, powders, and oils. "And these are the ingredients we are going to use."

The students were all summoned to the front, and everyone got to choose a range of perfumes and oils with which to personalize their soap. "Be extremely careful with the lye. It is highly caustic and could burn you," Dr. Holmes cautioned while handing out the chemicals.

"Now, as a special treat, whoever I judge to have made the best soap will get to have the rest of the day off and tour the soap factory that supplies my shops," Ms. Maris said.

Jack turned to David. "We have to win that prize—it's connected with a Ministry case. We think that Ms. Maris might have helped break criminal fish out of jail." After Jack had finished speaking he realized that his last sentence would sound insane. However, as usual David seemed to accept insanity with nonchalance.

"Okay, then. So you want me to help you win the soap-making competition?"

Jack looked serious and put his hand on David's shoulder. "No, David, I don't want you to help me. I want you to help everyone else in the class."

<hr>

The hour that followed went down in legend. Future chemistry teachers would whisper of the Great Soap-Making Disaster of 2016. Trainee teachers would be scared into learning their lessons by being told of the disaster that could befall them if they didn't follow health and safety procedures.[48]

〜〜〜〜〜〜〜〜〜

David wasn't normally allowed to help in Jack's experiments. In fact, during science lessons they had created their own game called "Statues," in which David tried to remain as still as he could and not knock anything over. But in this lesson David was set free and wandered amongst his other classmates, offering to help, lighting Bunsen burners, and carrying things.

Asking for David's help would be a bit like trying to solve the problem of a lost glove by cutting off one of your hands.[49]

Jack concentrated hard on making his soap but was constantly distracted by howls of pain and crashing noises. Jack looked up at the front of the classroom. Ms. Maris was watching him work. She smiled at him. But it wasn't a nice *How are you?* smile. It was a sinister *I know something you don't know* smile. She kept staring until Jack dropped his gaze and looked back at the experiment.

At one stage Jack looked up to see David carrying a tray. Jack normally *never* allowed David to carry trays. For other people a tray was a piece of equipment that enabled you to carry several things at the same time. For David a tray was

---

[48] Additionally, the disaster led to another rule being added. It was a simple rule that banned David from taking part in future experiments.

[49] Please don't try this at home. And for that matter don't go around to your friend's houses to try it either. Especially if their houses are nicer than yours or have white carpets.

a piece of equipment that enabled you to drop several things at the same time. Trays greatly increased David's efficiency at smashing objects.

As he walked with the tray he stumbled, and it went flying into the air. A beaker of lye landed on the back of a boy's blazer. The boy ripped it off and threw it away. It landed on a Bunsen burner and caught fire. Meanwhile another beaker of water had fallen from David's tray, causing a girl to slip and clatter onto a stool, smashing it to pieces.

David backed away from the mess, looking slightly sheepish, and knocked over a beaker on top of a tripod, which spilled a bubbling soap mixture onto the ground. Dr. Holmes rushed over to help, slipped on the liquid soap, and fell over.

"Someone put the fire out, at least!" groaned Dr. Holmes from the ground.

Dr. Holmes had made the crucial mistake of not specifying *who* was to try and put the fire out. David rushed over, grabbed the nearest beaker, and threw it at the fire. Unfortunately, the beaker had contained highly flammable ethanol and the fire leapt up. After a second's thought, David then grabbed a chemistry textbook and used it to beat at the flames furiously. Naturally, the chemistry book caught fire, causing tendrils of smoke to snake up toward the ceiling. There was a beeping noise from the smoke detectors and the sprinklers exploded into life, showering the room with water.

Jack looked up and saw Ms. Maris running out the door as if she was afraid of the water. If she was the woman who had walked into the sea, that seemed odd—why would she be frightened of a sprinkler? Did water have some kind of strange effect on her?

Jack was interrupted in his thoughts as the school's fire alarm went off, and they all left the room to make their way to the fire assembly point on the playing fields. On the way out Jack tried to help some of the wounded who had been hurt due to David's help. He felt more than a little responsible.

MINISTRY OF S.U.IT.S HANDBOOK

SOAP
THE CLEANSING PROPERTIES OF

Many people do not realize that many soaps contain a substantial amount of fat. And not some kind of weird or abstract fat, but pretty much the same kind of fat that you put on if you continue having large breakfasts consisting of piles of sausages, bacon, and poached eggs.

As everyone knows, you use soap by rubbing and jiggling it all over your body. Therefore, some scientists have conjectured that obese people would be self-cleaning if you put them on a trampoline.

25

AND WE HAVE A WINNER

The whole school had emptied out onto the playing fields at the sound of the fire alarm. Trudy wandered over to where Jack and David were standing.

"What's that?" Trudy asked, indicating the tub of orange goo in Jack's hand.

"We were having a soap-making competition," said Jack. He explained what had happened—including the fact that Ms. Maris, the woman from Neptune's Den and the Poseidon drilling company, had been the judge.

"And do you think you won the competition?"

Jack looked around at his classmates, most of whom were bruised, battered, or a little bit singed at the edges. "I think we're in with a good chance—at least partly because no one else bothered to bring their soap out here with them. They were mainly too busy nursing David-related injuries."

Dr. Holmes was hobbling across the playing field to where they were standing. Ms. Maris walked along behind him. Dr. Holmes looked at David with a mixture of suspicion and fear. "What on earth were you doing in there, boy?"

David stared blankly at Dr. Holmes. "Helping. I was helping."

"Well, thank you for your help. Thanks to you, if I have a career left, I'll probably be spending most of it filling in accident report forms."

"No problem." David smiled. "Always happy to help."

Jack decided it was a good point in the conversation to jump in. "This is my entry into the soap-making competition."

Dr. Holmes looked at Jack in disbelief. "Really? This is your entry?"

Jack nodded enthusiastically. "And given that no one else seems to have a completed entry, I would guess that means that . . ."

". . . you win." Ms. Maris finished his thought. "And perhaps you'd like to bring your friends here on the tour of the soap factory."

Dr. Holmes saw an opportunity. "Yes, please! Especially the boy David. Take him as far away from here as possible!"

Jack felt a brief moment of triumph. And then he realized something. It didn't matter what had happened. Ms. Maris was always going to name him as the winner. Because this hadn't been a competition. It had been a trap. And he had walked right into it.

———————

Ms. Maris's car was a large black Rolls Royce. A chauffeur got out of the car and opened the door for Jack, Trudy, and David to climb in. The back of the car was spacious, with two rows of seats facing each other. It was more like a living room than vehicular transport. It wasn't as fast as the Ministry cars, but it certainly smelled more fragrant. Jack wondered if things that were fast generally smelled worse. Certainly after he'd been out running, his P.E. clothes smelled worse than clothes he'd just been walking around in.

Trudy sat down beside Ms. Maris with Jack and David facing them.

"I think you'll enjoy the tour," said Ms. Maris. "We should be at the factory in about forty minutes."

The car started and Ms. Maris relaxed back in her seat. In the confined space of the car, the smell of Ms. Maris's perfume was incredibly strong. Jack pressed the button that rolled the windows down.

Jack had never been on a more awkward car journey. No one said as much as a word to each other. Jack wondered if they should confront Ms. Maris. Fix her with a stern glare and tell her that they knew what her evil plan was.

But then again, that was the problem. They didn't know what her evil plan was. They didn't have the first clue to what her evil plan was. And Jack didn't want her to realize that.

She'd tried to kill Jack with a bath bomb, so she must have thought they were dangerous. But why? And how had she known Trudy's name? And if she had broken the criminal fish out of the Ministry, what was she using them for? And why had she run so quickly when the sprinklers had gone off in the school?

For most of the journey David lay idly slumped in his seat. The feeling of tension didn't seem to bother him in the slightest. After about half an hour, David starting whistling tunelessly to himself. Everyone looked at him but he didn't notice and didn't miss a single note of his tuneless aria.

His whistling seemed to annoy Ms. Maris. Jack didn't mind it at all; he was used to David's little idiosyncrasies.

Ms. Maris leaned forward so that her nose was almost touching David's. She spoke slowly and pointedly. "I can switch the radio on."

David seemed to consider this for a minute. He sniffed and then said, "That's nothing to boast about. I can switch radios on too. And televisions. I think most people can. They normally label the buttons and everything."

Ms. Maris was completely flummoxed by David's reply. Jack had to look out the window and bite his lip to keep himself from laughing.

What Jack saw out the window surprised him. "What on earth is that?"

MINISTRY OF S.U.IT.S HANDBOOK

WHISTLING
SHEEPDOGS

Whistling is an extremely useful skill to master, mainly because it can be used to irritate other people. Some people over the years have claimed that it can also be used as a form of communication, as shepherds use it to tell sheepdogs what to do. This is clearly lunacy of the highest order.

If dogs got instructions to arrange fluffy things from whistling sounds, then your poodle would start plumping your cushions every time the kettle boiled.

The truth, of course, is that all dogs are highly organized and like things to be neat and tidy. This is why when you throw a stick a dog will bring it back to you at once. Dogs know that sticks shouldn't be left lying about and will return them so you can put them back in a tree where they belong. No other animal would do this.

Therefore, when a dog sees a sheep out of a pen, its natural reaction is to get it back to the place it should be.

You may be asking, if this is true, then why do shepherds whistle at their dogs while they work? The answer is, of course, simple. Looking at sheep will cause anyone to start falling asleep (see section **Insomnia: How to Get to Sleep**). The only reason the shepherd whistles is so the irritating noise will keep the dog awake so that it will not drift off into a doggy power-nap.

26

YOU KNOW THE DRILL

They were driving along the edge of Lough[50] Neagh, a huge inland lake right in the center of Northern Ireland. It supplied almost half of the country's drinking water and was well-known for its eel fishery.

But Jack wasn't amazed at Lough Neagh. Rather, he was amazed at what was in the center of it. There was an enormous tower that stretched up into the sky. Jack had to squint his eyes to see its top, which almost disappeared into the

---

[50] Lough is basically an Irish word for lake. So what's the difference between a lough and a lake? Well, because you find loughs in Ireland, they're generally a lot colder. (Unless of course you're reading this in Canada. In which case you beat us. Because Irish loughs may be cold, but you aren't able to play hockey on top of them.)

clouds. It reminded Jack of the impossibly tall filing cabinets from the quartermaster's store in the Ministry.

Jack pointed. "What is that?"

"Oh, that," Ms. Maris said casually. "Yes, I suppose it is quite impressive the first time that you see it. It's an underwater fracking drill—I also own Poseidon International Drilling Company. We're checking to see if there are any gas reserves under the lough."

"Do you need that large a drill?"

"Oh, yes, it needs to go very far under the water. Very far indeed."

David looked at all the clouds and stifled a yawn.

The car pulled over at the side of a large factory. The door was opened by the chauffeur, and Ms. Maris stepped out. "But let's not talk about the drilling platform now. You're here to see the soap factory, aren't you? You lucky, lucky people."

Jack, Trudy, and David followed Ms. Maris as she strode across the car park and into the reception area of the factory. "Now if you wait here, I'll go and get you some protective clothing for the tour." Ms. Maris walked over to a door, typed a code into a keylock, and disappeared. Jack, Trudy, and David sat down on a sofa the receptionist pointed out to them.

"This is a trap," said Jack.

"I know it's a trap," said Trudy.

"But does she know that we know it's a trap?" asked David.

"I think so," said Trudy.

"And we know that she knows that we know that it's a trap," said Jack.

"But does she know that we know that she knows that we know that it's a trap?" asked David.

"I don't know," said Jack.

Trudy stood up from the sofa. "I'm not sure that it matters anyway. We all know, is the point. She brought us here to try and get rid of us. We came here to try and find some evidence of what she's up to."

"Exactly," agreed Jack, "so we keep our eyes and our ears open on this tour, and if we see anything unusual, we let the others know."

"We're like flies walking into a spider's web," David said. Strangely he didn't seem that unhappy about it.

"Doesn't that worry you?" queried Jack.

"No, I'd love to be able to fly." David smiled, rather missing the point.

Ms. Maris arrived back and handed out white coats, safety glasses, and hard hats. Once everyone was suitably attired, the tour began.

⎯⎯⎯⎯⎯⎯⎯

As Jack walked around the factory he began thinking that Willy Wonka must have been a very skilled tour guide before he ever became a chocolatier. A tour around a factory was very hard to make interesting—especially when that factory made soap. At least at a chocolate factory you could be pretty sure if they gave you a goody bag at the end it would be full of some pretty delicious things. The goody bag they gave you at the end of the tour of a soap factory would be significantly less exciting.

However, Jack remained on edge throughout the tour. He suspected that it was all an elaborate trap and they might be attacked at any moment. Jack constantly looked around him to try to see how they would be killed. All the machinery had guardrails and stop buttons. The enormous vats of chemicals were far too high for them to be thrown into. In fact, there was safety equipment everywhere—sprinklers, fire blankets, foam extinguishers. If this was a trap, it was potentially the safest trap that Jack had ever been in.

There just didn't seem to be anything particularly unusual about the factory. Not that Jack had anything to compare it to, but it seemed to be a completely ordinary soap factory. The only unusual thing about the factory was the staff. They all seemed to be wearing a lot of perfume, just like Ms. Maris. It wasn't unpleasant; it was just a lot stronger than Jack was used to. The women all wore perfume. The men all wore aftershave— even the men with large beards were heavily doused in it.

It was strange to be disappointed that someone hadn't tried to kill you, and yet that was how Jack felt at the end of the tour.

"And this is the gift shop. Please feel free to take a few free samples, seeing as how you won the competition."

They were in a room with row upon row of containers filled with soap, bath bombs, moisturizers, and perfumes. Other tours of the factory had obviously just finished, as a number of other people were milling about and looking at the wide variety of bath products. Many of the people were clearly tourists, dressed as they were in brightly colored shirts and shorts. However, one man stood out as he was wearing a three-piece suit and carrying a briefcase with him. He seemed to be looking very closely at the bath bombs. There was something strange about the man; every time he looked at something, he then checked his watch and wrote something down in a tiny notebook.

David went over and smelled some of the containers. He almost instantly started sneezing and backed away without taking anything. At first Jack didn't touch anything, suspicious that maybe this was finally the trap, but then a thought struck him and he filled his pockets. Ms. Maris watched him making his choices and smiled.

"And that, I'm afraid, is the end of the tour."

Jack, Trudy, and David chorused "Thank you" like the polite little children that they weren't.

"Now if you just head out that door through the warehouse, I'll go and arrange for my car to take you home." Ms. Maris walked back the way they had come, leaving the children by themselves.

"So whatever's going to kill us is through that door," said Jack.

"Almost certainly," agreed Trudy.

David laughed. "Are you guys are certain about this? I think maybe you're just paranoid. This place is clearly just a soap factory."

David walked over and pushed the door open. Jack and Trudy rushed over but were too late to stop him.

SPIDERS
How They Really Catch Flies

As we all know, flies are deeply musical creatures. Many animals like music, but only flies spend their entire time humming as they fly around. Clever spiders have observed this. Therefore many of them have carefully spun the webs to be like the strings of a guitar. With their eight legs spiders can use the webs to play very high-pitched guitar solos that only flies can hear. Flies, assuming that there is some kind of music festival going on, will fly over to see what is happening, get stuck to a web, and then...well, then it ends very badly.

The proof of this is that a fly will still land on a web even if there are other flies already caught in it. The reason this happens is that the fly just assumes that the frantic movements of trapped flies are nothing more than flies dancing to the tunes.

Sometimes a spider will make an extra-special effort and dress some of the flies up so they look like festivalgoers, giving them little tiny Maroon 5 T-shirts and Wellington boots.

27

THE WAREHOUSE

"Nothing dangerous at all," said David.

He was right. The door hid nothing more sinister than a warehouse. On the far wall was a door marked *Exit*. They walked across the warehouse toward it. A number of forklift trucks stood idly by. On one side of the warehouse was an enormous set of shelves, which were stacked with mountains of soap.

"You guys are beginning to see plots in everything," said David. "Here's a good rule of thumb for you both. It you're investigating something, try putting it into a movie title, and if it sounds ridiculous, then you're probably barking up the wrong tree."

"What do you mean?" asked Trudy.

"Well, do you think they'd ever make a film called *Indiana*

Jones and the Soap Factory of Doom[51] or *King Solomon's Perfume Shops?*"

"No."

"There you go," said David. "That tells you that nothing suspicious is going on here. You guys really should listen to me more. You know . . ."

David was interrupted in his impromptu lecture as he suddenly fell over. Trudy and Jack were quite pleased, as they hadn't really been enjoying being told off by someone as strange as David. However, their enjoyment was quite short-lived as they were interrupted in their smugness by suddenly falling over themselves.

Jack tried to struggle to his feet but just slipped and slid farther across the floor. Trudy managed to get as far as her knees, but when she tried to stand up she collapsed again.

"What's going on?" yelled a panicked Jack.

"I think we've finally found the trap. They've covered the floor in some kind of extra-slippery soap. It's impossible to stand."

For a few moments they scrambled about, but the soap that had been used to coat the floor had been carefully chosen. It was the most slippery thing any of them had ever come across. Any effort at standing ended with a collapse, a

---

[51] George Lucas, if you're reading my book and you want to make a film about this, give me a call. I've got a cracking script already written. It all starts with . . . but I don't want to spoil it for you. . . . Just call. . . .

crash, and a few additional bruises. They gave up and concentrated on lying very still on the floor.

"I suppose it could be a lot worse," Jack observed.

"In what way?"

"Well, okay, we're stuck, but being on a slippery floor isn't exactly fatal."

Trudy snorted with derision. "I think you're missing the point, Jack. This isn't the fatal part; the fatal part is what comes next."

There was the sound of a motor starting. Jack tried to roll over and see where the sound was coming from. David spotted it first. "Over there—the forklift."

"They're going to run us over with a forklift!"

The forklift was being driven by one of the heavily aftershaved men from the factory. However, it wasn't moving toward them; it was reversing behind the enormous set of shelves that was loaded down with the mountain of soap.

"It's so obvious—they couldn't kill us by throwing us into a vat of chemicals or setting fire to us. That's far too unusual, and it wouldn't happen to three people at once."[52]

Trudy followed Jack's reasoning. ". . . But if we were crushed

---

[52] Villains often make the mistake of trying to kill their enemies in a ridiculously elaborate manner. Even if it actually works, frankly, it just isn't cost-effective. Imagine the price of sausages if butchers adopted this approach. "Well, Mr. Pig, I'm going to make you into sausages. But first I have put you inside a glass cage suspended above a pit of alligators. Now you'll notice that the wire holding up the cage has been coated in acid. . . ."

to death by a falling shelving unit—well, that's easy to accept. It would be seen as an unfortunate industrial accident."

The forklift truck started to push against the enormous shelving unit. Its engine took on a high-pitched whine as it strained against the weight of the metal and mountains of soap.

Jack, Trudy, and David struggled to get up or move out of the way, but they just lathered the soapy floor some more. Some nice bubbles floated up from the floor and caught the light, reflecting beautiful blues and purples. However, none of the three friends were really in a position to appreciate that.

"Jack, right about now we could use one of your oddball ideas."

"It's kind of hard to think clearly when all you have in your head is the prospect of death by soap avalanche."

"At least it'll be a nice clean death."

Jack and Trudy groaned. "David!" Jack yelled. "Now is not the time for that kind of stupid joke."

David looked confused. "What joke?"

"Oh right, sorry I forgot it was you."

There was a creaking sound as the shelving began to tilt and strain. A few of the soaps at the edge of the shelving began to slide slowly forward.

Jack slipped, banged his elbow, and then came up with an idea. "Guys, we aren't going to be able to get out of this one by ourselves. We need to call for help."

"Who's going to help us, Jack? All the people who work in this factory work for Ms. Maris." Trudy was very slowly trying to get to her feet.

"I'm going to call for someone I saw in the gift shop."

David was about to say something, but slipped again and winded himself. Trudy spoke instead. "Jack, we're halfway across a huge warehouse, the door is closed, and people are no doubt chattering in the gift shop. No matter how loudly you shout, they aren't going to hear you."

Jack look determined. "I've got a hunch, and if I'm right, I won't even need to raise my voice."

MINISTRY OF S.U.I.T.S HANDBOOK

FALLING OVER CONSTANTLY
THE YIPTAH TRIBE

As previously mentioned (see **Spiders: The Reason They Have Eight Legs**), the Yiptah tribe are a group of humans who lived in Indonesia and had eight legs. At first this seems like a brilliant advantage, but in reality it made them incredibly clumsy. It also meant that they had a lot of difficulty hunting animals for food. Every time the Yiptahs saw an interesting animal they might have had for dinner, they started to lace up their hunting shoes. However, by the time they had finally tied the fourth pair, their lunch had become bored and wandered off to do something else.

However, one day a particularly smart Yiptah tribeswoman decided to unlace all her shoes and make a lasso out of the laces. This allowed the Yiptah to capture animals without ever having to move at all. Soon the Yiptah, despite having eight legs, never moved from the tree stumps they were sitting on. They had become so skillful with a lasso that they would not move to get something, but would instead simply lasso it and pull it toward them.

As you can imagine, the lack of exercise made the Yiptah get very fat indeed. In fact, at one stage, if you had put them on a trampoline they would have been self-cleaning.

The Yiptah, however, eventually died out. One day the animals that were their prey figured out how to avoid getting captured by the Yiptah. They just started standing *slightly farther away*.

28

TAKE MY CARD

Jack didn't have much time left; the forklift's engine was revving and the huge shelving unit was beginning to rock backward and forward, ready to topple.

He tried standing, but predictably he slipped and fell, banging his elbow. Then he said *the words*. He did not say *the words* particularly loudly or quietly. He simply spoke them in a normal voice. *The words* had an amazing effect.

"I've just had a slip or fall in a workplace and it wasn't my fault."

Trudy and David looked perplexed. After all, no one could have heard Jack—he hadn't screamed or shouted. He had just spoken in his normal voice.

There was the sound of a scuffle. Behind the door that the children had used to get into the warehouse there was the sound of raised voices. One of the voices was insisting that the door was not the normal exit. The other voice was insisting that it didn't matter. There was a loud thumping sound, and the owner of the first voice came tumbling through the doorway. It was hard to tell from a distance, but his face seemed to bear the imprint of the combination lock off a briefcase.

The owner of the second voice came barreling through the door, adjusting his waistcoat. "Hello!" he called across the room.

Trudy shook her head in disbelief. "How on earth did you do that?" Trudy was even more amazed than normal.

Jack smiled. "I saw him in the gift shop and I thought he looked like a . . ."

The man in the three-piece coat strode over to the edge of the soap patch, carrying his briefcase. "Lawyer. My name's Dexter O'Neill."[53]

Jack heard the engine of the forklift truck being switched off. Clearly the factory workers wanted no witnesses to the children's "accident." Dexter O'Neill regarded the slippery patch of soap. "Take off your blazer and throw me the sleeve."

David took off his blazer and threw the sleeve at Dexter. The sleeve hit Dexter in the face, followed by the rest of the blazer. "Okay, you"—Dexter pointed at Trudy—"do the same thing, but this time hold on to the other sleeve of the blazer."

---

[53] In particular Jack had noticed the man continually looking at his watch as he did things. The only type of person who does this is one who bills by the hour. Novelists aren't concerned with time, as we don't bill by the hour. We generally bill by the word. Pumpkins. Rolodex.

One by one Dexter hauled them off the slippery soap patch, using the blazer as an improvised rope. When they were all safe he gave each of them a business card. "We're the biggest law firm in Ireland. Now this is a dangerous patch of soap with no *Slippery When Wet* signs up. That's definitely actionable—so we can sue the factory for your injuries. You guys get your parents to call me when you get home. All right?" Dexter smiled at them kindly. Then his face took on the cunning of a fox. He leaned close to them and whispered, "And try to limp a bit on your way out; I think they've got security cameras on the exit."

Jack's natural curiosity got the better of him. Just because someone saved your life, it didn't mean that you couldn't ask them questions. "What's a lawyer doing in a soap factory anyway?"

Dexter looked around to check that no one was listening. "Well, between me and three potential future clients, I got a phone call from a Mrs. Pearse today, who said that her bathroom had been blown up by a bath bomb. I reckon there's a big lawsuit in it."

Jack's eyebrows shot up so rapidly they almost left his forehead. Jack had realized that although a lawyer might not be able to hear a pin drop at fifty paces, he would certainly be able to hear someone falling with a potential to sue—this had been why he'd said the magic legal words. However, the only reason that the lawyer had even been in the soap factory was that Jack's mother had contacted him. Jack's mother had inadvertently saved his life. He made a mental note to inadvertently thank her when he got home.

"Anyway, that's a different case. You guys have had bad falls. Make sure your parents call."

"Um, couldn't you just hang out with us for a bit?" asked David, clearly not happy to be left alone in the warehouse.

The lawyer considered this. "Well, I don't really have anything else to do. . . ." Suddenly, Dexter's ears pricked up and he did possibly the best impression of a meerkat that Jack had ever seen. "Did you hear that?"

"Hear what?" asked Trudy.

Dexter pointed back through the gift shop door. "Someone in a café three hundred meters that way has just said that they've found a cockroach in their chips. I have to go."

Dexter sprinted back toward the gift shop while pulling a business card out of his pocket ready to hand it to his next client.

"That was brilliant," Trudy said to Jack. Jack smiled at Trudy's praise.

David brought them both crashing back to earth. "Don't want to rain on your parade, guys, but we're still in a warehouse with a man in a forklift truck who wants to kill us." As if on cue, the engine of the forklift revved up again. There was a grinding metal creak as it pushed one more time against the enormous shelving unit, causing it to rock and then tumble. Jack and Trudy each grabbed one of David's arms and pulled him backward. The shelving unit fell, creating an avalanche of soap in front of them. A fountain of soap and bath salts was thrown into the air.

It had missed them by mere inches. They dusted themselves off.

"Let's get out of here," said David, choosing exactly the right time to start making sense.

"Gift shop?" suggested Trudy.

Unfortunately, the factory worker who had been slightly concussed by Dexter's briefcase had managed to rouse himself and had locked the door to the gift shop behind him.

"We're still okay," said Jack. "I mean, there are only two of them. With The Speed we can probably . . ."

Jack's optimism was short-lived. The forklift truck had driven out from behind the shelving unit. Jack noticed that the two prongs that stuck out from its front were made of gleaming, shiny metal. Worse than that, they had been sharpened into deadly points.

"Oh, come on," complained Jack. "That isn't even practical."

"We can do this, Jack," said Trudy. "No forklift truck will ever be able to get us with The Speed."

"Umm. What about me?" asked David.

"Whoops," admitted Trudy. "I hadn't thought about that."

"It's going to be a problem, isn't it?" asked Jack.

Trudy ruminated on this. "That depends, Jack. How would you feel about being best friends with a shish kebab?"

The driver of the forklift truck pushed his foot on the accelerator and gained speed as he drove directly toward them.

Jack saw a sad look come over Trudy's eyes before The Speed descended on her and she ran straight toward the forklift. At the last second she dodged to the right. The driver tried to hit her by wrenching the wheel violently, but Trudy easily avoided this and jumped across the metal prongs.

The second factory worker advanced on her and swung a

punch. Trudy ducked and threw a single punch at him with her good arm; it caught him square in the stomach and he fell to the ground. Jack winced. He knew just how hard those punches of Trudy's could be.

The forklift driver wheeled his truck around and was heading straight for Trudy.

"Don't they give you any weapons in the Ministry?" David shouted at Trudy.

"Are you kidding?" Trudy laughed bitterly as she dodged another attack from the forklift. "Equipment is in short supply. I had to go to a hospital to even get this!" Trudy held up her damaged arm, showing the sling that held it in place. It was then that Trudy had an idea.

MINISTRY OF S.U.I.T.S HANDBOOK

LAWYERS
Their Hearing Capabilities

Many people think that lawyers spend years learning how to deal with the rules of courts, procedure, and other legal matters. Of course this is clearly untrue. After all, the law is a relatively simple matter—the rules are written down and you simply follow them. People don't have to spend years learning rules—otherwise games of Monopoly would be *even longer.*

The reason that lawyers spend so much time studying at university is that they are practicing at improving their hearing. This is why they study in old libraries—they sit quietly and try very hard to hear things that other people would never notice—the sound of insects scurrying, the sound of paint drying, the sound of hair growing. This means they eventually get to the stage where they can hear distant accidents and then offer to sue.

Even when their hearing improves to the level where they can hear a pin drop at fifty feet, they still try to practice every day. If you ever go to court, you will notice this as occasionally the judge will bang his gavel and shout "Silence in the court!" This is so all the lawyers present can have a few moments of listening practice in the middle of their otherwise busy day.

29

SURPRISINGLY ACCURATE

Trudy ran over to where the shelving unit had toppled and picked out a few large, square bars of soap.

Jack shook his head. "Trudy, now is not the time to be stealing soap."

A confused David looked at Jack. "Surely if there was going to be time specifically allotted to stealing soap, it would have been back in the gift shop? You aren't making any sense, Jack. I don't want to be critical, but you have quite poor planning skills."

The forklift driver had skidded to a halt and was turning around. He turned the forklift so the shiny metal skewers were pointing at Trudy again.

Trudy slipped her sling over her head. She flexed her injured arm once or twice and sucked in air at the pain. It seemed to be working relatively well.

"What is she doing?" muttered Jack.

Trudy carefully put one of the bars of soap into the divot in the sling that had been made by her elbow.

"I'm not sure that now is the time Trudy should be doing her laundry," observed David.

Trudy had grabbed the sling by the thin piece of fabric that had gone around her neck. Then she began swinging it around her head. The penny dropped for Jack. "She's made a sling out of her sling."

David looked at Jack. "That doesn't make any sense. That's just the same thing."

"David! Can't you see? She's made a *sling* out of her *sling*."

David stared blankly at Jack. "Now you're making *no sense* out of *no sense*."

As David and Jack squabbled amongst themselves, Trudy swung the sling faster. The forklift driver pushed his foot hard on the accelerator and was bearing down on Trudy. Trudy's eyes narrowed and she patiently waited as the forklift closed in on her.

Suddenly, Trudy let go of one end of the sling and the bar of soap zoomed out of it like a rocket. Being a square block, it lacked something in terms of being aerodynamic. It tumbled through the air in exactly the same way a clumsy tightrope walker would. And then BANG! It hit the forklift truck driver square between the eyes. A loud crack, a searing pain, the smell of strawberries and cream, and he was unconscious. He slumped over the wheel of the forklift and it swung abruptly to the right before encountering a pile of soap and toppling over.

Jack cheered and clapped. David tapped him on the shoulder. "Jack, she was making a sling out of a sling."

Jack was confused. "Yes, I know."

"Well, why didn't you just say that?"

Jack was about to start arguing with David; however, he was stopped by Trudy, who pointed out that they had more important things to do. "Come on, guys; we've got to get out of here."

Trudy ran toward the exit door followed by the two boys. She wrenched at the door handle but it remained stubbornly shut. "RATS!" she shouted.

Jack also tried it but it didn't move.

"Still shut a second after I tried it, Jack?" said Trudy moodily.

"Yes, that appears to be the case," Jack admitted sheepishly.

"We could use the forklift truck to crash through the door," suggested David.

Trudy shook her head. "The forklift's fallen over. Even the three of us together couldn't get it back on its wheels. We need something to blow the door open."

"Well, that wouldn't be a problem if we had a bath," said Jack. He took several bath bombs out of his pocket, which he had taken them from the gift shop. "I noticed these right at the back. They're the same type as the one that exploded in my bath. Add water to these babies and *boom!*"

"If we could find ourselves a bucket of water, we could lob the bath bombs in from a distance." Trudy and Jack busied themselves looking for a bucket or indeed some water.

David sighed and grabbed one of the bath bombs out of

Jack's hand. For a second Jack thought he was pretending to be a soldier from an old war film, pulling the pin from a grenade with his teeth before throwing it. And then Jack realized David had licked the bath bomb.

David threw the bath bomb in a curving arc. It had started to fizz slightly where he had licked it. Trudy, David, and Jack dived for cover.

Unsurprisingly, David was not the best shot in the world, and the bath bomb hit a few feet away from the door. However, as it crashed into the ground the chain reaction with David's saliva sped up and there was an enormous explosion. The wall blackened and the door tilted and fell off its hinges.

Jack, Trudy, and David got up off the ground. "That was amazingly brave," said Trudy. "How did you know that only a little water would cause a slower reaction?"

David looked at her. "Mieey tunnng hurtez. Eet is unnn firreee."

Little particles of the bath bomb were fizzing and causing minute explosions on David's tongue, which had swollen up to twice its normal size. Jack smiled. "That's the great thing about David—what he lacks in bravery he makes up for in stupidity."

David gave Jack a very stern look. He would probably have added a withering comment to this look if only his tongue hadn't been so badly swollen. After a while he stopped even trying to look stern with Jack, as he was mainly concentrating on breathing and not dribbling from the side of his mouth.

Trudy grabbed both of them by their sleeves and pulled them toward the door. "Let's get out of here. And possibly find some ice for David."

The only reason you could tell that David was smiling was that his tongue lolled to one side and slightly more dribble came out. "Thhenkk youb."

MINISTRY OF S.U.IT.S HANDBOOK

LICKING THINGS
THE REASON CATS ARE ALWAYS IN A BAD MOOD

If you have ever owned a cat you will have noticed that they seem to go through their lives appearing slightly grumpy. The reason for this is simply that cats clean themselves using their tongues.

If every meal that you ever had tasted of damp fur, you'd probably be in a fairly bad mood.

Therefore, if you want your cat to have a happy and sunny disposition, it is vital that you give him a line of credit at your local dry cleaner.

30
ECHOES OF THE PAST

It hadn't taken them too long to find a bus stop that would take them back to Belfast. David decided to go straight home, as he had had quite enough excitement for one day. More important, he wanted to lick the inside of his parents' refrigerator until the swelling of his tongue subsided.

⁙⁙⁙⁙⁙⁙⁙⁙⁙

Jack called his parents from the Ministry and told them he was going to go to Chess Club after school. "Well, okay," his mother agreed, "but try not to be late. We've got some news for you."

As Jack hung up he thought that was strange. His parents never had any news. Parents generally didn't. Sometimes they thought they did, but they were almost always wrong.

Jack walked over to Trudy, who was speaking to Grey.

". . . So you can see there's something very strange going on here."

Grey nodded. "Indeed. But knowing that something very strange is going on isn't enough. You've got to figure out what."

"Isn't there anything you can tell us to help?" she pleaded. "This is important to me. The aquarium is important to me."

Jack decided it was time to finally bite the bullet. "You've said that before. Why is the aquarium so important to you?" Jack screwed up his face in preparation for a punched shoulder that never came.

Trudy hung her head and spoke quietly. "A few years ago my mother went missing. The last place we knew where she was, was the aquarium."

Jack's eyes widened. "Your mother is missing? Why didn't you say anything before?"

"It's not . . . the kind of thing you tell people." Trudy's eyes went misty. "And before I met you . . . who would I have told? I've never been used to sharing my feelings."

Jack felt awful. He couldn't imagine what it was like not to have someone to share his worries and concerns with. All right, maybe David wasn't particularly useful at solving problems. But even being able to tell people your worries was a huge relief. "Trudy, you can tell me anything." He put a hand on her shoulder. Trudy was so upset she didn't even bother to shrug it off.

Jack turned to Grey. "Grey, this is the Ministry—you look into mysteries—can you help us find Trudy's mother? That's more important than all this fish nonsense, isn't it?"

"Well . . . umm . . . yes . . . but . . . ," Grey stammered.

Trudy eyed Grey suspiciously. Jack was surprised. Grey's voice was always crystal clear and steady. He wasn't the kind of man who stammered. Trudy fixed him with a steely gaze. "What's going on, Grey? If you're lying to me, I'll hit you so hard that the Tooth Fairy will need Virgin Galactic tickets to collect your teeth."

Even though Trudy was being deadly serious, Grey couldn't help smiling. "Trudy, sometimes you really remind me of your mother."

Two things happened simultaneously. Trudy's jaw dropped and Grey slapped a hand across his mouth.

Jack looked from Grey to Trudy and then back again. It took him slightly longer to realize what had happened. "Wait . . . wait a moment. How did you know Trudy's mother?"

Trudy's eyes stopped looking shocked and suddenly burned with flame. "Spill it, Grey. Right now." She said each word clearly and firmly. Her anger seemed to have banished her sadness for an instant.

Grey sighed and then dropped his hand from his mouth.[54] "I think I'd better take you to the Minister. He can explain this better than I can."

Grey led them along the corridors toward the offices of the Minister. Jack knew that this was going to be serious. Grey wouldn't have taken them to the office of the man who was in charge of the whole Ministry if this was a trivial matter. Trudy strode beside Grey, and Jack struggled to keep up.

---

[54] In many ways this spoiled the drama of the moment. Because he sighed with his hand over his mouth, it made a raspberry noise. Remember this, if you want to be dramatic in a similar situation. It's drop the hand first, *then* sigh.

Once outside the Minister's door Grey knocked, but Trudy was in no mood for waiting. She burst through the door, leaving Grey and Jack in her wake.

"You have something to tell me." Trudy pointed an accusing finger at the Minister. As usual he was dressed as a vicar even though he had no clerical training whatsoever.

The Minister looked over Trudy's head at Grey, obviously seeking some kind of explanation. Grey briefly described what had happened.

"Ahh," said the Minister, "that is unfortunate. Grey, you can leave us. I will explain."

Grey nodded and turned to go; however, Trudy wasn't going to let him get away that easily. "What? I want his explanation too. Anyway, how are *you* going to tell us how Grey knows my mother?" Trudy looked both confused and angry. It wasn't a pleasant combination for her or a safe combination for those around her. Jack knew better than to try and calm her down. He'd never seen her this furious before.

The Minister waved Grey out. "The reason I can explain how Grey knows your mother is that we all know your mother."

Grey closed the door quietly as he left. Even a nonlawyer could have heard a pin drop[55] in the room.

---

[55] It is worth noting that lawyers are actually the origin of the phrase "you could have heard a pin drop." Any normal person wouldn't care whether they could hear a pin drop or not. However, a lawyer would think to herself, "A dropped pin—if someone stands on one, it could turn into a lawsuit." Therefore, the *ping* of a pin dropping is like music to a lawyer's finely tuned ears.

"We all knew your mother because she worked here."

"What? You can't . . ." Trudy's voice trailed off as she tried to make sense of what she was hearing.

"She was one of the best agents that the Ministry has ever recruited."

"She was an agent? My mother worked here?" Trudy's face softened as astonishment replaced anger.

The Minister nodded. "Well, of course. Think about it. We came and asked you to be in the Ministry. That isn't the way it normally works. Usually recruits find their way here through curiosity and suspicion."

Jack's mind buzzed with questions that he wanted to ask. But this was Trudy's story and not his. He clamped his mouth tightly shut to try and prevent his curiosity from escaping.

Trudy kept talking. "Are you saying that I'm not . . . ?"

"Before you say anything more, I can assure you that as an agent you are exemplary," the Minister said.

Trudy stood up and slammed her fist onto the desk. "Why didn't you tell me this before? Do you know where my mother is now?"

The Minister's shoulders sagged. "Trudy, if I knew where she was, do you think I'd be sitting behind this desk? If anyone at the Ministry knew where your mother was, we'd be doing everything we could to rescue her. We don't know anything more than you do. She was investigating something at the aquarium one day and then she went missing."

A tear appeared in the corner of Trudy's eye. "I thought . . . I thought she'd abandoned us."

Jack looked at the floor. He'd never felt more helpless,

which was surprising considering how often he'd been rescued in the last two weeks.

The Minister's eyes became glassy. "This world is a strange place and anyone who tells you that they are sure of anything is an idiot. But one thing I am absolutely sure of—your mother would never, never abandon you."

Trudy spoke in a small, unfamiliar, trembling voice. "Why didn't you tell me this before?"

The Minister didn't answer Trudy's question, but he continued to stare directly at her. "What are you going to do now?"

"I'm going to the aquarium. And I'm going to start breaking things until I find my mother."

Trudy stood up to leave. Jack stood up with her.

"This isn't your fight," Trudy said to him.

"You're right, this isn't my fight," Jack conceded. "It's your fight. But you are my friend. And friends help each other."

Before Jack and Trudy could discuss this issue any more, the Minister spoke again. "This is why we didn't tell you before. Trudy, you are amazing. Even the Misery admires your use of The Speed. And Jack, you have the most amazingly twisted mind. You see things no one else does."

Trudy snorted at the compliments.

"But neither of you have the experience or skill that Trudy's mother had. You can't just rush into these things. This is why we didn't tell you what happened two years ago, Trudy. If your mother had gotten caught, you would have been caught too."

Trudy slumped back down in her chair.

"I know you don't want to hear this, but your mother wouldn't have wanted you to rush in and get yourself killed."

"I can't . . . I can't . . ."

"I know you can't just leave her. And we aren't asking you to. Just make sure you know what you're up against before you do anything."

Trudy looked at the floor. "Okay, okay," she whispered, then got up from her chair and slowly left the room. Jack slouched after her. Grey was waiting for them outside.

"He told you, then?"

"Yeah." Her eyes suddenly shot upward. "Why didn't you tell me, Grey?"

Grey breathed in. "Many, many years ago I joined the Ministry, just three months before your mother. And yet despite that she was ten times the agent I ever was. She outfought me, she outthought me; she could even make a better cup of tea than I could."

It wasn't so much that a smile spread across Trudy's face as it was that her frown weakened slightly. Grey continued. "She loved working at the Ministry. Some people said she loved helping people, and they were half right. She also liked smacking some sense into the bad guys. But there was one thing that she loved more than any of that. And that was her daughter."

Trudy sniffed and gulped. She started to say something but the words died in her throat.

"I wanted to tell you that she had gone missing while on an investigation. But your mother would never have forgiven me if you'd gotten caught in the same trap that she did. Your mother was headstrong too. And we couldn't afford to have you run into the aquarium with your fists flying. That wouldn't have gotten her back."

Jack decided it was time for him to say something. "That's all very well, but we have to do something now that we do know."

Grey nodded in agreement. "Of course you do. But fighting isn't going to be the solution—if it was, we'd have tried. You have to figure out what's going on—but that's not going to be easy. No one else at the Ministry has been able to figure it out—and we have been trying for years now."

Trudy threw her hands up. "How am I meant to think straight? How am I meant to do anything when my mother's an agent missing in action?"

Grey put a hand on Trudy's shoulder, but she shrugged it off. "Sometimes being brave isn't something you do with your fists. Sometimes being brave is something you do with your mind and heart."

Trudy looked up at Grey. For the first time since Jack had met her, she looked like a little girl. She said nothing for a minute then she spoke. "I'm sorry."

"Never be sorry for being passionate, Trudy. We should have told you sooner."

Jack looked into Trudy's eyes. "We'll find your mum."

Trudy said nothing but just nodded almost imperceptibly.

An idea occurred to Jack—he needed something to try and distract Trudy from what she'd just heard.

"Grey, a lot of the clues that we're dealing with point to some kind of water-based villain. You know soap, seals, aquariums. That kind of thing."

Grey nodded. "And?"

"Well, I was wondering if we could get any kind of water-based training. I don't know . . . swimming lessons."

Grey rubbed his chin. "I think there is something that the Misery might be able to help you with. Yes ... there are definitely a few skills that I'm sure he'd be happy to pass on."

If there was one thing of which Jack was certain, it was that the Misery wouldn't be happy about passing on skills. The Misery was never happy about anything.

MINISTRY OF S.U.IT.S HANDBOOK

SWIMMING LESSONS
INFLATABLE ARMBANDS

When you first go for swimming lessons, you are given inflatable armbands. This is typical of the kind of shoddy thinking that goes on in this world.

If you get in trouble when you are swimming, you won't panic while trying to keep your elbows above water. Generally speaking, elbows are fairly waterproof and can look after themselves.

The first person to invent the infinitely more sensible inflatable necklace[56] will no doubt become a millionaire.

[56] Patent pending.

31

PUPPET MASTER

Jack felt like a bit of an idiot standing in the middle of a dry corridor wearing a wet suit. Grey had sent them to changing rooms to get ready for their training. On the bright side, as Jack had hoped, the thought of training had seemed to distract Trudy at least a little.

Grey walked down the corridor with Cthulhu on one side of him and the Misery on the other. Jack was literally dumbfounded with fear. If the Tooth Fairy had been with them, they could have had the world's most terrifying picnic. As usual the Misery was dressed all in black, his long, lank hair hanging down in front of his eyes. Jack wondered if he could actually see anything through his heavy fringe.

Jack was so scared he had begun grinding his teeth. The Misery seemed to be arguing with Cthulhu.

"Okay, okay, I know your room is special. I just want to

borrow it. Anyway you owe me a favor—I rubbed out the chalk star and freed you."

Cthulhu made noises that sounded like mashed potato being forced through a plug hole.

"I will be with them the whole time. They won't be able to damage anything."

Cthulhu made a few cautionary squeaks.

The Misery nodded in agreement. "That's very reasonable. If they make a mess, I will wholeheartedly support your banishing them to a dimension where the only food is pain and the only drink is fear."

Cthulhu still looked as if he would refuse the request. A determined look came onto the Misery's face. "You do know the girl, Trudy—her mother is missing. Can you imagine how much pain it causes a child when they get taken away from their parent?"

Cthulhu's hoodless eyes got slightly bigger and appeared to water a little. He made a dull moaning noise.

The Misery nodded. "I know, I know, but it was the only choice you could make, and it was for everyone's good. Think of it like the best boarding school in the world—one with a near-inexhaustible supply of eels."

Cthulhu whimpered and his eyes watered more. Then something impossible happened. The Misery hugged Cthulhu.

Jack's jaw literally dropped. Although he had overheard their conversation, he really had no idea what they had been talking about. A boarding school with a supply of eels? And now two of the most terrifying people he had ever met were hugging. The day couldn't have gotten any stranger even if the Tooth Fairy had turned up and admitted that his favorite film was *The Fault in Our Stars*.[57]

Cthulhu noticed Jack and Trudy standing in the hallway. He pushed himself away from the Misery and shuffled backward as if embarrassed.

Jack tried to smile, but it came out more like a grimace. "Nice to see you again, Mr. Cthulhu and Mr. Misery."

The Misery snorted. Cthulhu ignored Jack and Trudy entirely and floated through a large door on their right. Grey spoke to the Misery. "Well done on persuading Cthulhu to lend you his room for the training."

The Misery sighed. "It wasn't easy, but he knows what it's like for a parent and child to be separated—so he's okay with it."

So was that why the Misery was so sad? Jack wondered. Perhaps he'd been separated from his parents? Jack was sure there was something more to this story, but at the moment he was still too terrified to start asking questions.

Grey turned to Jack and Trudy. "Good luck with the training. I'm sure the Misery will take care of you."

Jack prayed that the training would not be as intense as it had been the last time he had met with the Misery. The Misery gestured toward the door with his hand. "After you . . ."

Jack should have realized that when the Misery was polite it could not be the start of anything good. He also should have been looking where he was going instead of wondering why the Misery was being so polite.

---

[57] It wasn't. His favorite film was *Marathon Man*.

On his first step inside the room Jack fell straight down into murky green water. His head slid under the water. He panicked, turning and thrashing, unsure which was the way back up to the surface. He gulped down a mouthful of the fetid, stinking water.

Jack's panic was only relieved when a handful of his hair was grabbed and he was pulled to the surface. Jack gulped down as much air as he could until he felt like his lungs would burst. He found himself clinging on to the side of a hexagonal stepping-stone on which the Misery crouched.

"You seemed to be struggling for air under the water," the Misery observed.

Jack felt that this was rather a strange question. "Well, of course. I couldn't breathe."

"Okay, you were probably panicking too much. Sometimes that works, but not this time. We'll have to keep training."

Jack didn't understand what the Misery had said, but decided against asking for clarification.

Jack looked around the room. It was an enormous pool of green water surrounded by green cave walls. Dotted over the surface of the water were a series of hexagonal stepping-stones made of black rock. They varied in size considerably. Jack watched Trudy jumping from stone to stone with the surefootedness of a mountain goat.

A craggy, black island of stone was placed right in the center of the room. A swirling mist surrounded its edges. Cthulhu was floating in a cross-legged sitting position over the water toward the island.

Jack struggled out of the water and hauled himself up

until he was sitting on one of the stepping-stones. He shook his head to try and get the water out of his ears and then looked up at the Misery. "I suppose you think that was funny."

"Yes," the Misery agreed. "In the same way that I suppose that shiny disc in the sky at night is the moon. I suppose it because it's true."

"There was no point in doing that. You could have warned me."

The Misery shook his head slowly. "Do you like being wrong? I mean, do you try and achieve wrongness, or is wrongness just thrust upon you?"

Jack was confused again. This time a potent blend of curiosity and frustration made him ask a question. "What are you talking about?"

The Misery sighed. "When you fell in the water—that was training."

Jack rubbed the side of his face. It stung from where it had struck the water. "Training? Why does all training have to hurt so much with you?"

"Training is learning. Pain is stupidity leaving your body," the Misery said sternly. "Therefore it's something of a wonder to me why you aren't permanently in agony."

Jack could think of no response to this.

Trudy had stopped nimbly leaping from stone to stone and was standing on one leg on a hexagonal stone beside them. She decided to try and distract the Misery from his tormenting of Jack. "So is this the training, then?"

The Misery turned and looked at Trudy. He said nothing

for a few seconds. "You're smarter than that, Trudy. Why would I be training you to walk across hexagonal stones? Are you expecting to have to pursue someone across some particularly badly made crazy paving?"

"Well, no," admitted Trudy.

"The stepping-stones are here in case someone wants to come and visit Cthulhu."

"I thought they looked brand-new," Jack said, smirking. The Misery scowled at him. Jack stopped smirking immediately. Jack couldn't imagine anyone wanting to visit Cthulhu. Especially not in a room as unpleasant as this. "Do we have to train in water this dirty? There's stuff growing in it."

The Misery stared at Jack. "How do you think they keep swimming pools from having algae growing in them?"

Jack shrugged his ignorance.

The Misery smiled. "They put chemicals in the water that stop things from growing. Which is why they have to have a shallow end at the pool—because if you swallow enough of it, you'll stop growing forever."

Jack wasn't sure whether the Misery was joking or not, but made a promise to himself that the next time he went to swimming lessons he would be sure to keep his mouth clamped firmly shut.

The Misery looked around the room. "Okay, take a few minutes and look around the place and get your bearings—then we'll start the training." The Misery skipped off away from them. He moved lightly across the stones. Jack was surprised that he hadn't chosen to wear a wet suit. Instead he wore his usual baggy black sweater with a white letter *M* on the front.

Trudy smiled to herself and jumped lightly from stone to stone. The physical activity seemed to distract her from thinking about her mother.

Jack struggled to stand up. He decided that he had probably already found the best stone to stand on and didn't feel the need to leap to another.

He looked across the water. Cthulhu had floated onto the stone island and had just set up a small red-and-white-striped tent. Jack wondered if he lived inside it. Cthulhu sat on the ground in front of the tent, cross-legged. Jack was surprised when a dozen long, fibrous tentacles crept out from under the bottom of Cthulhu's dark robe, snaked their way across the island, and disappeared under the tent's bottom.

A few seconds later a range of puppets appeared in a small hole halfway up the tent. Jack realized what he was looking at. Cthulhu was giving himself a Punch and Judy show. Jack remembered Static with his sidekick Volty. The thought made him incredibly sad. He realized that both Static and Cthulhu shared something in common. They were so lonely that they had created imaginary puppet friends for themselves.

At that moment he heard a noise that sounded like an elephant[58] bellowing and something grabbed his ankle, pulling him off the stone and into the freezing water below.

[58] Or perhaps a woolly mammoth.

THE WOOLLY MAMMOTH
Why It Still Exists

Many people assume that the woolly mammoth became extinct. However, this would make no sense at all. After all, elephants currently exist and a mammoth was nothing more than an elephant wearing a furry sweater. Elephants would not simply cease to exist if Bill Gates used his money to set up a charitable foundation with the aim of ensuring that all elephants were wearing sweaters by 2020.

The truth is simple: Woolly mammoths and elephants are the same creatures. However, mammoths are the teenage version of the elephants when they decide to grow out a large, floppy fringe and have long hair.

This phase only lasts for a few years, which is why only the most dedicated naturalist will have observed a teenage, floppy-fringed elephant/mammoth in the wild. As an elephant/mammoth gets older, it becomes more conventional and decides to adopt the close-cut hairstyle of older elephants. (Just like a teenager getting a haircut in order to get his first Saturday job.)

Some elephants/mammoths would like to keep their longer hair, but these are rare—and even if they want to keep their hair, frequently it falls out through stress. Elephants never forget, which means they have an awful lot to worry about.

Suggesting that mammoths have died out is the equivalent of noting how many bald men there are around these days and suggesting that men with hair may be in danger of extinction.

32

TAKE MY BREATH AWAY

Jack's entire body spasmed with the shock. One minute he was feeling sympathetic toward Cthulhu and Static. The next he was submerged in water. It wasn't exactly the kind of thing that he had been expecting. He struggled to think. What had happened? What had grabbed his ankle? What was going to happen next? What had that noise been? He struggled to achieve any kind of rational thought. Unlike his previous dunking, which had just been unpleasant, this one was more confusing and shocking than anything else. He was so stunned that he forgot to even try and thrash his way to the surface.

The only thought in his head was *What is going on? What is going on? What is going on?*

Once more a pair of hands hauled Jack out of the water and made him grab the edge of a stone. Jack felt as if he should have been spluttering out mouthfuls of water. And yet for some reason he wasn't. Jack was still very confused as to what had happened. He pulled himself up and sat on the stone.

Floating in the water at the foot of his stone was a smug-looking Misery.

"What's going on here?" asked Jack.

The Misery didn't answer. He looked to Jack's left. Trudy was standing there glancing between a stopwatch in her hand and Jack. Something about Jack was confusing her.

"Do I have something dripping out of my nose?" asked Jack.

The Misery splashed the water at his feet and laughed. "No, Jack, and not only do you not have something coming out of your nose, but you don't have anything going into it either."

"Well, thanks... I think." Jack looked around the room, hoping to see something that would explain what was going on.

The Misery hauled himself up onto one of the stones, his baggy sweater sopping wet. He kept his eyes fixed on Jack while he spoke to Trudy. "How long now?"

"Five and a half minutes," Trudy answered.

"Impressive." The Misery almost smiled. Then he leaned forward across the gap between his stone and Jack's. He clapped his hands suddenly in front of Jack's face. "BREATHE!"

Jack hadn't stopped being stunned and confused, and the Misery's actions confused him still further. And then he realized something. He had stopped breathing. Jack gasped suddenly and took several deep breaths.

"What happened? Was there a...? Did I just...?" Jack stuttered, frantically trying to remember when he had stopped breathing.

"Focus, Jack," the Misery said. "If you become stunned again, you'll stop breathing."

Trudy was equally surprised. "Jack, you didn't take a single breath after you got out of the water. And your head was underneath for minutes."

"Is this magic water?" Jack asked, looking into the murky depths.

The Misery sadly shook his head. "Magic water? If you're going to ask stupid and inane questions like that, why don't you just become a talk-show host? It's ordinary water." The Misery considered for a moment. "Well, it's mostly water. I mean, Cthulhu lives here and you may notice that there isn't a toilet or even a bucket for that matter."

Jack frowned and then realized what the Misery was suggesting. He spat a few times to try and clear his mouth of any water he had swallowed. "This is all very confusing. Why did I stop breathing?"

"That was your training. Have you ever heard the phrase 'It took my breath away'?"

Trudy and Jack both agreed that they had. Jack thought back to how Trudy had seemed to stop breathing when she saw the amazingly beautiful marine biologist professor. Her breath had certainly been taken away then.

"You hear people saying things like that in pop songs. Or when they're talking about some fancy painting in an art gallery," Trudy suggested.

"Yeah, or if they're shocked. My dad always says that when he hears how much mum spent on shoes; it shocks him so much that it takes his breath away."

"And that's what I just did to you, Jack—I shocked you so much I took your breath away."

Jack laughed nervously. "But . . . no . . . I mean that's just an expression. When people say 'it took my breath away' they don't mean it literally."

"Please stop talking rubbish, Jack. All expressions have a basis in fact. Otherwise people would just be talking nonsense all the time, wouldn't they?" The Misery sighed. "Breathing is just a bad habit people have picked up over the years."

"Breathing is a bad habit?"

"Of course it is. It isn't an essential thing that we have to do. Not like drinking water. If you don't drink water you become dehydrated. You actually run out of water in your body. But that can't happen with air. There's lots of air in your body; you're surrounded by air, so why would you need to breath a lot of the stuff in? We don't *need* to breathe air in the same way that fish don't need to drink water."[59]

Jack was suspicious of this argument. "So why are you breathing, then?"

The Misery sneered at him. "Because I like having bad habits. Think about it—you breathe in and then you breathe out. Do you drink water and then spit it out straight away? What would be the point in that? Breathing is pointless."

---

[59] For those of you who are wondering, clearly fish don't need to drink water; otherwise goldfish would end up living in empty bowls.

Trudy chimed in with a question. "But wait a minute—don't we take in oxygen through our lungs? So don't we keep at least part of the air inside our bodies?"

"Stuff and nonsense. You really think that every time you breathe in you're keeping some oxygen inside? Think about it—if that were the case, then you'd be very slowly inflating yourself. After a lifetime of taking a little bit of oxygen in with each breath you'd be blown up to the size of a hot air balloon."

That seemed to make sense to Jack; after all, if you kept eating cake, you'd swell up to an enormous size. If you kept drinking water, eventually you'd burst. And yet every moment of every day you were meant to be taking in more and more air and yet you didn't get any larger.

"So breathing is a bad habit?"

"And it's very addictive. Most people find it almost impossible to give up. So the only way to get people to stop doing it is to distract them. Like if you're on a diet and you do things to take your mind off food because of how hungry you are."

"So technically I could just stop breathing forever now?"

"Maybe, but I wouldn't try it. You've been breathing all your life and it's very addictive. Often when people stop breathing altogether they can die of shock."

"So we can use this skill to go underwater without needing to breathe? Just like using The Speed?" asked Trudy.

The Misery shook his head. "This is a lot more difficult than using The Speed. It's relatively easy to make yourself sad. It's a lot harder to surprise yourself. It's also vitally important to make sure you're surprised and not panicked."

"Why's that?" asked Trudy.

"Well, a surprise or a shock takes your breath away, so you don't need to breathe, but have you ever seen people panicking? They breathe really quickly—hyperventilate—which fills their lungs with water. So panicking actually makes things worse. That's why people drown. If you fall in the water and you're surprised it'll be fine, but if you panic instead then you're a goner."

"And surprising yourself is the only way to take your breath away?" Jack wondered out loud.

"Obviously not," snapped the Misery (a touch harshly, Jack felt). "If you can spontaneously fall in love, that also takes your breath away."

Jack scratched his head. "Is it easy to fall in love?"

The Misery stared off into the distance; for a moment he seemed to forget that Jack and Trudy were even there. "It's easy to fall in love. Almost impossible to get over it." His voice trailed off into silence.

The room went completely silent. A single tear looked as if it was about to fall from the corner of the Misery's eye. Trudy looked as if her heart was about to break. Jack, on the other hand, was considerably less sympathetic. He wished that people weren't as complicated as this. He'd just found out what made Trudy so sad and suddenly it turned out that the Misery also had a tragedy in his past. Jack felt a little left out—his life was annoyingly tragedy-free.[60]

"Anyway, you losers can practice by yourselves for a

[60] Which, incidentally, is the only reason Jack had never won a television singing competition.

while. I've got better things to do." The Misery's expression darkened—he was clearly embarrassed that he had shown any kind of vulnerability in front of Jack and Trudy.

Jack felt his curiosity taking hold of him. Maybe he could figure out a clever way to ask the Misery what he meant about falling in love. He thought carefully about framing a question. "Look, Misery, before you go, I was wondering what you meant by . . ."

Jack didn't get any further with his question. The Misery reached forward and gave him a small push in the center of his chest. Jack's arms windmilled and he fell backward into the water. The Misery streaked out of the room so fast that his slipstream nearly knocked Trudy from her stepping-stone.

Jack pulled himself up out of the water and back onto a stepping-stone again. "Why does everybody have to have a secret past?" he muttered as he hauled himself out of the water.

Trudy glared at him.

"It isn't my fault! I'm just curious!" Jack observed.

Jack comforted himself with the thought that even if Trudy and the Misery had secrets in their past, at least some people were more straightforward. After all, Cthulhu was an evil interdimensional being who wished to destroy life and send all humanity into gibbering insanity. Jack felt fairly sure that Cthulhu wasn't going to suddenly reveal a secret hidden motivation or mysterious backstory.

Jack looked across to where Cthulhu was sitting on his island. He had stopped playing with his hand puppets and was looking mournfully into a strange leather-bound book.

"OH, COME ON!" Jack shouted at no one in particular.

FALLING IN LOVE
How Easy It Is

Anyone who has ever listened to a pop song or watched a Hollywood movie will know that falling in love is easy. However, it used to be even easier in the olden days. Hundreds of years ago when everyone lived in a castle (or at least anyone that really mattered), the only thing you needed to do to fall in love was to put an ad in the local newspaper reading, "Young woman who has had hard life, but remains cheerful, kind, and pure of heart seeks Prince Charming for marriage and happily ever after. *(Please note Duke Charmings and Earl Charmings need not apply.)*"

If the world had remained like this, the algorithms that are used to make Internet dating sites function would be considerably more straightforward.

The evidence for this is quite clear in the historically based story of Cinderella. Even though Cinderella had met Prince Charming only once, she knew that he was the ideal man for her, and they lived happily ever after.

It is with some reluctance that we note that "ever after" in the case of Cinderella lasted for only three weeks. The part of the story that is often overlooked is that running in a single glass slipper is a health and safety nightmare. While she was running, the single slipper she was left with shattered, lacerating Cinderella's foot. She was then forced to run along behind the mice that had been pulling her carriage. Her foot got infected with mouse poo and she died of septicemia weeks after marrying the prince.

It should be noted that the prince could have found Cinderella much sooner if only he had been bright enough to notice the fact that she was wearing glass shoes. Then instead of having to search the kingdom he could just have searched the client lists of the kingdom's registered podiatrists.

The moral of this story is that if you are going to a dance wearing glass slippers, then it is almost always advisable to take a pair of flip-flops with you for the walk home.

33

PRACTICE MAKES PERFECT

Jack still didn't have all the answers he wanted. "So when the Misery shocked me—how did he do that?"

Trudy laughed and pointed to a small black box that sat on one of the hexagonal stones. "Nothing special—he just used that MP3 player to make the bellowing noise. Then he jumped out of the water and grabbed your leg. You should have seen your face."

Jack carefully leapt over to the stone where the MP3 player sat. "How about some music while we're practicing?"

"I really wouldn't do that if I were you. That belongs to the Misery and we don't have a good track record of looking after his property."

Jack decided to ignore Trudy's advice. "I'm not going to damage anything; I'm just going to play some music!" Jack skipped through the tracks on the MP3 player. Pressing the arrow keys, he moved it away from the sound effects list it was currently on and found listings for some albums.

"Most of these are really depressing songs."

Trudy frowned. "It belongs to the Misery—what did you expect?"

Jack finally found a track he recognized and put it on. It was by one of those bands that wore so much dark clothing and makeup that when they played together, there was a distinct chance they would cause a singularity and collapse into a black hole.

A tinny sound echoed across the room. "Wait a minute— I'm going to pump the bass right up."

Jack slipped as he twiddled a knob on the MP3 player, knocking it into the water. He froze in terror at what he had just done. A deep bass note echoed through the water.

Trudy was about to shout at Jack, but she was stopped by a piercing scream. It sounded like the shattering of a thousand panes of glass fed through a heavily distorted amplifier system. It was a sound of impossible, interdimensional evil in distress. Jack and Trudy both clapped their hands over their ears to try and shield themselves as much as possible. They both turned to see Cthulhu howling.

Cthulhu dropped the leather-bound book he had been looking at and bolted across his craggy island. With his robes billowing about him, he half hovered, half flew across the surface of the water.

Jack braced himself, ready for Cthulhu to hurtle into his body. However, Cthulhu wasn't aiming at Jack but at the door, which he crashed through, splintering it into a thousand pieces. Slowly Cthulhu's screams quietened as they echoed down the corridor outside.

Trudy looked at Jack sternly. "I told you not to play with the MP3. See what's happened now? The Misery is going to kill us."

Jack wasn't sure what actually had happened. The dull bass guitar music was still echoing from under the water. "The MP3 player's still working, though."

Trudy listened and realized Jack was right. She dived into the water and kicked downward. After a minute she broke the surface and was holding the player, which was even louder above the surface. She pressed the Stop button and set it on one of the hexagonal stepping-stones. "I thought Cthulhu was mad at us for breaking the MP3 player—but that wouldn't make him run away, would it? I wonder what it was that made Cthulhu so upset?"[61]

Jack shrugged. "Maybe it was the music. Squid ears probably work differently from ours." Then a thought occurred

---

[61] For those of you who are wondering why the Misery's MP3 player was waterproof, the reason is simple. Not only did the Misery like to listen to his music by himself, but he also liked to listen to it when the sky was dull, overcast, and full of rain. Frequently in a graveyard, if there was one nearby that was not too full of teenage Goths. The popularity of the Goth movement in recent years, combined with the increasing fashionability of being cremated, has led to an increasing problem of graveyard overcrowding. This is a serious matter that will soon have to be addressed by the Supreme Goth Council. Because it's almost impossible to be moody and alone when sitting in the dining area of a Subway sandwich shop.

to Jack. He carefully hopped from hexagonal stone to stone toward the green island.

"Jack!" Trudy called after him. "I really hope you aren't doing what I think you're doing."

Jack's mother had often told him that curiosity killed the cat. However, she had never said that "curiosity would inspire the potential wrath of an interdimensional creature of almost impossible evil." Which was a shame, as that would have been the more accurate advice.

A final bound took Jack sprawling onto the rocky shore. He stood up and looked at Trudy. "Maybe what made him fly into that rage was something he read in the book. Aren't you a little bit curious about what can make an interdimensional being, composed of equal parts squid and evil, sad?"

"Jack, this is Cthulhu we're talking about." Trudy pretended to be weighing two options up in her hands while she talked. "So, while yes, I'm curious as to what he was looking at, on the other hand I'm not curious about what I'd look like with all my internal organs hanging off the outside of my body. Which is what Cthulhu would do to us if he found out we were looking at his stuff."

Trudy's colorful turn of phrase almost turned Jack's stomach.[62] But the one thing that Jack couldn't stand was an unsolved mystery. "Keep a lookout for me—I'm just going to take a quick peek."

Trudy's mouth narrowed in anger, but then she bounded

---

[62] Which at this stage was, thankfully, still on the inside of his body.

over to the splintered door. She stuck her head out of the now-empty doorway, and kept watch down the corridor.

Jack opened the book and flicked through it. The first page he turned to was a photo of a long, thin lake taken from an airplane. Jack had expected it to be a picture of something stomach-churning or a story that was beyond rational human understanding. Confusingly, the photo was neither of those things. Which was annoying, because instead of satisfying his curiosity this had just made it worse.

Jack looked at the next page. It was another photograph of the strange lake. And then another. And then there were some shots of the lake from the ground. There wasn't anything particularly interesting about the pictures, although a few of them seemed to focus on floating logs, or dark shapes looming out of the water. Unfortunately the photos were all blurred or out of focus, and Jack couldn't quite make out what the dark objects were.

Jack carefully put the book back where he had found it and then jumped from stepping-stone to stepping-stone until he was standing beside Trudy.

"What was in the book?" she whispered.

"Just photos of some large lake."

Trudy looked puzzled. "Like Lough Neagh? Where the fracking was? Do you think Cthulhu's involved in this somehow?"

"Maybe." Jack shrugged. "But I don't think we should be expecting Cthulhu to be doing anything that aligns with sanity. He drives people insane for a hobby. Maybe he's just trying to do a really slow, relaxed job with us."

SQUIDS
THEIR ABILITY TO HEAR AND HOW IT RELATES TO JELLY

As has been previously discussed, squids have no ears and therefore have limited ability to hear. However, this does not mean that they are entirely insensate to the world of noise.

If you have seen squids at aquariums, you will have noticed that they are wobbly and flexible, in many ways like a large bag of be-tentacled Jell-O. (It is worth noting that be-tentacled Jell-O does not actually exist. Although if it did, it would be awesome and terrifying at the same time.) This means that they can sense vibrations through the water. Naturally, they find deep bass sounds most disconcerting indeed, which is why so many of the larger squids live on the ocean floor. The ocean floor, with its freezing water and lack of sunlight, is not a nice place to live. However, many giant squid swim down there purely to get away from the deep booming bass sounds that the engines of ocean liners make.

Interestingly enough, this is also the reason that teenagers stop having Jell-O at birthday parties. Young children tend to enjoy plinky-plonky piano music. However, as they become teenagers they enjoy music with a larger bass range. In the same way that squid find bass sounds uncomfortable, there is a risk that if you play bass music to a Jell-O, it will shake itself to death and splatter everyone in the room.

This can be the only reason why parents stop serving Jell-O at children's birthday parties. Having said that, the only thing that is more awesome than Jell-O would be a Jell-O that exploded and splattered everyone in the room. However, parents don't seem to understand this.

34

FIRST PIECE OF THE PUZZLE

A Ministry car dropped Jack off at home. His parents were just finishing their tea when he went in.

"Good day?" his mother asked.

"Yeah, fun."

Jack's father set down a plate of sausages, mash, and beans that had been kept warm in the oven in front of Jack.

"Great, I'm starving."

Jack reached for a knife and fork and caught a look at his hands. Before they had left the Ministry Jack had been sure to check that his hair was completely dry. Anything else would have been a dead giveaway. Jack had seen the people who went to Chess Club, and he was pretty sure that none of the matches they were involved in were strenuous enough to require a shower afterward.

Therefore Jack was sitting at the table with bone-dry

hair. But his hair wasn't the problem. The problem was his hands. Jack had spent a good few hours splashing around in the water in Cthulhu's room and, like when he stayed in the bath too long, it had made his hands and fingertips wrinkle up like those of an old man. He looked as though he'd had a hand transplant from someone twice his grandmother's age.

Jack quickly jammed his hands into his pockets. He then sat there nervously trying to figure out his next move. Jack's mother was the first to notice that something was wrong. "Aren't you going to eat anything?"

On hearing Jack's mother, his father looked up as well. "Yes, I thought you said you were starving."

Jack looked from one parent to another. He couldn't think of anything to say. They were waiting for him to make the next move. And then a thought occurred to him.

"Have you hired a lawyer?" he asked.

Jack's mother and father looked at each other, even more confused. "How did you know about that?"

Jack explained about the trip to the soap factory but didn't mention how the lawyer had saved his life.

"Nice to see that he's doing his research." Jack's mother looked impressed.

Jack's father thought briefly and then spoke. "Maybe he'll get us a really big settlement."

Jack's mother nodded. Her eyes glazed over slightly. "... And then we could get the kitchen redone as well as the bathroom."

"Yeah, yeah," Jack's father agreed even though he really

wasn't listening. He was lost in his own dreams of a big monetary settlement. "... And I could get a motorbike."

"... And we could go to Las Vegas for a holiday...."

"... And we could get one of those really powerful Dyson vacuum cleaners...."

Jack's mother snapped out of her dream for a minute. "A Dyson vacuum cleaner?"

"I like vacuum cleaners," Jack's father answered sheepishly.

"Well ... okay," Jack's mother reluctantly agreed. "And we could get a new car, something really sporty...."

"... And a ..."

When he was sure his parents were far enough buried in their thoughts of millions of pounds, Jack took his hands out of his pockets and picked up his dinner plate. "I'm just going to eat this in my room while I'm doing my homework," Jack half-lied.

"Whatever ..." His father waved him away.

"And we could get a sun parlor like the Smiths next door."

"We could get one even bigger than the Smiths next door."

"Great idea ... With a hot tub...."[63]

---

[63] For those of you who were wondering what Jack's father's mustache was thinking about while his mother and father were doing their daydreaming, it would have been contented with a small purpose-built mustache comb and a lifetime supply of Captain Fawcett's Moustache Wax. Like all the best mustaches, it was a mustache of humble and simple tastes.

Jack left and made his way up to his bedroom without further incident. After he had finished his sausages and mash, he considered going back down to the kitchen to see if there was any dessert in the offing. However, when he looked at his hands they were still wrinkled and white.

For a moment he was extremely upset that he would be missing pudding. His father made a mean trifle. On the other hand, trifle could be distracting, and Jack wanted to spend some time thinking. He felt as if they had all the pieces of the jigsaw puzzle.[64] Now they just had to put them together.

[64] For those of you who have never seen a jigsaw puzzle before, they look a bit like what happens to an iPad's screen if you drop it from a significant height.

JIGAW PUZZLES
THE ORIGIN OF THE JIGSAW PUZZLE

Although many people don't realize it, a great number of popular toys were in fact invented by people who absolutely hated children.

The perfect example of this is the jigsaw. A better name for a jigsaw would be a "broken picture." However, this would have been an unappealing name and would not have sold well. Therefore the evil scientist who came up with the jigsaw came up with a more fun and friendly name.

But why is the jigsaw an evil toy, you ask? Have you ever noticed that when you make a jigsaw it is incredibly frustrating when the very last piece is missing? And it is always the *last piece* that is missing, never one of the first pieces. Many people assume that it is a coincidence—but it is not.

The jigsaw was designed by Professor Heinrich Thunderbolt using five-dimensional quantum mathematics. This means that it is always the last piece (instead of the first piece) that will be missing—thus maximizing a child's frustration. Professor Thunderbolt had a vendetta against children and toys in particular. The cause of Professor Thunderbolt's frustration is currently unclear.

35

TWO BUCKETS
THURSDAY

The next morning when Jack's alarm went off, he jumped out of his bed and bolted for the bathroom. Of course, after the nasty explosion with the bath bomb, it wasn't in the best shape. His mother had put out two buckets into the bathroom to substitute for the damaged fittings.

One of the buckets had been filled with hot water and was for washing yourself. The other bucket was filled with something that wasn't hot water and was most definitely not for washing yourself. It was vitally important to remember which one was which.

Jack picked up a sponge and started to wash his face. It was the natural sponge that Trudy had bought him from Neptune's Den. Thankfully it didn't seem to have any of the unpleasant effects that the bath bomb had.

And then Jack remembered something strange. He

remembered from a science class earlier in the year that they had been studying all the different kinds of life there were on the planet. Amongst all the strange animals they had studied were sponges. This was because the sort of natural sponges you bought in places like Neptune's Den weren't inanimate objects—when they were in the sea they had actually been living animals.

The thought freaked Jack out slightly and he dropped the sponge into the wrong bucket. "Well, we won't be using that sponge again," Jack muttered to himself.

But the more Jack thought about it the more he realized that there was something very odd indeed about using an animal to clean yourself. You wouldn't have used a swan's neck to dry under your armpits. You wouldn't have used a hedgehog to comb your hair or a bristly caterpillar to brush your teeth.

If Jack had suggested that people start using a chinchilla as a washcloth, he would just have been stared at. And yet sponges, which had once been live animals, were used in this way. Jack looked at the sponge absorbing the "not-water" in the bucket and another thought occurred to him. The realization shocked him and he took a step backward, knocking a tub of his mother's moisturizer off the edge of what remained of the bathtub.

And then it all came together—the clues connected in his head. Jack grabbed a towel and dried his face as he ran back to his bedroom and pulled on his school uniform.

As usual, when Jack got on the school bus he made the mistake of trying to explain his thoughts to David. "You'll never guess what, but there's a connection between sponges, moisturizer, and wet, wrinkly skin."

David looked at Jack. "Yes, they're all things you find in the bathroom."

Jack considered trying to explain the more sinister connection. Then he thought better of it. He could wait until they got to school and spoke to the more sensible Trudy. "So, David, any good documentaries on television last night?"

"Of course there was." David smiled. "There was this brilliant one about paper clips. . . ."

Jack sat back and listened to David as he recounted ten amazing facts about paper clips.[65]

―――――――――

The minute Jack and David walked into the school Trudy came over to him. "Jack, I don't think I can stand this any longer."

"Stand what?"

"I went home last night and sat with my father, watching TV. Every day since my mother went away we've said less and less to each other."

Jack frowned. "That must be awful."

"Awful would be like a holiday. To start off with he was depressed, but he still talked. But slowly, as time has passed

---

[65] Basically a paper clip is just a broken piece of wire. You'd be surprised how many inventions are just other inventions that have been broken or damaged. The first sandpaper was just flypaper that had been dropped at the beach. A sprinkler system is just a leaky hose, and Post-it Notes were originally dollhouse wallpaper, but they couldn't get the dollhouse wallpaper paste to be strong enough.

he's said less and less. On Monday when I came home he said 'Hey there, Trudy.' Then Tuesday it was just 'Hey there.' Yesterday it was just 'Hey.' We have to find my mother."

Jack wondered how he would feel if his parents stopped talking. Okay, for a few weeks it might have been a bit of a relief. But after a while he knew it would make him miserable.

Jack asked David to give them some space. David nodded silently and trotted off to class.

"Jack, this is driving me insane. Waiting isn't something I'm good at."

"Well, hopefully you won't have to wait for much longer. I think I've figured some of this out."

"Tell me." Trudy's voice was filled with hope.

Jack started explaining. "You remember the old woman from the aquarium? The one who walked out into the sea."

Trudy nodded. "The one you said that looked like the grandmother of Regina Maris."

"Mmm-hmm. The thing is I was completely wrong. That wasn't any relation of Regina Maris. That was Regina Maris."

"But you said she was far too old."

"But think, Trudy. If you swim for an hour in the sea, your skin goes all white, old looking, and wrinkly. Now imagine how much worse the effect would be if you actually lived in the sea."

"But that makes no sense. When we saw her at the school and at the shop she looked young, pretty, stunning even."

"And that's the genius of her plan. Because she spends so much time in the sea she should be permanently wrinkly and old looking. But think about it: If you wanted to appear young, what kind of a shop would you go to? One with row upon row of moisturizers. She's using all those moisturizers to counteract the wrinkly-skin effect of living under the sea all the time."

"Neptune's Den."

"Exactly. And that's not all—what's the most striking thing about Neptune's Den?"

Trudy thought for a minute. She cast her mind back to the shopping center. Then it occurred to her. "The smell."

"Exactly."

"But it sells perfume, so you'd expect it to smell, wouldn't you?"

The more Jack spoke the more connections came together in his head. "No! The exact opposite. You'd expect a perfume shop to not smell of anything. Think about it—if you were trying to sell something that smelled nice, you'd want to sell it in a shop that didn't smell of anything."

Trudy snapped her fingers, realizing exactly what Jack was getting at. "Because if the shop smells constantly of perfume, how is anyone supposed to tell whether they like the one perfume they're actually trying on?"

"Exactly, it'd be like a gourmet restaurant making the most delicious and subtle food ever and then insisting on coating everything in KFC gravy."

"Although that would be amazing," offered Trudy.

"Well, yes, that would be amazing," admitted Jack. "But it really isn't the point."

"So wait a minute," Trudy said as she thought through what Jack had said. "Why do shops like Neptune's Den smell so strongly if they aren't trying to sell perfume?"

"I think Regina Maris lives in the sea. So think about fish

that also live in the sea. What's the most distinctive thing about them?"

Trudy answered more quickly this time. "The smell."

"Exactly. Anything that lives in the sea starts to smell when you take it out of the sea and put it on the land. I think Regina Maris and her workers are some kind of undersea race. The smell in Neptune's Den and those kinds of shops is to try and disguise the fish smell. It also explains the names of Neptune's Den and Poseidon drilling."

Trudy exhaled slowly. "It almost all makes sense—and if they're living under the sea they'll mainly be eating fish . . . like the Professor—and remember how he smelled?! But if they live under the sea, then why come onto land at all? And what's the fracking about?"

Jack's face fell. "I still can't figure out those parts yet. But there's one thing I'm sure of. It involves sponges." Jack explained to Trudy his revelation about sponges. "For some reason they sell natural sea sponges in those shops. We know that they need the moisturizers to get rid of the wrinkles the water causes. We know that the bath bombs can be turned into weapons. We know that the soap and perfume are there to hide the smell of fish. But I can't figure out why on earth they'd be selling sponges."

Trudy gave Jack an enormous hug. He still wasn't used to Trudy's hugs yet. Although Trudy tried hard to be affectionate when she was hugging, it still felt a little bit more like the beginning of a wrestling move rather than a reassuring gesture. Jack knew she was doing it because they were closer to solving the mystery of what had happened to her mother.

As they were hugging Edwyn walked past them wearing

a *Static Rules!* badge he'd clearly made himself. "Why don't you two just get married already?"

Trudy turned around and gave Edwyn a smack around his ear. Jack noticed that he was heading along the corridor that led out to the playing fields.

"Where are you going?"

"Haven't you heard? They're going to turn on the fracking drill. They're having a ceremony out back."

"I've got a bad feeling about this," Jack said. "What if the fracking is the secret to all this? Maybe we should have stopped them before they could turn on the drill."

"There's only one way to find out." Trudy grabbed Jack's hand and pulled him out the back door toward the playing fields.

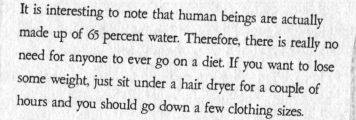

MINISTRY OF S.U.I.T.S HANDBOOK

HUMAN BEINGS
Percentage of Water

It is interesting to note that human beings are actually made up of 65 percent water. Therefore, there is really no need for anyone to ever go on a diet. If you want to lose some weight, just sit under a hair dryer for a couple of hours and you should go down a few clothing sizes.

Alternatively, just go and sit outside in the sun and do a bit of evaporating. This is why people who lie about poolsides in bikinis and small swimming costumes are always so thin. They're just desiccated.

36
CARNIVAL

The playing fields were full of children running from stall to stall. It was as if a carnival had been set up overnight. There were ring toss games, cotton candy sellers, even a small Ferris wheel. Right in the center of the carnival the enormous fracking drill stood, surrounded by the corrugated iron maze. Jack shivered a little when he saw it. Even though the gate remained locked there was something scary about knowing that it contained two Minotaurs. Both vain, but one considerably more dangerous than the other.

Jack and Trudy wandered around the stalls trying to find something that was deadly and that would threaten the populace of Northern Ireland. Trudy paid a pound at the stall where you burst balloons with darts to win a prize. With her natural physical skills, she easily won a teddy bear that was almost as big as Jack. Thankfully it was nowhere near as deadly as the cuddly bear that served as the Ministry's most deadly operative. Trudy shoved the bear into Jack's arms, not giving him a chance to refuse.

Trudy sniffed the air as she walked away from the stall. "Perfume," she mouthed silently. Jack nodded. Clearly all the carnival employees were in the employ of Regina Maris.

"What is this all in aid of?" Trudy asked.

Jack had no answer. In one corner of the playing fields a television screen the size of an advertising billboard crackled into life. There was a brief flare of static[66] and then an image of a woman's face appeared. The crowd began to wander toward it.

The face was of Regina Maris. Jack studied her closely. On the enormous screen he could see that although the moisturizers from Neptune's Den had done a good job, there were still some small telltale signs of wrinkling from all the time she spent underwater. He was certain that his theory was right.

"Welcome to a wonderful day for Poseidon International Drilling Company." Ms. Maris's voice boomed out from two huge black speakers that had been placed at either side of the television screen. "All across Northern Ireland we are holding gala events to mark the turning on of our exploration drills. We hope to find large deposits of natural gas across the island. If our efforts are successful the costs of energy will drop dramatically."

Ms. Maris paused dramatically, expecting applause.

---

[66] Like, you know, actual static. Not the superhero Static. It's all in the capitalization.

Although there may have been applause at other locations, the school playing fields were largely quiet. Generally school-children are fairly unconcerned with the price of energy. Jack was reminded of the pirate Blackbeard Junior, who had been building wind turbines. What was it with evil villains and energy efficiency? Maybe running evil organizations used a lot of power. He wondered if pirate ships were all packed full of fiberglass insulation to save on heat loss and running costs. Still, it was nice to think that you could be a maniacal evil genius, but at the same time be environmentally responsible.

Ms. Maris continued her speech with a dramatic flourish. "So without further ado, we will turn the drills on!"

The image of Ms. Maris's face disappeared and was replaced with dozens of smaller images of drilling rigs across Northern Ireland. Right at the center of the screen was a live feed of the large drill in the middle of Lough Neagh.

Jack felt as if his body was deflating at the noise of dozens of drills whirling into action at once. He couldn't help feeling that he and Trudy had failed. Whatever evil purpose the drills had been created for would now be achieved.

After a few minutes the screen crackled with static again and Ms. Maris's face appeared. "All the drills are active. Our quest for gas has begun!"

Jack raised an eyebrow. This didn't sound like normal supervillain gloating.

"Of course, the drills move through the earth and dirt slowly, so it will be several days before we have any results to speak of. In the meantime, the giant screens around the country will continue to broadcast live pictures from all our fracking sites so you can follow the excitement." The screen again switched back to the drilling sites.

Jack and Trudy let out relieved sighs. The drills weren't immediately effective. They still had some time to stop Ms. Maris's evil plan . . . whatever that was.

David bounded over to them. His face was covered in cotton candy and he had a toffee apple sticking to his elbow for some reason. "I don't find this as exciting as some people," he observed looking around at the other children. "I mean, it's just pictures of giant drills, which I find boring."

Trudy and Jack laughed. David just looked at them quizzically. "You made a joke," said Jack. "Giant drills. Boring. Because they bore holes in the grou—never mind."

The school bell rang for the first class of the day, and teachers appeared to herd children away from the carnival. It was then that the earthquake struck.

MINISTRY OF S.U.IT.S HANDBOOK

EARTHQUAKES
EARTHQUAKE-PROOF BUILDINGS

Earthquakes, scientists have reliably informed us, are caused by plates sliding against one another. This is why dishwashers always have sturdy racks to prevent this from happening halfway through the rinse cycle.

Architects the world over have spent years trying to design earthquake-proof buildings. Some of these are designed so that they wobble and shake, but absorb the energy and don't actually break apart. Following on from this advice, if you want to try to eat something during an earthquake that won't cause you any damage, Jell-O is a good idea, peanut brittle—not so much.

As usual, architects are going about this in entirely the wrong way. Rather than trying to design houses that don't fall down in earthquakes, they should design houses that would fall down, but that could be easily rebuilt.

All houses should therefore be built of LEGOs. Then if your house fell down during an earthquake, it wouldn't make you sad. In fact, you'd probably be slightly excited while you figured out if you'd rather live in a fire station or a spaceship.

37

WHOLE LOT OF SHAKING GOING ON

David fell over before the ground even started shaking.[67] But after a few seconds everyone was rocked from side to side. Jack would have tumbled too, but Trudy, with her excellent sense of balance, grabbed hold of him and held him upright.

"They're trying to shake Northern Ireland apart," Jack said. "I can't believe we didn't stop them. I also can't believe that evil villains keep trying to move Northern Ireland. It fits quite snugly where it is." Jack briefly wondered if Google Maps would be annoyed that they'd have to change all their databases if half the island was destroyed.

---

[67] After the event Jack wondered if David's clumsiness could actually sense an earthquake ahead of time and was falling down as a preemptive measure. It was a bit like a dog barking before a storm, or cows lying down on grass before it started to rain.

Trudy didn't speak to Jack right away. She was looking around and taking in her surroundings. Clearly she was thinking about something.

Jack looked around the crowd—everyone was falling over. Almost everyone was screaming. Interestingly enough, the only person who wasn't crying out was David. He was used to feeling like an earthquake was going on beneath his feet and falling over. To be honest it was nice for him to see other people fall over for a change.

Trudy finally broke her silence. "You're wrong, Jack. This earthquake isn't their plan. This is something different."

"How can you be so sure?"

Trudy pointed at Ms. Maris's staff, who were manning the stalls. "Do they look triumphant to you?"

Jack admitted they didn't. Some were cowering under carts of toffee apples while others were holding on to their stalls for grim life. Trudy rammed her argument home by pointing at the screen. The pictures of the drilling rigs across all of Northern Ireland seemed to be shaking with the tremor of the earthquake. But the one that was shaking more than most, with the metal of its platform distorting and bending, was the drill that had been in the middle of Lough Neagh.

The picture on the big screen distorted into static for a moment, before cutting to a shot of Regina Maris screaming at an assistant. "Find out what this is at once. Our plans will not fail!" Ms. Maris's face was twenty feet across on the enormous screen. She turned and for a minute Jack felt as though she was looking directly at him. He gulped, but then quickly recognized that Ms. Maris had just realized the camera was still on her. She sneered and then reached out with a gigantic hand to cover the camera lens. The screen went black.

***

The tremors had almost completely stopped. Jack reached down with the hand that wasn't holding the enormous bear and hauled David into an upright position.

"Was that an earthquake?" David asked.

Trudy nodded. "I think so."

Although it had been terrifying, very few people seemed to have been hurt. Because they had been out on the playing fields, no one was hit by any falling debris.

After a short time one of the caretakers brought the headmaster an enormous megaphone. It made the headmaster look ridiculous. Jack couldn't help imagining him as one of those dogs that comes home from the vet with a gigantic cone around its neck.

"Please listen up, everyone." A hush descended. "Now, it doesn't seem like anyone is hurt; however, we can't be sure that some kind of structural damage hasn't been done to the school. Therefore, we are sending you all home for the rest of the day. Those of you who can't contact your parents will be kept until normal dismissal time and supervised by myself."

Jack snorted to himself. He was pretty sure that all the children there would make sure they could contact their parents whether they had to use Morse code, smoke signals, or semaphore. No one would want to spend an afternoon on the playing fields being supervised by the headmaster.

DOGS RETURNING FROM THE VET

THE CONE—COLLARS PUT AROUND THEIR NECKS

Often people believe that vets put cones around dogs' necks to stop them from chewing on their stitches when they have had an operation. This is a patently ridiculous suggestion. Dogs would have no interest in stitches unless they were bone-marrow flavored. In fact, dogs have little interest in stitching or in any kind of crafts whatsoever. This is why you will almost never see a dog knitting.

The real reason that vets put cones around dogs' necks is that after they come out of surgery dogs are frequently feeling a bit depressed and lonely—the cone-collar acts as a megaphone, amplifying the dog's barking so that people pay it more attention than normal.

Cones are incredibly effective and often make a Chihuahua sound like a Great Dane.

38

CHARADES WITH SEALS

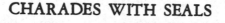

Naturally Jack and Trudy didn't even try to contact their parents. Instead they phoned the Ministry and asked for a car to be sent to collect them. Many of the other children were impressed when the gleaming luxury car turned up and took them away.

"Lucky they can't smell the inside of it," said Jack as he clambered inside, holding his nose. "So what do we do now?"

Trudy thought. "We go to the aquarium. That's where this all started; it's where my mother went missing."

"But what are we trying to find out when we get there?"

"We know that Ms. Maris is behind this all. And we know that she came out of the sea. Wherever she came from that's the problem. So that's where we head for."

The aquarium was full of people when Jack and Trudy

arrived. Jack was pleased. With that many people wandering about, there would be less chance of them being attacked
by any kind of aquatic creatures. Trudy marched up to the
woman sitting behind the ticket desk. "Free entry, please."

Jack frowned. Trudy hadn't mentioned anything about
this approach.

The woman at the ticket desk smelled strongly of perfume
and moisturizer. "I'm sorry, there isn't free entry for anyone."

"Oh, I'm sure there is for us," Trudy said. "We're friends of
Regina Maris's." With that Trudy ceased talking and nimbly
jumped over the metal turnstile. Jack realized that this was
not going to be a quiet reconnaissance-type mission. This was
more a type of *Go in, shoot up the place, and blow everything to
smithereens* mission. Jack couldn't help thinking that it would
have been substantially easier to achieve that kind of out-
come if they had brought guns or explosives with them.

Jack smiled apologetically at the woman behind the
ticket desk. "Sorry my friend's a bit rude, but you know, we
think you are probably working for the baddies." Jack sniffed
the woman's heavy perfume. "Yes, you're almost certainly
working for the baddies." With that Jack tried to jump over
the turnstile. He almost made it, but at the last minute his
foot caught on the metal bar and he went sprawling across
the floor.

He got up and rubbed at his sore knee. The woman at the
ticket desk was still looking at him. "We're the good guys. I
know it doesn't seem like it, but there you are," Jack added
before running off after Trudy.

Trudy had already made her way through the aquarium

and to the seal sanctuary. She was crouched down looking through the Plexiglas and had attracted the attention of several seals who were gathering in a semicircle.

"H-...h...have y-...you learned anything f-...from them?" Jack panted as he caught up.

Trudy stared blankly at Jack. "Well, no, because I don't actually speak seal."

"Ahhh," said Jack, "maybe I could try. I can speak starfish and I have a smattering of porpoise. I think they both have a lot of the same vocab, although the grammar is completely different."

Trudy gave Jack a withering look and then punched him in the arm. It had been a while since she'd punched him in the arm and Jack felt slightly nostalgic. Trudy stood up from the clamoring seals. "Be serious, this could lead us to whoever kidnapped my mother."

"Right," Jack agreed. "Serious."

A large, burly man wearing an aquarium T-shirt was moving toward Jack and Trudy. "Speaking of serious, how are we going to deal with this?"

"I'll do the rough stuff." Trudy moved in front of Jack. "You try and communicate with the seals."

Jack decided to get as close to the seals as possible. He clambered over the Plexiglas barrier and managed to lower himself gingerly into the concrete tank, sliding down the walls slowly. He sat down cross-legged on the ground so close to the seals that he could feel their fishy breath on his face. But how could you talk to a seal? Unlike the spider he'd found in his bathroom, the seals were relatively poor at charades, flippers not being amongst the most expressive of appendages.

In the background Jack could hear the noises of a brief scuffle. He jumped slightly when the aquarium employee came falling over the Plexiglas barrier and his head bounced off the ground. The employee moaned once and then lapsed into unconsciousness.

Trudy nimbly leapt over the barrier and landed with a neat forward roll. "Well, that was a bit of an anticlimax." She ran over to see how Jack was getting on. "So what have the seals told you?"

"How come you defeated that guy so quickly?"

Trudy appeared to be wrestling with a dilemma. "I'll be honest with you: It's probably a bit easier to fight when you aren't *helping*."

"Oh," said Jack, a bit crestfallen.

Trudy tried to cheer Jack up. "But you're the one with the weird outlook on life. You're the one who can figure out how to talk to seals."

Jack looked even more crestfallen.

"So you haven't figured out how to talk to the seals, then?"

"I appear to be struggling with that."

The seals were gathered around the pair, barking loudly and insistently. One bit Jack on the ankle. "Ouch—not helping!" he complained. The seal then rushed over to the side of the sanctuary that faced the sea. All the other seals joined it quickly.

"I think they want us to let them out," Jack observed.

Trudy looked at the seals. "I don't think so." Trudy pointed to the far side of the Plexiglas wall. "That's where the gate is.

If they wanted out, they'd be gathered around that. They're pointing out to sea."

Then it clicked for Jack. "Of course they are; that's where I saw the wrinkled version of Regina Maris walking out to."

"Then that's where we go." Trudy ran quickly over to the gate in the far side of the Plexiglas wall, undid the bolt, and threw it open. The seals barked loudly and clapped their flippers in thanks[68] before scooting through the gate, across a small plateau of rocks, and into the sea.

Trudy and Jack ran through the gate and walked over to the rocky outcrop that led to the sea. They watched the waves below them. Jack and Trudy took off their blazers and shoes. Jack looked at Trudy. For once she looked nervous.

"You okay?" asked Jack.

"We need to shock ourselves enough to take our breath away—and it's got to be shock, not panic—otherwise we might drown. I'm not good at this. I'm not easily shocked."

Jack smiled and then pushed Trudy incredibly hard, causing her to tumble into the waves.

Jack couldn't believe what he'd done, and he jumped in after her.

---

[68] It should be noted that seals are actually amongst the world's best clappers. The reason for this is that it used to be the case that, when seals went to the theater, they were always in the royal box. Because other people would watch and see what the people in the royal box enjoyed, the self-conscious seals clapped very hard for every act and became extremely skilled at this. The reason seals were allowed to sit in the royal box will only become clear later in our narrative.

SEALS
Their Ability to Play Party Games

The evolution of the seal has rendered it relatively poor at many parlor games. Their flippers mean they are poor at charades. Their lack of manual dexterity also means they struggle at tiddlywinks. This, along with the fact that they are hard to buy presents for (socks and gloves being almost definitely out), means that seals are rarely invited to Christmas parties.

If you want a game that you can play safely with a seal, Monopoly is generally a good bet. They can roll dice with their noses and move the little metal iron with their flippers. Having said this, no matter how many times you explain the rules to them they spend almost all the game trying to buy the Waterworks and then, once they have it, they just look pleased with themselves and bark loudly.

For this reason seals will almost always refuse to play the *Star Wars* edition of Monopoly, which lacks a Waterworks square.

39

WHAT'S IN STORE?

Jack's instinct had been right. After years of being called Moody Trudy and making people terrified, the one thing that was going to shock her more than anything else was someone being brave enough to deliberately push her into the sea.

Jack's idea had worked perfectly. He was so shocked that he had been brave enough to actually go through with his plan that it had taken his breath away too. Once underwater Jack realized that the look on Trudy's face was less than pleased. Jack suspected that once they were back on dry land he would be getting a severely punched shoulder. However, in the meantime they had other business to take care of. Jack pointed in the direction he had seen Regina Maris walking into the sea. Jack swam ahead with Trudy following.

It was a strange feeling, swimming under the sea with no need to breathe. Jack tried not to think about it too hard. He knew that the value of the shock would only last for so long and he wondered when the effect would run out. More important, he wondered if, when the shock did wear off, he would have enough time to swim to the surface before drowning. He really wasn't a particularly strong swimmer.

Luckily they did not have to swim that far—two hundred meters offshore Jack felt Trudy tugging at his ankle. He turned around to make a face at her—his ankle was still sore from where the seal had bitten it—but Trudy was pointing at an old, rusted, massive anchor abandoned on the seabed. It took Jack a few seconds before he realized that anchor looked a bit like an enormous arrow.[69]

As they swam closer to the anchor it became apparent that hidden behind it was a small, dark hole. Jack looked up at the surface of the water, nervously wondering when his shock would run out. Trudy kicked her feet and swam into the blackness.

The underwater tunnel was truly terrifying. Without any sunlight it was impossible to tell how far they were swimming. It was also impossible to tell when the tunnel turned, and Jack was continually scratching his hands or face on small outcrops of sharp rock, causing him to flinch in pain. After three or four minutes there seemed to be a dim light

---

[69] It should be noted that all anchors look like the shape of an enormous arrow. This is to make a hundred percent sure that sailors know which way they should throw them over the side of the boat.

up ahead. Trudy kicked hard and broke the surface seconds ahead of Jack.

They bobbed in a pool of water in the middle of an enormous cavern. It was a strange experience. Anytime Jack had seen anything like this in films the heroes always breached the surface of the water panting and gasping for breath. Because of the Ministry technique they had learned, not only did they not feel out of breath, they hadn't even started breathing again.

They hauled themselves out of the water and sat on either side of the pool.

"Have you started breathing again yet?" asked Trudy.

Jack looked down at his chest, which still hadn't started to rise or fall. "I don't think so. The shock can't have worn off yet."

They sat in silence for a while.

"Oh! There we go!" Trudy smirked. "Just started breathing again."

Jack had obviously been considerably more shocked than Trudy, as it was several minutes more before he started breathing again. "That feels weird now."[70]

Trudy stood up and started walking back into the cavern.

---

[70] If you are wondering how weird it felt for Jack, it's the same kind of feeling that you get when you suddenly realize that your tongue is clearly too big for the inside of your mouth and you can just feel it all lumped up in there. And it means that you become incredibly self-conscious about it, and when you try and talk you start mumbling and ... oh no, now it's happened to me.

It was much bigger than they had first realized. Jack almost hurt his neck rotating it to try and take in the full view of a cave the size of an aircraft hangar. He should have been filled with a sense of awe, but actually found himself wondering how they managed to keep it all clean. The cave was filled from top to bottom with bladed weapons and armor made out of seashells.[71]

Trudy picked up a large trident and weighed it in her hand. "These are weapons. For . . . for some kind of invasion army."

Jack found several large cartons filled with sea sponges and starfish. "And these sponges must be what they sell in the shop. Not sure what the starfish are for . . ."

Unsurprisingly, Trudy was much more interested in the weapons. "Regina Maris must have some kind of aquatic army of an undersea people."

Jack thought about what kinds of creatures lived under the sea. "Maybe mermaids and mermen. Are they real?"

Trudy shrugged. "We can ask Grey when we see him next."

"Okay, so if it is angry merpeople, they're going to invade the land but . . ."

Trudy threw the trident at the cave wall, where it cracked the stone and stuck fast. "But what?"

Jack shook his head to clear it. "It can't be as simple as

[71] This sentence makes no sense. Seashells are fish armor. Therefore, what I've essentially said here is that it was filled with armor made out of fish armor. Which is a bit redundant when you think about it.

that, can it? I mean, if it's creatures from the sea, then why were the seals pointing them out to us? There must be something more to their plot."

"Like what?"

"Umm, I haven't figured that part out yet."

Trudy tutted disapprovingly. "That seems to be happening a lot to you lately. Maybe you're losing your touch."

Jack really hoped he wasn't. The key thing he was bringing to their partnership was his ability to think in strange spirals. If he lost that, there really wasn't much else he could bring to the party. "We can figure this out back on the surface. This is obviously some kind of a giant storeroom.[72] Someone will come back to get this stuff at some stage."

Trudy was still wandering around. "Just a few more minutes."

Jack realized that Trudy was looking for any clue that her mother may have been held captive in the room. He helped her look for fifteen minutes before he knew that the search was hopeless.

"I don't think we're going to find anything; we need to go," Jack said reluctantly. Trudy hung her head and walked back over to the pool, where Jack was waiting for her.

---

[72] Jack is wrong. It was just a very large storeroom. A giant storeroom is one where you store giants, or one where giants store their possessions. You can always tell if it's a giant storeroom as they have special velvet compartments for giants' cufflinks and hens that lay golden eggs. Generally speaking, a giant storeroom will also smell slightly of beanstalk.

This time she approached him cautiously. "I won't be shocked if you push me this time, so how do we take our breath away?"

Jack thought hard. He looked at the hole in the ground and wondered if there was an easy way he could shock himself breathless. As usual, when you concentrate on one thing really hard, it allows the sneaky thoughts in your brain to creep up and catch you unawares.

While Jack was staring at the pool of water and thinking about how to surprise himself, a thought crept up on him that stunned him. His jaw dropped and he looked at Trudy. "I know what the fracking is about!"

"What? No . . . you can't—you weren't even thinking about that. . . . How did you manage?"

Trudy's jaw dropped at Jack's revelation. The pair were stunned into silence. Complete silence. You couldn't even hear the sound of breathing in the cave.

Jack and Trudy smiled at each other and dived into the water.

GIANTS
BEANSTALKS

Many people have assumed that Jack from the story of Jack and the Beanstalk was an early Ministry agent. In point of fact, that Jack was not a Ministry agent—rather he was a fugitive from Ministry justice.

Although that Jack has been portrayed as a hero, he was a villain. He broke into a castle (trespassing), stole a bag of gold coins (burglary), and abducted a goose that laid golden eggs (kidnapping).

Jack then proceeded to cut down the beanstalk, murdering the giant.

Possibly the worst part of the story is Jack's obsession with money. If he hadn't been bothered about stealing the gold coins, Jack would still have been the possessor of the world's largest beanstalk. Not only would this have made his fortune, but with the enormous beans he could easily have solved the problem of world hunger.

You may wonder, if Jack did all these awful things, why the stories about him are all so positive. The answer is simple. Golden eggs can be used to bribe journalists and buy an awful lot of enthusiastic press reviews.

It is also interesting to note that Jack made up a lot of the giant's dialogue himself—the giant, being dead, was not in a place to contradict him. However, Jack was rather slipshod in some of his claims, which should prove that he was lying. For instance, Jack claimed the giant shouted, "I'll grind your bones to make my bread."

As we all know, giants are all excellent bakers; in fact, it has been suggested that it is their love of baking that causes them to grow to such enormous sizes, swollen by their colossal yeast intake.

As an excellent baker, a giant would never use bonemeal to make bread—bonemeal would not cause the bread to rise like yeast does. So if the giant was using bones to make anything, it must have been a flatbread.

Therefore we can assume that the giant said something like, "I'll grind your bones to make tortilla wraps" at worst.

40

THE HORN OF A DILEMMA

On the way back Jack didn't find the tunnel as scary. He knew that the darkness would only last so long. As long as you knew something would end, it was never that bad.

As he turned the corner he could see Trudy shadowed against the light at the end of the tunnel,[73] pulling her arms against the water faster. Jack churned the water with his feet but struggled to keep up. He saw Trudy up ahead, swimming out of the tunnel and into the sea. Reaching the end of the tunnel, he adjusted himself, ready to swim up, and felt Trudy's foot kick him in the head.

---

[73] Some people wonder where the phrase "the light at the end of the tunnel" comes from. It comes from when people are in tunnels and they see the light at the end of that tunnel. Some people wonder about the stupidest things.

Jack looked up and made a face, ready to complain, but he quickly saw that Trudy had accidentally kicked him while dodging a deadly predator. Trudy had missed being skewered by a long, spiraling horn by mere inches. The horn was the length of two men and was connected to a huge, gray-and-white speckled[74] whale-like creature. Jack recognized it from one of the aquarium posters. It was a narwhal. It was sometimes called the unicorn of the sea. Jack was therefore suspicious of narwhals, as Grey had previously told them that unicorns were known to kill bunny rabbits for amusement.

The narwhal circled and came charging back toward them with its deadly looking horn. Jack needed to think quickly. He wondered whether it would be more unpleasant to die from drowning or skewering. Then Jack briefly thought about how often his thoughts weren't either helpful or constructive.

Trudy dodged behind the large anchor that marked the tunnel's entrance. Jack kicked hard off the seabed and just managed to float up as the horn swished underneath him. Jack looked down and saw Trudy mouth "GUARD" at him. He nodded in agreement. Obviously this narwhal was working for Regina Maris.

---

[74] Jack wondered why it was gray-and-white speckled. It was a strange pattern for a fish. In many ways it reminded Jack of a dappled horse. He was right in assuming that there was something "horsey" about the narwhal. . . .

NARWHALS
Why Unicorns Are Almost Extinct

Many people are amazed that both the narwhal and the unicorn share an incredibly similar horn. In fact, many scientists claim that in the olden days people only imagined unicorns and assumed they existed because they found narwhal horns on the beach. Of course, this is typical of scientists, who are always mouthing off regarding things about which they know nothing. There are three reasons why the narwhal tusk/unicorn horn suggestion is ridiculous.

(a) Because we all know unicorns used to exist.

(b) Just because someone finds something on a beach, they don't automatically jump to the conclusion that it must have fallen off a horse. If this were the case, most people would spend their holidays wandering around the place looking for a horse that had lost a single flip-flop.[75]

---

[75] If only a single flip-flop was lost, they would probably be looking for a particularly unfortunate pirate horse.

(c) If people had assumed that narwhal horns were from unicorns, they would have had to imagine a strange and magical creature existed that really, really enjoyed beach holidays. None of the legends about unicorns involve sunbathing for a while and then wandering up to the arcade for a round on the bumper cars and a game of skeeball. Therefore the narwhal tusk/unicorn horn hypothesis is patently ridiculous.

As always, the truth is considerably more intriguing. The fact is that the reason that narwhal tusks resemble unicorn horns is simple. Narwhals used to *be* unicorns.

As you know from **Unicorns: Why They Are Evil**, unicorns love killing bunny rabbits and skewering three or four on their cruel, spiraling horns. For a long time the bunny rabbits were few in number and were easily overpowered by unicorns. The bunnies' only defense was being able to nibble unicorns a bit. But very few creatures ever die of a fatal nibbling.

Then one day a particularly intelligent and interspecies-lingual bunny rabbit called Fluffy Bubkins was having a chat with a well-traveled parrot. The parrot, called Tony (because not all animals have to have ridiculous names), was telling Bubkins about having seen a shoal of piranha in a river in Venezuela eat a cow (who was a friend of his) in a matter of seconds. Bubkins swiftly realized that nibbling could be used as a deadly form of attack, but only if you had enough creatures *all nibbling at the same time*.

Bubkins therefore spoke to all his rabbit friends and told them to have as many children as possible. That way they could form rabbit "shoals" and when a unicorn attacked, they could swiftly nibble him to death.

This approach worked, and soon there were tens of thousands of bunnies across the countryside forming themselves into bunny defense leagues. The bunnies were so successful in their nibbling tactics that land-based unicorns became almost entirely extinct. The only unicorns that survived were those that took to the water and eventually evolved into narwhals. Bunnies don't follow unicorns into the water, because when their fluffy tails get wet they become frizzy and positively unmanageable.

Fluffy Bubkins decided that, in honor of the cow that had died and inadvertently inspired the idea of bunny shoals, they would name all future bunny houses after him. The dead cow's name had been Warren.

41

AN INCONVENIENT TOOTH

Jack bent his back and avoided being skewered by the skin of his teeth.[76] Moving underwater was tiring and slow. Every single move felt as if he had weights tied to his arms and legs. He wasn't sure how much longer he could dodge, and his muscles were beginning to ache. He needed to come up with a plan.

Trudy already had put into action a plan that was working extremely effectively. The last time the narwhal had tried to skewer her she had dodged under it, waited until it was almost past, and grabbed hold of its tail. Without any

---

[76] Some of you may wonder where the expression "skin of his teeth" comes from. It's perfectly reasonable to wonder about this. It's a much more complicated expression than "light at the end of the tunnel." So go ahead and wonder about it. I'm not going to stop you.

kind of a neck the narwhal couldn't turn and attack Trudy. She actually seemed to be enjoying herself being pulled around by an enormous, fishy, underwater Jet Ski.

Jack looked around to see if he could find something to use as a sword to battle the narwhal's tusk. Jack fancied himself as a pretty good sword fighter, as he had attended his school's fencing club for almost three weeks. He would have stayed for longer but they made you fight sword battles while wearing a mask instead of wearing a large floppy hat with a ridiculously ostentatious feather in it. And surely half the fun of sword fighting was the big, feathery hats?

The narwhal passed him again. This time the horn caught the edge of his shirt, tearing a hole in it. Jack nearly gasped, but stopped himself in the nick of time. Gasping is generally considered a good way to show surprise. However, gasping underwater was generally considered a good way to drown. Jack gritted his teeth and tried to concentrate in spite of the danger—now was the time for him to come up with a brilliant plan.

The last pass of the narwhal had been too close for comfort. Jack decided to use The Speed. Even if he was underwater, the extra boost it would give him would be helpful.

He searched his memory for a sad thought, and his mind seized on the pain he had experienced when he had lost his first tooth. So many adults had told him it wouldn't hurt, but, as was frequently the case, they weren't telling the truth. The memory was especially sad now, because not only did he remember the pain of losing the tooth, but also the fact that he now knew what the Tooth Fairy really did with the teeth.[77]

Jack felt The Speed descend on him. But this time it was not only The Speed, but also a brilliant idea. A brilliant idea inspired by the loss of his first tooth.

The narwhal was circling, preparing itself for another attack. Jack kicked his feet and windmilled his arms, propelling himself toward the huge anchor that marked the entrance to the underwater tunnel. He knew that the narwhal was following him and only hoped that he could make it in time.

Kneeling on the sea floor beside the anchor, Jack found the end of the long, rusty, snapped metal cable that was attached to it. His fingers had begun to wrinkle and it was difficult work underwater, but he tied the end of the cable into a rudimentary knot. He had seconds before the narwhal was upon him.

Jack looked up and realized the narwhal's horn was only inches away from his eye. If it hadn't been for The Speed, he would have ended up wearing an eye patch.[78] As it was he managed to pull himself down using the anchor, allowing

---

[77] It is interesting to note that at the moment Jack was thinking this, his first baby tooth was part of the C key on a piano onstage in the Ulster Hall and was being used to play "Sono Andati?" from *La Bohème*. Which is a very sad song indeed.

[78] Jack later reflected to himself that, what with the pirates he'd had to battle the previous week, Ministry work seemed to entail a high risk of losing eyes. He decided if he made it to a third week in the Ministry he would almost definitely buy himself a pair of goggles.

the narwhal to sail over him. Once the narwhal had passed, Jack threw the knotted end of the cable, praying that his aim would be good.

The knotted loop caught on the end of the narwhal's horn and tightened as it swam rapidly away. The cable underneath Jack's feet was dragged through the sand on the seabed, silently snaking away.

Now Jack had to pin his hopes on the cable's running out before the narwhal could slow itself and turn. Jack watched the narwhal still swimming on; there were only a few feet of cable left. The slack left the cable, and there was an audible *ping* as the narwhal stopped, pulled backward by the cable around its horn—the cable that was attached to the anchor.

As Jack looked up he heard a popping noise.[79] The sudden stop had worked so well that the narwhal's tusk had neatly popped right off. Trudy had let go of the narwhal's tail and was giving Jack a thumbs-up. A narwhal without a horn doesn't look particularly threatening. The narwhal didn't even seem to be in pain, just slightly sheepish and embarrassed. Using The Speed, Jack swam rapidly through the water and caught the sinking horn. Holding the blunt end, he pointed it menacingly at the narwhal. The large, de-horned, gray-white fish knew when it was beaten and swam off.

---

[79] Many of you will have wondered where Jack got this amazing plan from and how it was related to the loss of his first tooth. The answer is simple. Imagine that the narwhal horn was Jack's wobbly tooth, the cable was a piece of thread, and the anchor was a door handle. I'm sure you can put it together yourselves from there.

THUMBS-UP SIGN
GLADIATORS

Everyone knows that the thumbs-up sign originates in ancient Rome. When a defeated gladiator had done a good job and the emperor wanted him spared he would give the victorious gladiator a thumbs-up sign to spare his life.

This was why gladiators were extremely upset when Tiberius "Thumbless" Severus became emperor.

Tiberius was famous for two things. One was presiding over the most deaths in the gladiator arena. The second was for the time as a child when he had tried to feed an alligator by hand.

An interesting footnote is that Tiberius also had the slowest time of any Roman emperor for completing the Rubik's Cube.

42

A CONVENIENT TOOTH

Trudy was the much stronger swimmer and made it back to shore before she had totally overcome her shock and started breathing again. Jack took slightly longer and so had to swim the last fifty meters on the surface. It was made harder by the fact that he was using one arm to carry the narwhal horn.

Trudy waded out the last few meters and stood, dripping, on the shore. "Are you really keeping that thing?"

Jack looked at it. "Yes. Firstly, because it's pretty awesome looking. And secondly, because the next time we get attacked by an evil narwhal we'll be able to fence with it."

Trudy squinted skeptically. "You are full of brilliant ideas, Jack. But sometimes it seems like the top layer of ideas you're filled with is mostly made up of the stupid ones."

Jack tried to look annoyed, but it was difficult to muster up a stern look when you are wearing a dripping school uniform and carrying a narwhal tusk.

Jack and Trudy put their shoes back on and made their way back to the aquarium. They could hear a dull ringing noise from inside the building. "What's that sound?"

"Sounds like bad news for us," Trudy guessed. "They couldn't attack us with giant crabs when the aquarium was filled with visitors and tourists. So they've set off the fire alarm. Once the place is empty, the giant crustaceans can come out to play."

As they walked farther through the aquarium, Jack could barely believe what he saw. There were still some staff/henchpeople in the aquarium. It was just that none of them were conscious. Their bodies lay slumped, battered, and bruised every step of the way. There wasn't a single one of them who was capable of standing up, much less trying to fight two Ministry operatives.

"This is a bit of good luck," said Jack as he got used to the scene of carnage.

Trudy, however, was less sure. "Maybe we don't have to fight the henchpeople. But what happens if we have to fight the thing that fought the henchpeople?"

Jack looked at the crumpled forms of the aquarium employees and felt his blood run cold. As they turned the corner into the foyer the alarm stopped ringing for a very scary reason.

The fire alarm in the foyer had stopped ringing because an enormous man had reached up to the wall and crumpled the red metal ringing bell with one enormous hairy hand. The bell folded into a ball as if it were made of tinfoil. The other enormous hairy hand was around the neck of a barely conscious aquarium employee.

The enormous man looked at Jack and smiled. He dropped the red bell, threw the aquarium employee over the back of the ticket kiosk, and strode over to where Jack and Trudy were standing. He was still wearing the pink tutu that was far too small for him.

"Thought you'd lose me?" the Tooth Fairy asked. "I always get my teeth." The Tooth Fairy had pulled his pincers out.

A feeling of panic rolled over Jack and he broke out in a sweat. Perspiration rolled down his forehead. In his head he saw images of chomping apples and chewing bacon sandwiches floating away from him. The future held no solid food for him. He would have to cope with a world made up of soup for lunch and liquefied sandwiches sucked through a straw for tea. And then a thought occurred to him.[80]

Jack stepped forward with the narwhal horn out-stretched. Trudy reached out to pull him back, but he shook her off. Surely Jack couldn't be thinking about fighting with

---

[80] Few people realize that humans generally think better when they are sweating. This means that you should never put someone who is calm in charge of your army. Calm people never panic and therefore think things through slowly. People who are panicking think quickly, have a dozen ideas racing through their minds at once, and then can easily pick the best one. (Of course, panicking is still potentially fatal if you're underwater.)

the Tooth Fairy? The narwhal horn was long and pointed, but the Tooth Fairy was practically invulnerable.

Luckily Jack wasn't thinking about fighting—he was pretty sure that even if you skewered the Tooth Fairy with the largest narwhal horn in the world he would just shrug, put a Band-Aid over the hole, and then tear out your incisors.

Jack had decided to make another bargain. "You could have my teeth. . . . Or alternatively, you could have this instead." Jack waved the narwhal horn enticingly. "Potentially the largest tooth in the world."

The Tooth Fairy's eyes focused on the narwhal horn, which he hadn't noticed until then. His eyes bulged disturbingly (as his tutu also generally did). Then he put on an emotionless poker face—the Tooth Fairy was a shrewd businessman as well as a psychopathic maniac.[81] "What's to stop me from taking your teeth and then just relieving you of that?" The Tooth Fairy pointed to the horn.

Jack shook his head vigorously. "Because I know you, and that isn't the way you work. You're insane, but you're fair. That's why you have the contract clause about teeth under pillows belonging to you put into people's birth certificates." Jack held the narwhal horn toward the Tooth Fairy. "You

---

[81] This is called a tautology. A tautology is when you say the same thing twice but using different words. So for example a shrewd businessman is pretty much exactly the same as a psychopathic maniac. Other tautologies would include an evil gym teacher or an annoying daytime television host.

wouldn't just take this from me. You're are a psychopath, but an *honest, decent* psychopath."

The Tooth Fairy's mouth wrinkled in annoyance. Then his face assumed an expression of grudging respect. He ran this fingers through his beard thoughtfully. "All right, boy, we can maybe figure out a deal."

〰〰〰〰〰〰〰

"And if you just sign here, and initial here."

Jack did as he was told on the last of the paperwork that the Tooth Fairy had put in front of him.

"And now your teeth are your own again."

"Thanks," said Jack, who felt it was safe to smile again. "And this belongs to you."

The Tooth Fairy took hold of the narwhal horn[82] and looked at it lovingly. "Think of the number of piano keys that I'll be able to make with this."

Jack decided to test his luck. "Look, I don't suppose you can give us a lift back to the Ministry?"

The Tooth Fairy shook his head. "Not this time, sunshine. I'm the Tooth Fairy, not a taxi service." He took out the golden key ring made from a tiger's tooth, spun it once around his finger, and strolled out to his black Ford Cortina.

Trudy and Jack breathed a collective sigh of relief.

"I really don't know how you do it," Trudy said.

"Mmm," Jack agreed. "To be honest, I'm really not a hundred percent sure myself."

---

[82] As was noted earlier, the walrus is the Tooth Fairy's second-favorite marine animal—clearly the narwhal is his first favorite.

THINKING QUICKLY
WHY PERSPIRING IS HELPFUL

Many people wonder why we think so much more quickly when under pressure or perspiring. The answer is of course obvious to anyone who has ever seen a brain.

Brains are incredibly wrinkly things. This is one reason why it is often assumed that old people have great wisdom. Because many of them are so wrinkly that they actually look a bit like brains.

Any neurologist worth their salt will tell you that the more wrinkly the brain the more intelligent the creature. The brains of rats and mice are quite smooth compared to dolphin and human brains. Wrinkly brains have more surface area and therefore more space to do the actual thinking on.

When you sweat or perspire, your head gets wet. As we know, when parts of the human body get wet enough they start to get wrinkly. Therefore when your brain sweats a little, it gets a little bit more wrinkly and you get a little bit smarter.

This is why panic, which creates sweating, helps people think a little bit faster.

Interestingly enough, this is also the origin of the phrase "Go and stick your head in a bucket of water." These days many people use the phrase as an insult. However, in the olden days people knew that wrinkly brains made you think better. Therefore it wasn't really an insult and would probably have been best translated as—"I disagree with your theory; please go and wash your brain until it is more wrinkly so you may rethink your philosophy."

The wrinkly brain is also the reason many people do their best thinking in the bath. Please see **Archimedes: Eureka Moment**.

It is also why many people find it almost impossible to think intelligently about anything in the morning before they have had their first shower.

43

THE WORLD'S LARGEST PLUG HOLE

Trudy and Jack called for a Ministry car and were taken back to the headquarters in the museum. Trudy kept badgering Jack to tell her what he had figured out when they had been in the underwater cave, but Jack refused to say anything. "I'll explain when we see Grey. I have questions to ask and I don't want to have to repeat everything."

Trudy clenched her fists in annoyance.

Grey was waiting for Trudy and Jack in the passage room of the Ministry. "You had something that you wanted to see me about?"

Trudy looked expectantly at Jack.

"Yes. I think I've figured out what all the fracking is about."

"Well, we know that it can't be about finding gas under the ground," said Grey.

Jack had figured out what the drilling was about, but wasn't sure what made it particularly unlikely that it was about gas apart from the lack of gas tanks at the drilling locations. "Why not?"

"Well, isn't it obvious?" asked Grey. "I mean, think about things that are filled with gas. They either float, catch fire, or smell bad. And Northern Ireland doesn't do any of those things. So there can't be gas underneath it."

Jack considered Grey's argument. It seemed sound, although Jack could have argued that occasionally bits of Northern Ireland caught fire and other bits smelled bad.[83] However, he decided that this was not the time to start an argument of this nature. "I think I have most of this figured out. We're fighting some kind of undersea army this time. That explains the sponge and soap shops. But why would they be drilling holes in Northern Ireland?"

Trudy thought about this. "Because they're trying to find something underground?"

"No." Jack shook his head vigorously. "They aren't digging underground—that's what the pirates were doing. These bad guys are drilling *through* the ground. And they're drilling the biggest hole right in the center of Lough Neagh. Why there? And if it's sea creatures that are attacking us, why would the seals be on our side?"

---

[83] In fact, often the parts that caught fire also smelled bad. They smelled of burning Northern Ireland. Which was a bad thing.

Trudy and Grey stared at Jack blankly. They were failing to make the connection. Jack sighed and rooted through his schoolbag. He took out a copy of the atlas they used for geography. He flicked through the pages until he came to a map that showed a picture of Loch Ness in Scotland. He paused for a moment as he realized Loch Ness was shaped like the bodies of water he had seen in Cthulhu's book. A thought occurred to Jack. Could Cthulhu be related to the Loch Ness Monster? It was an intriguing thought. That would have explained all the photographs in Cthulhu's book and the strange shapes rising out of the Loch.

Jack shook his head. Now was not the time to be solving the age-old mystery of the Loch Ness Monster. He hadn't been looking for Loch Ness in the book. He kept flicking pages until he came to the page that showed a map of Northern Ireland. "We already know that the pirates have dug around the edge of Northern Ireland. Now what's this?" Jack stabbed his finger into the center of Northern Ireland.

"It's Lough Neagh." Trudy studied the picture more closely. "Have you ever noticed that Lough Neagh seems to have five points to it? If you squint, it's almost star-shaped?"

Jack ignored Trudy's suggestion.[84] "But doesn't it remind you of anything?"

"Umm, well, I suppose it looks like a big lough."

---

[84] Although Jack ignored this suggestion, luckily he remembered it later, as it would prove absolutely vital.

Jack ignored her sarcasm. "It's a big hole in the middle of Northern Ireland. Like a plug hole in the middle of a basin."

Trudy thought about Jack's recent adventures with plug holes. "Are you suggesting that underneath Northern Ireland there's an enormous spider waiting to burst out?"

"Not at all," said Jack. "That would be ridiculous. But there's no other country in the world that has a hole that large in the center of it. We're like a land doughnut."[85]

Grey's forehead wrinkled. "Jack, are you suggesting that someone is going to eat Northern Ireland? Even with all my experience in the Ministry I think that's fairly unlikely."

Jack exhaled impatiently. "Okay, that was a bad simile for me to use."[86] Jack tried to think of a better simile. "Do you remember the *Titanic*?"

Trudy and Grey nodded. Every schoolchild in Northern Ireland knew the story of the *Titanic*. In many ways Northern Ireland was a strange place. Other countries tried to ignore their major disasters. Germany rarely mentioned the World Wars, England tried to pretend that the last time the World Cup had been played was in 1966, and Ireland frequently tried to pretend that Jedward were from Australia. For some reason Northern Ireland's people were proud of their disasters, and every schoolchild was forced to spend at least three weeks of their lives undertaking a project to find out about the *Titanic*.

---

[85] This was a bad simile for Jack to use.

[86] Told you so.

"We did a project about it in elementary school," said Trudy.[87]

"What happened to it?"

"It hit an iceberg. So what's your point?"

"And what happened to it when it hit the iceberg?"

Trudy was getting fed up with the succession of questions but answered anyway. "It put a hole in the hull and the ship sank."

Jack nodded. He pointed to the center of Lough Neagh. "And they're drilling a hole here. Right in the center of an enormous body of water. What do you think's going to happen?"

It took Trudy a moment to understand what Jack was saying. Then the enormity of it all hit her. "They're going to try and sink Northern Ireland!"

Jack nodded solemnly. "Exactly."

Grey let out a long whistle. "That makes sense."

"That's why the seals are on our side. Seals live in the sea, but they also need bits of land to live on. That's why they were trying to help us. I think we're up against an army of merpeople. Mermaids and mermen."

Trudy spoke. "And you think they kidnapped my mother?"

Jack looked at Trudy. "Your mother must have been at the aquarium because she realized something was going on

---

[87] This was further proof that Northern Ireland was a truly unique place in the world. Nowhere else would a maritime disaster that killed hundreds of people be considered something good to teach elementary schoolchildren about.

with the seals. They tried to tell her, but before she could get back to the Ministry she must have been caught by one of those crabs."

Trudy's face dropped. "That's how Regina Maris knew my name—the staff must have recognized me. They guessed we were from the Ministry and used us to get the crab into the prison tanks to break out the criminal fish."

Jack nodded. "Exactly. I think they wanted the hammerhead sharks and the sawfish especially. Think about it. They're building things under the water—imagine how helpful fish with tools for heads would be."

"I think you're almost right, Jack," said Grey. "But it isn't merpeople. Merpeople aren't evil and they're generally friendly with seals—they used to use seals to carry mail to humans. No, if the seals were being captured, it must have been because the merpeople were trying to warn us what was going on. I think a different kind of undersea denizen is behind this plan."

"Who?" Jack asked eagerly.

Grey fixed Jack and Trudy with a deadly serious stare. "The Atlanteans."

SEALS
Their Use as a Postal System

There are rumors that a time existed before there was such a thing as e-mail. If you believe this (many don't), there were different ways of sending mail. A long time before the post office existed, kings and queens used to send mail to each other via pony couriers and carrier pigeons.

However, on occasion messages would need to be sent under the sea to the merpeople. Therefore a messenger was needed that could carry a letter over land and then through the sea. Naturally, seals were chosen for this duty.

Seals were expensive to train and hard to keep, therefore only kings could afford to use them as messengers. Many kings were proud of their seals and would take them to the theater with them. This is where seals learned to clap so well.

The tradition of using these aquatic mammals as a postal service is where the expression "sending a letter with the royal seal" comes from.

44

THE MYSTERY OF ATLANTIS

"The Atlanteans?" Jack asked.

"Who are they?" Trudy quizzed.

Grey explained the story of the Atlanteans. "A long time ago in ancient Greece there was an island called Atlantis. It was populated by a race of people called the Atlanteans. At the time there were a lot of ancient islands that ruled themselves. The Atlanteans lived not that far from the island of Crete—you know, where the Minotaur was from."

Jack and Trudy looked at each other and nodded. That explained why the maze that surrounded the fracking platform was guarded by the effectual and the ineffectual Minotaur. The Atlanteans must have gotten the idea from the Cretans.

"The Atlanteans were a proud race. They had technology that no other island had at that time—airships, plumbing, water-powered computers. But as with all technologically advanced races they got lazy and other nations started catching up with them."

"Doesn't that happen to all countries in the end?"

"Yes, Trudy, but the Atlanteans were too arrogant to accept it. So they took steps to try and avoid it. They used their plumbing systems to build enormous baths."

Jack was unsure as to how this would help. "Baths? So they could be really clean?"

Grey looked at Jack. "Sometimes I wonder if you're even paying attention, Jack. Baths and water make you wrinkly. The more wrinkly the brain gets the more intelligent you get. Do you ever wonder how the Romans managed to take over most of Europe? It was all the baths they built. They bathed all the time, their brains got extra wrinkly, and they outthought their opponents."

Jack remembered doing a project on the Romans in elementary school and remembered that they had seemed extra fond of their baths. In fact, from what he remembered of their empire it seemed to mainly consist of a lot of straight roads connecting enormous public bathing facilities. "Did that work?"

"For the Atlanteans? For a while, yes. But as I said the clever Romans copied their system. And the ancient Greeks did even better by inventing the shower, which allowed you to directly wet your brain in half the time. Soon the Atlanteans were being outthought by half the Mediterranean. And that's when the queen of Atlantis came up with a scheme to make the Atlanteans the smartest race ever. She decided to sink the entire island of Atlantis. That way all their people would be underwater forever, their brains could permanently wrinkle, and they would become a nation of geniuses."

Trudy interrupted. "That really doesn't sound that smart to me. I mean, wouldn't they have just drowned?"

Jack thought about the Queen's plan. He looked at Grey. "She didn't tell any of the Atlanteans about her plan, did she?"

Grey smiled at Jack. "You're still a smart boy, Jack. Of course she didn't. If she had told anyone, it would never have worked. She secretly arranged to borrow the team of laborers who had just finished digging the foundations for the labyrinth from King Minos of Crete. They set about digging an enormous hole in the middle of the island of Atlantis. Down and down they dug until they hit water. An enormous waterspout sprang up from the ground and the entire island sank."

"So why didn't the people drown?" asked Trudy again.

"Think about what the Misery told you recently. Imagine how shocked the people were. The sight of their houses, their island, their very world sinking. It simply took their breath away."

It made perfect sense. As usual Jack really wished that it didn't, but it did. "Didn't they ever start breathing again?"

Grey shook his head. "It was an such enormous shock it took years before they got over it. By that time most of the Atlantean people had developed gills alongside their usual lungs. And so the Atlanteans became an amphibious race. Fiercely intelligent thanks to their wrinkly brains. Capable of the most incredibly complicated plots."

"Why didn't you mention the Atlanteans before?" Trudy snapped. "That would have been helpful."

"There are hundreds of creatures living under the sea. Apart from the Atlanteans and merpeople there are selkies, sea monsters, kelpies, Nerieds. . . . It wasn't until Jack mentioned trying to sink a country that I realized it had to be the Atlanteans behind this."

"But that still leaves us with one big question," said Jack.

"Yes—why are the Atlanteans trying to sink Northern Ireland?" asked Trudy, finishing Jack's thought.

"I don't know," Grey admitted. "That's still part of a mystery that you need to figure out."

"Well, we can do that at any stage," said Jack. "I think it's probably more important that we figure out a way to stop them from drilling that hole in the middle of the country."

"Good point," Grey agreed. "I don't want all my suits getting wet."

"So we go to Lough Neagh?" asked Trudy.

Jack looked at his watch. "Not tonight, it's time we were going home."

Trudy scowled. "You're putting off saving our country because you want to get some sleep?"

"I wouldn't want to save the world without adequate sleep. I'd get all grumpy. Anyway, if we're going to attack Lough Neagh, we're going to need a plan. There's an entire factory staffed with Atlanteans there. There's no way we can possibly attack them by ourselves. And I'm guessing that the Ministry won't have any spare staff to help us out."

Grey looked sympathetic, but ultimately his answer was unhelpful. "With overtime rates what they are at the minute? Not a chance, I'm afraid."

Trudy looked stubborn. "We might be able to find my mother."

"I know, but just wait one more night." Jack consoled her. "There's no point in finding her if we get captured and thrown into the same jail cell."

Trudy hesitated, but finally agreed.

"I'll sleep on it and I'm sure that I'll have come up with a plan by tomorrow morning."

"You had better, Jack Pearse. You had better."

Jack's mouth contorted into a nervous smile.

MINISTRY OF S.U.IT.S HANDBOOK

WATER-POWERED COMPUTERS
Their Usefulness

Many people have suggested that the creation of water-powered computers would be useful in modern society. It would mean that computers would be environmentally friendly and not use as much costly electricity.

This is true, but it misses the most significant advantage of the water-powered computer. Which is simply that no one would shout at you if you spilled your juice on it. Because for once you wouldn't actually have destroyed the computer— you'd just have made it *slightly more powerful*.

45

BLACK BAG OPERATION
FRIDAY

Jack sat down to breakfast the next morning. He had a bacon sandwich. He had a glass of milk. The one thing he didn't have was a plan. He briefly considered going back upstairs to stick his head into a bucket of water to see if that helped.

Jack wasn't sure if he was more scared of being drowned when Northern Ireland sank or of Trudy, who was quite possibly going to murder him for not coming up with a decent plan.

"You're not eating your bacon sandwich," Jack's mother observed.

Jack considered explaining to her that the reason he wasn't eating his bacon sandwich was because he was terrified. On reflection he thought that this would probably worry her unnecessarily.

Jack then considered his bacon sandwich. He might have

been terrified, but if he didn't eat the bacon sandwich, he would have been both terrified and hungry. There didn't seem to be any sensible argument in favor of that, and so he devoured the bacon sandwich in four bites.

"Anything planned at school today?" his father asked.

Jack thought for a few seconds. "Swimming lessons," he said.

"That'll be fun," his mother said, putting Jack's plate into the dishwasher.[88] "I always loved swimming."

Jack secretly thought to himself that if he didn't come up with a plan sometime soon, his mother might get quite bored of swimming after a while.

"Right, I'm off to school." Jack grabbed his schoolbag and made for the door. Just as he was about to turn the door handle he turned and looked at his parents. "Dad, do me a favor—could you get the inflatable crocodile down from the attic at some point today and blow it up?"

Jack's father looked sideways at Jack. "Umm, why exactly?"

There was steel in Jack's eyes. "Just in case, Dad. Just in case." Jack left the house to get the bus.

Jack's mother and father looked at each other in silence.

"Our boy is either a genius or a complete idiot," observed Jack's mother.

Jack's father pondered this. "Is that inflatable crocodile still up in the attic?"

---

[88] She was careful to ensure that it didn't slide over any other plates and thus cause an earthquake.

"I think so, but I'm pretty sure it has a hole in it."

"Okay." Jack's father stood up from the breakfast table. "In that case I'm going out to the garage to fetch the puncture repair kit."

Jack's mother arched an eyebrow. "Why?"

"Well, if he's a genius, it would make sense for me to inflate the crocodile in case he's right."

"Okay, and what if he's an idiot?"

"Well, in that case an inflatable crocodile[89] will be a nice friend for him to play with."

Jack's mother couldn't fault her husband's logic.

———

Jack wandered along the street toward the bus stop, desperately riffling through his brain for a plan, but none came. He stopped in the middle of the pavement and closed his eyes, willing a brilliant idea to come. Sadly, brilliant ideas refuse to be cajoled in this way and every single one of them refused to appear.

"Well, that didn't work," said Jack as he opened his eyes again. Jack was slightly surprised when he opened his eyes. He had a general rule of thumb that every time he opened his eyes the world would become at least marginally brighter. On this occasion it wasn't true. It was every bit as dark as it was when he had them shut.

Jack was a child of the computer generation. He decided

---

[89] It is worth noting that if inflatable alligators had been available during the reign of Emperor Tiberius, then many more gladiators might have gotten out of the arena alive.

to try a reset by closing his eyes and opening them again. That didn't work either. Suddenly Jack smelled a strong whiff of perfume and felt as though he was being bundled off his feet and carried into a car. The reason that he felt as if this was happening, was because this was precisely what was happening. He tried to call out for help but his cries were muffled by the bag that had so recently been put over his head.

〰〰〰〰〰〰〰〰

Jack sat silently. From the perfume smell and the squashed feeling he could tell that two large Atlanteans were on either side of him in the car. Jack had seen movies where people who were kidnapped, blindfolded, and put into cars were able to tell which way they were traveling by listening to the sounds they passed. Jack discovered that this was made considerably more difficult when the driver of the car was listening to an audiobook.

On the bright side, listening to the audiobook took his mind off what was happening to him. It was an especially good book about a man who was having a particularly bad day. First his house was knocked down and then the Earth exploded. The man in the book was called Arthur Dent, and a lot of strange things happened to him. Jack thought of all the strange things that happened to him and wondered if perhaps Arthur Dent might be a Ministry operative. Maybe the audiobook was actually based on the real-life adventures of an English member of the Ministry. Of course then Jack realized that the book couldn't possibly have been based on a real-life adventure. Because in the book the Earth had exploded. And if that had happened in real life, he was pretty sure that he would have noticed it. Jack was interrupted from his thoughts and pulled out of the car. Part of him was terrified at being completely in the dark about what was going to happen next, and part of him just wanted to hear the end of the audiobook.

He was half marched and half lifted along some rough ground, then into a building. He could hear the door slam behind him. Once they were inside the building there was an overpowering smell of soap, perfume, and moisturizer. After being hauled down a few more corridors he was pushed into a seat and the bag was pulled off his head. He looked down into his lap and saw that his hands were secured with plastic ties.

Looking up, he was unsurprised to see Regina Maris. She was just finishing coating her face with moisturizer. Rubbing the last remnants away with a white cloth, she smiled at Jack, showing rows of pearly white teeth.

"I suppose you have questions to ask me."

ATLANTEAN MOISTURIZER
THE WORLD'S BEST MOISTURIZER

The Ministry has recently come to be aware that the world's best moisturizer is made by the Atlanteans. The moisturizer is mostly made from normal ingredients; however, it also contains pieces of starfish. The starfish's ability to regenerate is thus communicated to the skin and helps it revitalize and renew itself.

This is clearly the only reason that the seafloor is not absolutely strewn with starfish, especially considering how difficult they are to destroy.

(EDITOR'S NOTE: Now that this information has come to light it is essential that we update the section **Aquatic Animals: The Starfish.**)

46

THE WRONG ANSWERS

"As a matter of fact, I do have some questions to ask you. Do Arthur Dent and Ford Prefect get rescued after they were thrown out of the spaceship's airlock?"[90]

Unsurprisingly, Jack's answer confused Regina Maris. "What are you talking about?"

"We were listening to an audiobook in the car and I was just wondering how it ended."

Jack had expected his answer to infuriate Regina Maris, but instead she just laughed. "Yes, *they* said you'd be the funny one."

"Who said that?" Jack was confused but also quite pleased that someone thought he was the funny one.

---

[90] For those of you who think that I'm going to reveal the answer to the question, you are quite mistaken. You're just going to have to read *The Hitchhiker's Guide to the Galaxy* yourself.

Regina went over to a desk and tapped something into a computer that made a gurgling sound as it worked. She pointed at something on the screen that Jack couldn't see. "Years ago I wouldn't have had a clue who you were. But villains aren't as far behind the times as you think. I've checked you out on the evil genius message board."

"What? There's no such thing."

"How naive, Jack. There's a message board for everyone on the Internet. There's a message here from BlackbeardJnr1680. He just posted it last week."

Jack eyes narrowed. So Blackbeard Junior hadn't been trampled to death by a dinosaur after all. And now he was giving out information about the Ministry. This was going to make things a lot harder.

"He says that you're funny, but not desperately effective."

"Hey," complained Jack. "That isn't fair."

"Apparently you're always getting beaten up in fights and have to get rescued by your much stronger and more able companion, Trudy."

"Hey," complained Jack again. "That's reasonably fair . . . but it still isn't a nice thing to say."

Jack tried pulling at the plastic cuffs that were securing his hands. They stretched slightly but still held him fast.

"But there are more interesting things here than that."

Jack frowned. "Like what?" He didn't like the idea that people were writing about him on the Internet.

"Well, it was Blackbeard who suggested that if anyone was going up against the Ministry, they try and capture you first. Even if you can't punch your way out of a paper bag, he says that you have an uncanny knack of seeing through evil plots."

"Like a group of Atlanteans trying to sink the whole of Northern Ireland?"

Ms. Maris looked up from her computer. "So Blackbeard Junior was right. You have figured out our little scheme."

"It wasn't that hard . . . although I haven't quite figured out why you're doing it yet."

Regina Maris stood up from her chair and wandered over to where Jack sat helpless. She put her face right in front of his. "So you now expect me to gloat about my entire plan?"

"From my limited experience it does seem to be how these things work."

Regina Maris considered for a moment. "BlackbeardJnr1680 warned me about this. He said that gloating was what caused his downfall."

Jack decided to try reverse psychology. "Well, yes, but Blackbeard Junior is nowhere near as smart and pretty as you. I'm sure you're going to defeat us without even trying."

Regina Maris walked away from Jack and considered his words. "I know what you're doing. You're doing reverse psychology."

"Yes," agreed Jack. "Reverse psychology is exactly what I am doing." Jack was now trying reverse reverse psychology.

Regina sighed. "Lonely is the head that wears the crown."

Jack knew what each of those words meant, but the order that Regina had put them in seemed somewhat confusing to him. "Umm, what do you mean?"

"I'm a queen, Jack. I'm queen of Atlantis."

"Right, good. You seem to be making sense again. Carry on."

"And it isn't easy being the queen of an entire race. Apart from anything else you have to appear royal at all times. Which means you have no one to confide in."

"Must be hard."

"You have no idea how hard. If I talked to my servants or soldiers about my problems, they would think I was weak."

"That is a problem," said Jack, pretending to be sympathetic as he tried to wriggle out of the plastic cuffs.

"I mean, I used to have a little glove puppet that I talked to, but then I lost it one day."

Jack stopped wriggling his wrists. "Oh, come on! Does everyone have a glove puppet for a friend these days?"

Regina squinted at Jack. "What are you talking about?"

"Nothing, it's just sometimes my life seems to be bizarrely repetitive. Everyone who is lonely seems to be relying on a puppet these days.[91] Anyway, I might not be a puppet, but you can talk to me."

Regina weighed up Jack's offer. "Well, okay, you aren't going anywhere."

Jack smiled inwardly. That was exactly what Blackbeard Junior had thought, and Jack had escaped from him.

"You already know we're Atlanteans and that we're planning to sink Northern Ireland?"

---

[91] Jack did not realize how important this realization was, but ultimately it would be a thought about glove puppets that would save Northern Ireland.

"Yes, but why? I mean, you have an entire seabed to live on. Why would you want to sink one small country?"

"Your country is only a start." Regina sighed and began her story. "I am descended from a long line of Atlantean queens. My adopted name, Regina Maris, translates as 'queen of the sea.'"

"Did Atlantis always have queens, never any kings?"

"Well, of course we only had queens; after all, we were very smart," snapped Regina. "Anyway, one of my ancient ancestors decided to turn us into a race of superintelligent people by sinking the island. Unfortunately, she hadn't thought the entire plan through."

"So it didn't work, then?"

"Oh, it worked. But it was only after we became super-intelligent we realized that living under the sea wasn't such a brilliant idea after all."

Jack remembered animated cartoons about undersea worlds. As far as he recalled, living under the sea was basically one long carnival with singing crabs and slightly annoying, forgetful fish. "What was wrong with living under the sea?"

"Lots of things. Haven't you ever noticed that builders never work when it rains? Well, it's even worse when you're actually under the sea. Cement doesn't set, trying to get the electricity done is almost impossible, and you can forget anything that requires welding."

"So your houses are pretty poor, then?"

"What with the problem of actually building anything we mostly live in caves. And on top of that we basically live in an enormous toilet."

"I'm not sure I entirely understand that."

Regina Maris was clearly warming up to her subject. "Think about it—where do you think the water goes when you flush your toilet? Into the sea. It's very unpleasant. And to make matters worse, our own plumbing is awful."

"Why's that?"

"Because when you're underwater it's pretty much impossible to tell where a pipe is leaking from."

Jack was beginning to see that living underwater clearly wasn't that fun, no matter how good crabs were at playing the xylophone. But there was still one thing that was confusing him. "Okay, I can see how all that would be very annoying, but I'm not sure why any of this would make you try and sink a country."

Regina Maris ignored Jack and carried on complaining about the problems of undersea life. "And the water gets into food. There's no such thing as concentrate for diluting. It's all prediluted the minute you open the bottle. And as for trying to read a book, well, forget about that, unless you're willing to spend an entire weekend laminating it page by page...."

Jack coughed loudly. "Excuse me, I was just wondering why any of this would make you try and sink Northern Ireland? I mean, you know how awful it is to live underwater. So why would you do that to us?"

Regina Maris smiled cruelly. "Because we really don't care about you. But if we sink your country, it goes to the bottom of sea with houses and buildings already built. With a plumbing system that's been built in the air so we know that it's going to work. With roads, electrical wires,[92] walls, fences, and infrastructure."

Jack realized what she was saying. "You sink the country and then you steal our houses and homes."

"Pre-cise-ly," said Regina, sounding out every syllable in the word. "It was an idea we came up after spending decades living with hermit crabs."

"But thousands of people will die."

"Oh, no . . . *hundreds of thousands* of people will die. Some might be shocked and have their breath taken away—but not all of them. But that's the beauty of our plan: We won't even have to clear up the mess."

"What do you mean?" Jack asked.

Regina Maris smiled the most sinister smile Jack had ever seen. "Because the land will be on the bottom of the ocean, and corpses float."

"You'll never get away with this," said Jack, although he wasn't altogether sure that she wouldn't. After all, she seemed to have it all very well planned out.

"But don't you see, Jack? We already have. We kidnapped you as a hostage. Your friend Trudy will never attack when she knows we have both her Ministry partner and her mother at our mercy."

The mention of Trudy's mother enraged Jack, and he jumped from his chair and swung his cuffed hands at Regina.

---

[92] Interestingly enough, the electrical wires weren't really being used for what the queen of Atlantis thought they were. But their real purpose wouldn't be revealed until Ministry of SUITs 3. . . .

She moved effortlessly out of the way, then tripped Jack, sending him sprawling to the ground. "Is that the best you can do?"

Jack struggled to his feet. "Where is Trudy's mother? Tell me!"

Regina snorted. "I'll do better than that. She's being held by a scientist that works for me. And that's where you're going to be going soon." Regina put her hand flat on Jack's chest, and a sharp shove sent him tumbling back into his chair. "Forget about trying to save Northern Ireland. Forget about trying to save Trudy's mother. Forget about trying to save yourself. Soon all of you will be drowned. And if the fracking plan works in Northern Ireland, then we'll start sinking the rest of the countries of the world!"

"The pirates thought that their plan was foolproof. But it wasn't," Jack snarled.

Regina smiled. "Yes, my Internet friend BlackbeardJnr1680 admitted that. But our plan goes back a lot longer than Blackbeard. It's been right under people's noses for thousands of years and no one even noticed it. And on top of that we freed the criminal hammerhead sharks and sawfish from the Ministry for a reason. Apart from finishing the drilling platform in Lough Neagh, they've also been building something of an insurance policy."

Jack started to speak but couldn't think of anything to say.

Regina Maris then said something very odd indeed. "You people are so foolish. After all, you still think that the Giant's Causeway is the result of a volcanic eruption, don't you?"

UNDERWATER BUILDING
ADDITIONAL CONTRACTORS

It is amazing that so many people are unaware of the underwater races such as the Atlanteans and the merpeople. After all, so many fish and aquatic animals have clearly been adapted and trained by the Atlanteans to become builders. The most obvious of these is the crab, who comes complete with a hard hat and his own pliers/snippers.

However, the crab is far from being the only creature adapted for building. A person would have to be idiotic not to realize that animals such as the hammerhead shark and the sawfish could not have turned up by accident. They have been specifically bred by the Atlanteans to look after carpentry.

It is also worthwhile noting that there is even a fish called the carpet shark. Just because you live all your life underwater, it doesn't mean that you don't like soft furnishings.

47

CRAZY AND CRACKED

If there was one thing that schoolchildren in Northern Ireland did nearly as many projects on as the *Titanic*, it was the Giant's Causeway. It was a large formation of hexagonal-shaped stones on the north coast of the country. It was called a causeway because it looked like a road that led under the sea.

"But the Giant's Causeway *is* the result of localized volcanic activity," Jack said automatically, remembering his third-grade project. "Lava flowed over the land, then as it cooled, it cracked into symmetrical shapes."[93]

"You really believe that explanation?"

---

[93] Secretly Jack was wondering to himself if the Causeway had really been a causeway built by a giant. Although it was kind of all over the place, so it would have to have been a giant with poor building skills.

Jack felt slightly unsure. "Well, my third-grade teacher did."

"How many volcanoes are there in Northern Ireland?"

Jack paused and did a very short mental calculation in his head. "Well... none."

"So how did the lava get there? Did a giant carry it?"

Jack refused to even dignify this with a response. It was one thing being lectured by Grey about these kind of things. It was quite another being lectured by a mean Atlantean queen who was trying to drown everyone.

"And anyway, have you seen the Giant's Causeway? It's all hexagonal shapes. Have you ever seen footage of a volcano exploding? Lava rolls over the landscape at random, burning, killing, forming odd shapes. If lava formed perfectly symmetrical, hexagonal shapes, they would never have found the lost city of Pompeii, would they? They would just have assumed that for some reason someone had decided to cover an area of Italy with the largest-ever piece of crazy paving. Even if an archaeologist had dug it up he would have been stumped, wondering why someone decided to put a patio over a city."

The more Jack thought about it the more the explanations he had been given for the Giant's Causeway seemed ridiculous. After all, when you heated something until it turned molten and then let it cool, it never formed a perfect hexagonal column. If that were the case, then Rice Krispies treats would be considerably more uniform that they were.[94]

---

[94] And not nearly as much fun.

Jack's curiosity overtook him. A few moments ago he had promised himself he would just be silent and give Regina Maris the cold shoulder. But now he found himself asking questions again, so great was his curiosity. "So *was* it a giant that built it, then?"

"Why would a giant make a bridge out of dozens of tiny stones? The stones are just big enough for a human foot. A giant would spend his entire time tripping and falling into the sea. No—quite clearly the Giant's Causeway was ..."

Jack completed Regina's sentence, "... built by Atlanteans."

Regina clapped her hands slowly. "So the boy that BlackbeardJnr1680 thought was so bright finally figures it out."

Jack had just remembered the stepping-stones in Cthulhu's room. But of course the stones of the Giant's Causeway weren't placed so that people could jump between them. Instead they ran down to the waves of the sea and then continued on underneath them. Jack had a horrible thought. "So that's what the Causeway is for—it's like a ladder out of the sea for you. It's built so you could attack with an invasion army."

"It was built millennia ago, shortly after Atlantis sank beneath the waves. We decided that we would try and invade Ireland."

Jack cocked his head to one side. "Well, obviously it didn't work. So what went wrong?"

"Nothing went wrong," Regina said in an irritated voice. "We were just early. We had been looking for a country to sink and use as our home. Preferably a smallish island with ready-made buildings we could use. We had already figured out that trying to build a new city underwater was pretty much a nonstarter. We thought Ireland might fit our requirements. And so we created the Causeway. We couldn't just use a conventional port. Islands are always expecting to be invaded by sea, so ports tend to be surrounded by castles, cannons, and men carrying pointy sticks."

"But there was someone waiting for you, wasn't there? There are always people at the Giant's Causeway." Jack was proud of himself.

"Jack, don't be an idiot. There are always people at the Giant's Causeway because they come to see the Giant's Causeway. Before we built it there was no reason to go there at all. And so our people arrived and started marching down Ireland trying to find the buildings with the plumbing we so craved."

"What happened?"

"Well, not much. They didn't come across many buildings and very little plumbing of a satisfactory nature."

Jack couldn't understand this. "But there are lots of buildings."

"Not back then there weren't," Regina sighed. "It took Ireland a lot longer to get their buildings, you see. What my ancestors hadn't figured out was that the difference between living under the sea and living in Ireland is that living under the sea is *slightly wetter*. But very much with the emphasis on the word *slightly*. That meant it took a lot longer for Ireland to get around to erecting a satisfactory number of buildings."

This Jack could understand—it rained a lot in Ireland. Occasionally there would be two or three weeks without a single drop of rain, but even when that happened it was only because you knew the weather was building itself up to give you a really thorough drenching. "So your ancestors went back into the sea?"

Regina smiled confidently. "Not at all. They decided that eventually when enough buildings were in place they would sink the island and claim it for their own. The Atlantean army disguised themselves using perfume made of natural flowers and marched right to the center of Northern Ireland. There they spent nearly a hundred years digging out an enormous round hole. That way, when Ireland was ready, all they had to do was to drill down in the center of that spot and the water would flood in, sinking the country."

Jack tilted his head quizzically. "But Lough Neagh isn't a round shape. It's got knobbly bits. It almost looks like a star shape."

The queen's brow wrinkled. "We know. But we aren't sure how that happened. Someone must have done more excavations after we left Lough Neagh to reshape it. Although we really aren't sure who. . . . After all, who would want to make it that shape? And we needed an entire army to dig it in the first place. So whoever changed the shape . . . Well, they must be a creature of enormous power. Anyway, despite the change in shape it's still an enormous hole, so it still fits our purposes."

Cogs and wheels where whirring in Jack's head. He was

thinking of a dozen things at once. "So why are you fracking on different sites at the same time?"

"The biggest hole will be in the center of the country, with dozens of smaller holes around it just to make sure that when it sinks it doesn't overbalance and capsize."

Jack had a theory, but he needed to check one more thing. "And why did you cause the earthquake?"

The smug look vanished from Regina's face. "What? We thought that was you. It wasn't us."

The Atlanteans hadn't caused the earthquake. Just as Jack had suspected. But then what had caused it? Was there yet another villain out there? Perhaps the one who had changed the shape of Lough Neagh after the Atlanteans had dug it?

Regina went back over to her desk and used an intercom to call for some burly Atlantean guards. "Anyway, Jack, I enjoyed our chat, but until my scientist comes to collect you I'm afraid you're going to have to be locked in our dungeon."

Jack wasn't worried. The minute he got into the dungeon he would merely put a pillow over his head and summon the Tooth Fairy. He was willing to risk his teeth if it meant saving the entire population of the country.

The guards grabbed an arm each and began hauling Jack out of the room. Just as he was being dragged through the door Regina shouted after him, "And don't think you'll be using the pillow trick to summon the Tooth Fairy. BlackbeardJnr1680 mentioned all about that on the evil villain Internet forum."

GIANTS
FINN McCOOL

The giant who *claimed* to have built the Giant's Causeway was called Finn McCool. Giants are notoriously boastful people in general.

However, the truth was that giants very rarely achieve anything. Although they will claim to make bread out of ground bones and build causeways, the truth is considerably more pedestrian.

Most giants spend at least fifty percent of their entire lives trying to find shoes that fit them.

48

A WELL-DESIGNED DUNGEON

The guards threw Jack headfirst into the dungeon. Jack gritted his teeth and prepared for his head to hit the ground. When it happened, the ground made an odd splashing noise. The floor of the dungeon was covered in a foot of water. Jack spluttered and stood up. Being wet wasn't fun, but he was quite pleased that he hadn't been knocked unconscious. That had happened a lot in his last adventure, and he was pretty sure that concussions weren't good for you at all.

One of the guards stood at the entrance to the dungeon. "So, do you like our dungeon?"

Jack looked around. Although the dungeon was in a modern soap factory, they had gone for the "classic dungeon chic" look. There were green, slimy stone walls with manacles and chains hanging from them. The ceiling was low and there were no windows. The water was filthy, with pieces of sticks and seaweed floating in it. In fact, the only indication that he wasn't in a castle sometime in the twelfth century was that there was a modern porcelain toilet in the corner.

"It's a very nice dungeon," Jack said to the guard. "The architect really did his job well when he was designing this. I mean the décor—it really says 'dungeon' to me."[95]

"Thank you," said the guard.

"And it's not very often you get an en suite dungeon."

The Atlantean guard knew that Jack was making fun. "Listen, you may take toilets for granted but you wouldn't if you lived in the sea. Using a toilet under the sea is like staring terror in the eye. Is the flush going to empty the bowl or cause what's in there to spiral out upward into the room?"

When it was described that way Jack thought that maybe he understood why the Atlanteans were so grumpy all the time.

The guard shuddered. "When we get a building on dry land, it's such a relief to get a toilet that actually works that we end up putting them in every room. Our bedrooms are en suite, the warehouses are en suite. Even some of the en suites are en suite."

"Well, thanks," said Jack. Just because you'd been captured by someone who was trying to drown your entire country there was no need to be rude. "I mean, it's a lot better than a bucket."

---

[95] For those of you who are wondering, Jack's mother watched far too many surprise property-makeover shows. Jack always wondered how people got away with breaking into someone's house and changing everything without their permission, and then were never arrested. Jack had an idea that you would be able to get away scot-free if you burglarized Fort Knox, as long as you left a few throw pillows and a cast-iron pergola in place of all the gold.

The guard nodded and slammed the door shut. Jack was left in the cold, dank room. There was hardly any light. The only reason he could see anything at all was that the dungeon door didn't fit the doorframe perfectly. It was made of a series of wooden planks that had swollen and twisted due to the constant damp. Through the cracks in the door small slivers of light illuminated the darkness.

It took Jack's eyes a few minutes to adjust to the low level of light, but he soon found he was able to get about easily enough. The only problem now was how to escape. With no pillow he had no idea, no clue.

Jack took one of the longer pieces of stick that were floating on the water and started poking about with it. He had hoped that there was something useful hidden under the water's surface that he could use to escape. Sadly, after twenty minutes of trying he found nothing but more water. Although, for some reason, like all boys, he had felt strangely at peace with himself while poking the water with a stick.

Jack sighed. He felt like slumping down in the corner of the room. However, if he had done that, his head would have been underwater and it wouldn't have been much fun.

All he had in the room was a toilet—and it was almost impossible to escape a room only using a toilet. If only the Misery had taught him some magical shrinking trick, then perhaps he could have flushed himself to safety. It wouldn't have been a hygienic way to escape, but Jack was so desperate to escape he was willing to try anything.

But in order to try and do something he needed an idea. Jack went over to the toilet, put the lid down, and sat on it.

He could feel frustration welling up. Here he was half sub-merged in a dungeon and soon his country was about to sink like the *Titanic*.

The *Titanic* ... that was it!

Jack stood up and kicked the pipe that led away from the toilet. He kicked it three times quickly. Then three times more, slowly. Then finally three times quickly. As Jack kicked the pipe another piece of the puzzle fell into place—he realized why the seal had been rapping its flipper against the Plexiglas. It had been sending the same message that he had.

Then he sat back down on the toilet to wait. Wait and hope.

MINISTRY OF S.U.IT.S HANDBOOK

BOYS
THEIR NEED TO POKE THINGS
WITH STICKS

Stick poking is a habit with a long and honorable tradition dating back millions of years. The habit originated shortly after an early Stone Age man was trampled by a mammoth. It happened as follows:

"Ugg, don't go near that mammoth; it might only be sleeping."

"Don't be ridiculous, Lug; it's dead. Look."

STOMP STOMP STOMP STOMP STOMP

And so Lug went back to his tribe to tell them how the mammoth in question hadn't actually been dead and how Ugg wouldn't actually be needing his space in the cave that night.

Cavemen scientists worked around the clock in a desperate attempt to solve the problem of unnecessary mammoth stampings. The caveman opposition pointed out in the caveman Parliament that mammoth stampings had risen by sixty percent in the last two years.

In the end the cavemen scientists designed the stick. With a stick a caveman could establish how lively a mammoth was simply by poking the mastodon[96] from a safe distance.

This is engraved in men's collective memory. Women do not tend to suffer from the same problem because during cavemen times everything was dreadfully sexist, and so the women were not allowed to go hunting. Instead they had to stay at home, look after the children and the crops, and make sure that the cave was pretty.

[96] Okay, technically a mammoth isn't a mastodon. But I just wanted to use the word because I like it. It kind of rolls off the tongue. *Mastodon*.

Therefore, they were never actually supplied with sticks to poke anything with. Occasionally a woman would get hold of a stick and use it to poke one of the children—but this was frowned upon in caveman society.

Although many people in modern society see stick poking as anachronistic and out-of-date, it has helped in many of the great scientific discoveries of the age. Before Oppenheimer split the atom he spent a considerable amount of time poking the atom with a stick. Before Einstein stated that energy is equal to the speed of light squared, he spent literally years poking both energy and the speed of light with a stick. Probably most important is that before the apple actually fell on Sir Isaac Newton's head, he had spent almost half an hour poking it with a particularly long stick.

Men still remember all this stick poking on a subconscious level and in times of stress or danger resort to the habits of their forefathers. This is part of the reason all fathers have an area of their garage or shed where they keep pieces of wood of different sizes. They're never quite sure why they have them—but they always somehow feel that "they might come in handy" someday.

49

A SCUTTLING NOISE

Jack had almost given up hope when he heard a scuttling noise outside his cell. There was a moment of silence and then an observation hatch in the center of the door opened. An eye appeared at the hatch. Then another and another. Jack's plan had worked perfectly!

Jack was feeling incredibly proud of himself. He'd remembered that giant spider Ministry operatives were located underneath baths across the country and used the plumbing system as a way to communicate with one another using Morse code. Jack, like many other twelve-year-olds, didn't in fact know much Morse code. But he did know one piece. Three short dots. Three long dashes. Three short dots. The sign for SOS—the international distress signal. But how had he remembered this? Simple—in his elementary school project about the *Titanic*, he had learned that it was one of the first ships to use the SOS signal—before that, ships had signaled distress with CQD.[97]

Jack heard the bolt securing the door sliding back, and standing there in front of him was an enormous spider. Jack walked out of the room. He was getting very good at escaping from locked rooms and decided he might change his name to Houdini.

After confirming that there were no guards in the corridor, Jack turned and spoke to the spider, hoping it could understand English.

"I need to get a message to my Ministry friends."

The spider read Jack's lips and then waved its arms/legs to get him to stop talking. It mimed banging on some pipes and then pointed at itself.

"You've already contacted them?" Jack guessed.

The enormous spider nodded.

"Right, then, the only thing left to do is to escape."

The spider nodded again and scuttled down the corridor, leaving Jack with no option but to follow it.

---

[97] CQD stood for "Come Quick, Danger!" Actually that isn't true at all, but the real explanation is a lot more dull. . . .

MORSE CODE
FREQUENCY OF USE

Many people assume that Morse code is rarely used in the modern world. The truth is that it is all around us, but people do not notice it.

Many people, for example, do not realize that tap dancers are not only dancing, but also telling a story in Morse code. It is always nice to go up to them afterward and say, "I loved the dancing, but the story was even better."

Most drumming is too regular to be able to communicate a message. However, experimental jazz is played without sheet music and their drummers sound almost entirely random. Their drummers use Morse code to signal to the others what to play next.

Interestingly enough, the most common phrase of Morse code used by jazz drummers is *"Gary, please ... we all like a saxophone solo, but three hours is long enough. Please stop, as we all want to go home."*

50

CHARADES AGAIN

At first the spider seemed to be moving incredibly quickly, but every dozen yards it had to stop and remember which leg was supposed to move next. This caused it to dash quickly for a short space of time, stop for a few seconds to think, and then run again.

Jack realized that this was the way ordinary spiders ran as well. Previously he had assumed that it was because they were stopping to look around them, but he now realized it was almost certainly because when you have eight legs, it's probably very difficult to keep them in sequence.[98]

---

[98] It should be noted that it's difficult enough to keep your legs in sequence when you only have the two of them. This is why, when they're marching, soldiers have someone shouting "left, right, left, right" beside them just to make sure they're getting it in the right order.

The spider led Jack to the warehouse where he had nearly been crushed by the enormous shelving unit. All the soap, moisturizers, and perfumes had been removed and replaced by spears, tridents, seashell armor, and boxes upon boxes of explosive bath bombs. A dozen burly Atlantean warriors stood in the center of the room guarding it.

"Looks like they're getting ready for a battle," Jack said to the giant spider. The giant spider bobbed its body up and down, nodding enthusiastically.

Even using The Speed Jack would never have been able to take on a dozen warriors in full battle armor. If Trudy were here, maybe they would have had a chance. But at the moment his partner wasn't Trudy. It was a giant spider. Maybe he could use that to his advantage. . . .

"All right, giant spider . . . ," Jack said.

The spider waved a long, hairy leg in Jack's face before he said anything further. It then used its long legs to spell out the letters *T I M*.

Jack wondered if it was trying to spell *time*. Maybe it was telling him to hurry up? Then he realized what it meant. "You're called Tim. I get it. Okay, sorry about the 'giant spi-der' thing. It's just that we hadn't been formally introduced." The spider stood up on its back legs and performed a small

---

It's also why they don't have a 100-meter conga line at the Olympics. They did try it in 1928 when the Olympics were in Amsterdam. However, the experiment wasn't repeated after a conga-line pileup seriously injured sixteen people. Which is a shame, as it was a lot of fun and they were only people who did P.E. for a living. . . .

bow, and then Jack had to shake each of its "hands" in turn, wasting a considerable amount of time that they probably didn't have to spare.

"And my name is Jack. I work for the Ministry."

Tim mimed banging on pipes again.

"Right, they told you that using Morse code on the pipes."

Tim nodded.

"Okay, well, now that we know each other, here's my plan. I'm going to run in there and distract those guys. While I do that I want you to shoot webs out of your wrists and catch them."

Tim lifted up two long appendages and appeared to be holding his head in his hands.

"What? Can't you do that?"

Tim shook his head and pointed around the back of himself.

Jack caught on almost immediately. "Ahh, I get it—the webs don't come out of your wrists, they come out of your bottom."[99] Jack paused to think about this briefly. If they had bothered to make Spider-Man anatomically accurate, it would have been a very different film indeed. "Right, can you shoot webs out of your bottom at them?"

Again Tim shook his many-eyed head. Jack put his hands out palms upward in a sign of frustration. Tim thought to

---

[99] It should be noted that spiders do not actually shoot webs out of their bottoms. They come out of the spinneret glands at the bottom of their abdomens. However, after all the time wasted with introductions Tim decided to let this point of detail go. They clearly didn't have the time to spell out "spinneret" or "abdomen."

himself and suddenly stood up on just two legs, spreading the others out across the corridor.

Jack tried to guess what he was doing. "What are you pretending to be? Ummm . . . a web?"

Tim collapsed back onto all eight legs and bobbed his head up and down.

Jack tried to understand what Tim meant. "Wait a minute—I get it. You can't shoot things with your silk, can you? You can only spin a web."

Tim nodded vigorously.

"Right, well, I'm not sure if that's actually much use to us." Jack wondered about Spider-Man again. He wouldn't have been considered much of a crime fighter if he couldn't have webbed people. He would just have had to call them names until they chased him, hoping they would follow him into a web he had previously spun. It didn't seem very heroic.

Jack wasn't feeling very heroic himself. He needed to figure out a way to make himself invisible. If only he'd bought a clipboard with him he would have been able to stroll across the warehouse nonchalantly. Although having a giant spider with him might have made him a bit more memorable than he wanted to be.

Jack turned to Tim. "Maybe we could make a run for it?"

Tim just frowned at Jack.

"Oh. That's right; you aren't the world's best runner, are you."

The problem was that the guards weren't busy. If they were distracted somehow, then maybe he could . . . An idea struck Jack.

"Wait here," he said to Tim, and then he strolled into the

warehouse. The guards began to walk toward him. They looked suspicious. Jack walked straight toward them. He thought that if he approached them they wouldn't suspect he was up to anything—hopefully the guards weren't aware of who he was.

One of the guards called out to him. "There aren't any tours of the factory today."

"I'm not here for a tour. I'm working with Regina. . . ."

The guard captain interrupted him. "Working with Regina. Don't be ridiculous. You're only a child. There are child labor laws, you know."

Jack had feared something like this would happen. He should really have had a lie prepared for this eventuality. However, as he hadn't, he panicked and tried the first lie that popped into his head. "Um, no. Well, I'm not really working with her as such. It's more . . . umm . . . Bring Your Daughter to Work Day?" Jack offered. It sounded stupid even to him.

The guard captain was confused. "But Regina doesn't have any children."

Jack actually felt relatively relaxed as he told more lies. The first one had been so ridiculous that he knew it couldn't get any worse.[100]

"Well, yes, you're right: Regina doesn't have any children. Which is why I'm actually the neighbor's child. You know she nipped next door to borrow a cup of sugar. But in this case it was a . . . well, a cup of Me."

---

[100] This is a vital life lesson to learn. When you're doing something, always do it very badly the first time. That way even if you only try a *tiny bit* the second time it's still going to seem like an improvement.

Jack expected the guard captain to see through this patent lie, but instead he merely asked another question. "But you're a boy and you said it was Bring Your Daughter to Work Day."

Jack sighed and pretended to be exasperated by the question. "Well, yes, but my sister wasn't there because she's on a school trip to Russia. So I was the next-best thing." The guard captain was about to ask another question, but Jack decided it was time to put his plan into action. "Anyway, Regina told me to come down here because she has a special task that needs to be done and she wants a few volunteers. So . . ."

The Atlantean guards all stiffened at once. Before they had been lounging about, leaning against the walls, and chatting. But in mere seconds they became incredibly busy. Some polished their armor; some sharpened their swords; others started sorting the bath bombs by color, size, and texture. The guard captain himself took a map out of an oyster shell pocket and started looking at it. "Sorry, we'd love to volunteer, but we're all very busy."

"Very busy . . ." the men behind him all chorused.

Jack smiled to himself. This was exactly the behavior that he had been banking on. He'd seen the same reaction at home. His father could have been sitting on the sofa, idly staring into space, literally doing nothing. However, the minute Jack's mother asked him to do anything, he managed to instantly become busy with something else. Fixing a pair of glasses, wiring a plug, or repairing a radio that hadn't worked for over a decade.

"Okay, I'll let her know how busy you are," Jack said as he edged his way toward the exit from the warehouse.

"Very busy . . .," the guards muttered.

Jack took a last look at the guards. They intently focused on trying to look busy. Jack waved to Tim, who scuttled as quickly as he could across the floor. Jack prayed that none of the guards would look up before he made it to the door.

Jack held the door open and Tim scuttled through it. None of the guards had noticed. Jack breathed a sigh of relief. Tim held up a leg for Jack to high-five.

"Right, we don't have time to waste. We've got to get back to the Ministry and let them know what's going on."

Jack and Tim ran across the factory's car park. Jack saw a Ministry car pulling up. "Wow, that was quick. I hadn't even called for one yet."

MINISTRY OF S.U.IT.S HANDBOOK

SUPERHEROES
ANIMAL POWERS

Over the years you may have noticed that when superheroes get the powers of animals they are almost always the useful powers. Like the ability to fly, shoot stingers, or climb up walls. They almost never have the powers of less exciting animals such as llamas or cows.

Of course, the truth is that occasionally in bizarre scientific experiments people do get their DNA spliced with duller animals and go on to try to become superheroes. It's just that if you are Alpaca-Man and your only power is having really touchable, soft fur, your adventures generally aren't that exciting and so you tend to get reported about less in the popular press.

It's interesting to note that one of the most bitter heroes that has ever existed was Cow-Man. Occasionally in comic books you can see him standing in the background in his black-and-white Holstein jumpsuit. He'll be the one chewing the cud and muttering to himself, "*One of these days a world-destroying deity will turn up who is lactose intolerant and then they'll be begging for my help.*"

What made it even worse was that he'd never been invited to a dinner party or asked to play spin the bottle (please see **Being Sick: Location—Your Own Mouth**).

51

THE CAVALRY ARRIVES

Trudy and Grey stepped out of the Ministry car.

"I escaped being captured." Jack felt proud of himself.

Trudy didn't look impressed. "Do you ever think that maybe you wouldn't need to escape all the time if you weren't so dreadfully easy to capture?"

Jack decided to ignore what Trudy had said and pretend that she had been congratulating him. "You're right, Trudy, I am excellent at escaping. But I think saying that I could be the next Houdini might be going a bit too far."

Trudy punched Jack in the shoulder.[101]

---

[101] It is interesting to note that one of the ways that Houdini used to get out of straitjackets was to dislocate his shoulder. Given the repetitive strain injury that Jack will eventually develop from Trudy continually punching him in the shoulder, this is a skill that Jack may well gain over the years.

"There'll be time enough for patting each other on the back later. Did you learn anything new?" Grey asked.

Jack told them about his confrontation with the evil Regina Maris, queen of the Atlanteans. He explained her plot.

"And they did kidnap your mum," Jack finished.

"You saw her?" asked Trudy.

Jack shook his head sadly. "I'm afraid not. She's being held elsewhere by some kind of scientist, but when we capture Regina we can make her take us there."

"Brilliant, Jack. So what's the plan?" asked Trudy.

Jack suddenly remembered that last night he had promised to come up with a brilliant plan to save the day. "Oh, the plan . . . yes . . . well . . . thing is, I was too busy escaping with Tim here to actually come up with a plan. I mean, we have to destroy the drilling platform and all, but beyond that I haven't really dreamt anything up."

Jack was expecting a severely punched shoulder, and he gingerly edged away from Trudy. However, Trudy was so focused on rescuing her mother that she didn't even have time to get angry. "Right, well, the first thing we need to do is get some kind of explosives."

"Well, if we could defeat some Atlantean warriors, we could use the bath bombs from the factory."

"Easy enough," said Trudy. "Then we need some way of getting them out to the drilling platform without them getting wet."

"Tim, do you think you could swim out to the platform spinning us a silk thread?" asked Jack.

Tim bobbed his head up and down.

Jack turned to Trudy. "We can use that to make a zip line."

"Great, then we have everything we need to take these Atlanteans down."

Jack smiled to himself. "What do you know? I had a plan after all."

Trudy arched an eyebrow at him. "You had a plan?"

Jack stopped smiling. "We. We had a plan."

"Let's go." Trudy strode off toward the exit from the warehouse with Grey and Tim following.

"Back into the lion's den, then?" Jack said to no one. Then he ran after the others.

Before opening the door to the warehouse, Trudy turned and spoke to Jack. "Okay, so what are we up against?"

"There are a dozen Atlantean warriors. And I don't just mean guards, I mean proper warriors. With armor and nasty-looking swords."

"What do you think?" Trudy asked Grey.

Grey pulled himself up to his full height. "I don't know. A dozen trained warriors? I'm pretty useful with The Speed myself, but it's going to be risky."

"Risky's fun," Trudy said. But she didn't look as though she was thinking of fun at all. Jack felt nervous—if Trudy wasn't confident about a violent encounter, then he should be very worried indeed.

Trudy reached out for the door handle, but it turned without her touching it. The heroes jumped back and flattened themselves against the wall.

An Atlantean captain walked out and spoke to his troops, who were still inside. Luckily, he kept his back to Jack and his friends. "We're going to need to mobilize. So start packing up the weapons and bring them out here. The transports to pick them up should be here shortly." The captain put a wedge under the door, keeping it open, and walked back into the warehouse.

Trudy, Jack, Tim, and Grey quietly sneaked to the far side of the warehouse. Grey stretched and performed a few lunges, using his umbrella like a sword. "Okay then, guys, time to think about something sad."

Jack sighed and started thinking as hard as he could.

"Wait!" Trudy said. "I think I've got a better idea. Maybe we can get the bath bombs without having to fight anyone."

Jack stared at Trudy with concern. There was something seriously wrong with her if she was suggesting that violence wasn't the best way to achieve something.

"Grey, do you have any matches?"

Grey found a box in his pocket. "What are you thinking about?"

"Something happened at school today that's given me an idea," Trudy smiled.

The Atlantean warriors had been busy. Half a dozen blue plastic containers on wheels had been rolled out into the car park. Three of them contained plastic bags full of bath bombs. "Grey, Tim, I need you to roll these over to the far side of the car park," Trudy said. Grey and Tim both nodded and started pushing the carts.

"What are we going to do?" asked Jack.

"We're going to take on the Atlantean warriors," Trudy explained.

"I was worried you were going to say that."

For the life of him Jack couldn't figure out what Trudy's plan was. They were going up against a dozen soldiers who had probably spent half their lives training at fighting. He didn't see how two schoolchildren with a matchbox could possibly defeat them.

Trudy walked into the warehouse. Jack reluctantly followed. Luckily, the warriors were all standing thirty feet away at the shelving unit. They were loading more carts full of weapons and bath bombs.

"Hey, guys," Trudy called.

"That's a good idea, attract their attention," Jack muttered to himself.

The Atlantean captain and his guards turned and looked at them. He was slightly confused. "Is that your sister, then? Is she back from the school trip?"

Trudy was confused and turned to Jack for an explanation.

"Don't ask. They just think I'm Regina Maris's neighbor's son. You were on a trip to Russia. And you were my sister as well . . . apparently."

"Oh," said Trudy. "Well, that explains everything."

The Atlantean captain was clearly beginning to suspect that something was wrong. He drew a vicious-looking sword from its scabbard and began walking toward Jack and Trudy.

Trudy took out the matchbox.

"Trudy, if you're thinking of burning the factory down, I think we'll have been sliced up long before that actually works."

Trudy struck a match and let it burn. A tendril of smoke snaked up to the roof. "I'm not going to burn anything down. Quite the opposite." Trudy pointed to the roof.

Jack looked up. Trudy was indicating the smoke detectors and sprinkler system that dotted the roof. The tendril of smoke set a detector off, and a siren rang out. "Figured it out yet, Jack?" Trudy asked.

One of the sprinklers popped open, then another and another. It reminded Jack of David and the soap-making carnage.

The Atlantean captain stopped walking and looked upward, his brow wrinkled in confusion.

Jack realized what Trudy's plan was. "The bath bombs!" The plan was genius, and Jack was a bit miffed that he hadn't thought of it himself. Of course, because it was a Trudy plan, it was genius and incredibly violent and dangerous all at the same time.

There were still dozens of containers of explosive bath bombs dotted around the warehouse. The sprinklers were now deluging the room with water. The bath bombs started to fizz.

Trudy and Jack looked at each other and spoke at the same time. "RUN!" They had made it halfway across the car park when an enormous explosion sent them sprawling. Grey and Tim ran over and helped them up.

Trudy dusted herself off. "Well, I think that's the Atlantean army sorted out."

The factory was burning fiercely but at the same time giving off a delightful aroma. Grey sniffed the air. "Vanilla and honey, I think."

Jack sniffed. "And maybe a dash of hibiscus?"

Grey, Tim, and Trudy all stared at Jack in disbelief.

"What? I'm beginning to like all these lotions and bath oils, okay?"

Atlantean soldiers were stumbling out of the wreckage and collapsing on the ground. Their weapons and armor were in tatters. Being involved in a massive explosion has a tendency to take the fight out of people.

"You've just created the world's largest scented candle," Jack said to Trudy.

"This is no time for congratulating ourselves. We're only halfway home. There's still the drilling platform to be taken care of," Grey said.

Trudy agreed with Grey. "And we've got to find out where my mother is."

Jack noticed a speedboat skimming across Lough Neagh. "Look!"

Sitting in the speedboat were three Atlantean warriors and Regina Maris. However, she had changed out of her business suit and was wearing regal armor, dripping with pearls and gems. "The queen of Atlantis," Jack whispered.

"Let's get her," said Trudy.

MINISTRY OF S.U.IT.S HANDBOOK

OYSTERS
THE CREATION OF PEARLS

Oysters are a perfect example of a creature who so nearly got it perfectly right. Generally speaking animals don't want to be eaten. We can't blame them for this. It is perfectly normal behavior. I would not be keen on being eaten myself.

However, where most animals make a fatal mistake is that they taste very pleasant indeed. Not, however, the clever oyster. The oyster has deliberately gone out of its way to look and taste disgusting.

And yet pride is the oyster's downfall. If only the oysters had carried on looking and tasting repulsive, human beings would never have bothered them. But oysters figured out a way to create pearls and had to show that off to the world. The only reason people ever started eating oysters was that they were secretly hoping that they would find a pearl. However, not wanting to appear greedy, they pretended that wasn't what they were doing at all——they just pretended they really loved the taste of oyster.

If you don't believe this, watch people actually eating oysters. They generally add lemon juice and Tabasco sauce——the kind of flavors you would add only if you were trying to mask the real taste.

52

THE ZIP LINE

The plan was simple enough to initiate. Tim climbed to the top of a nearby cell tower and tied off a section of silk line. Then he clambered back down and took to the water, trailing the line behind him. Unfortunately, Tim wasn't the best swimmer and would occasionally forget the order his legs should kick or stroke in. When this happened he would start twirling around like the blade in a blender.

However, he eventually reached his target, climbed up one of the legs of the drilling platform, and tied the silk line off. Tim had created what was possibly the world's longest zip line. Jack wasn't keen on using the zip line. He'd been on one before and didn't really understand why people found them fun, unless of course your idea of fun was mind-numbing terror.

Trudy slung a bag of bath bombs across her shoulder and clambered up the cell phone tower. "This is going to be fun."

"I certainly wouldn't say *fun*," Jack grumbled, climbing up behind her. "Although I suppose at least if we fall in the water it'll give us a soft landing."

Grey brought up the rear. "I'd really try to avoid that. Remember, you're going to be carrying a bag full of bombs that explode on contact with H_2O. So if you do fall into the water, you're going to find yourself becoming part of the world's first human fireworks display."

"Thanks, Grey," said Jack, "that's a helpful thing to think about. I'll just jump onto the zip line as soon as I can stop my hands from shaking."

Trudy gazed out over the vast expanse of water. "Grey, I suppose the Ministry has managed to capture all the water monsters and sea creatures that used to terrorize ships, haven't they? I'm slightly worried that the Atlanteans might have a few tricks up their sleeve."

Grey thought for a minute. "Mostly," he said.

Trudy winced. "Mostly? That isn't reassuring. Might we end up fighting the Loch Ness Monster?"

Grey glanced down at his feet, slightly ashamed. "Actually, no one in the Ministry has ever figured out what the Loch Ness Monster really is. So that's a possibility. The other worry is that we never actually captured the Kraken—although he did seem to stop attacking ships several millennia ago, so we probably don't have to worry about him."

Trudy shook her head. "Great, so on top of Atlantean warriors we might be up against aquatic monsters."

"I can't be sure," Jack admitted, "but I've got a feeling that if there are any aquatic monsters they might be on our side."

Grey pursed his lips. "And what makes you think that?"

"I'll explain later when we have more time."

Trudy looked with skepticism at Jack. "Then the only thing we have to fear is falling!"

Jack took a deep breath and held his hands out in front of him to see if they'd stopped shaking. Trudy laughed and, using a handstrap that Tim had knitted out of silk, she kicked off from the cell tower. She went hurtling across the sky. The spider-silk zip line was so thin it almost looked as if she were flying.

Jack counted to five and threw himself off the tower with reluctance. The feeling was amazing. His stomach came up into his mouth. He felt terrified and exhilarated at the same time. Halfway across the zip line Jack looked over to the far shore. Standing there was someone who looked as if they had a squid on their head. And they seemed to be dumping buckets full of slithering eels into the water. Jack smiled to himself. It was the last piece of evidence he needed to feel that he had solved another mystery.

Unfortunately, the sight had distracted Jack slightly, and he felt his bag moving on his shoulder. One of the bath bombs slipped out of it and fell to the water below him. The resulting explosion showered him with kelp and lough water. Jack prayed none would get onto the remaining bath bombs. He just managed to hold on to the handstrap by the smallest of margins.

Trudy had already landed by jumping nimbly onto the

platform. When Jack reached the end of the zip line, she helped him off. Grey was not far behind them, and Tim caught him easily, using just four legs.

Jack thought that for once everything might go according to plan.[102] "So what's next?" Jack asked Trudy.

"We take the bath bombs and pour them around the drilling platform. With any luck the explosions will cause the platform to fall apart. With no platform, no drill and no sinking Northern Ireland."

It seemed like as good a plan as any. "Well, there are four of us. One for each corner of the platform . . ." Jack was interrupted by an imperious and commanding voice.

"I'm afraid that your plans won't come to fruition. Mainly because you're going to be lying at the bottom of the sea." It was Regina Maris, the queen of Atlantis. Jack hated to admit it to himself, but she did look very impressive wearing full royal armor, with blue conch-shell shoulder pads, pearl adornments, and chain mail made from thousands of tiny cowrie shells. At her belt hung a sword that had clearly been fashioned from the long, flexible snout of a swordfish.

While Jack was busy being afraid of the queen, Trudy was more surprised. "You've come here to face us alone? I thought the water was supposed to make your brain wrinkle more in order to make you smarter."

The queen's nose wrinkled in anger. "It does and it did."

---

[102] I think it's fairly safe to assume here that Jack will turn out to be very wrong indeed.

346

"Then is there something wrong with your counting? You're outnumbered four to one."

"Yes, unfortunately I had to send the royal guard to start the drill working—there's only fifty more feet before it's through to the ocean. So they're in the command room. But I don't think I'll need them."

"Oh, really?" Trudy clenched her fists.

"Of course not. I mean, a large insect, two children, and a middle-aged man in a cheap suit."

"Children?" Trudy spat the word at the queen and was about to launch herself into battle when Grey tapped her on the shoulder.

"Trudy, I don't think you can really be annoyed at that. I mean, technically, you are a child."

"Look . . . ," said Trudy.

"Now, come on, there's limited point in arguing over that. You fit right slap-bang into the middle of what is defined as a child."

Jack had deliberately been avoiding getting involved in the argument, as it seemed as if it had been personal between the queen and Trudy; however, he found himself getting drawn in. "Grey, is this really the time for worrying about precise definitions of what people should be insulted by?"

"Jack, we're Ministry operatives. Just because we're in a life-threatening situation doesn't mean that we have to get sloppy about our definitions. You are most assuredly both children." Grey paused and took a deep breath before turning toward the queen and scowling. "On the other hand, I do not think that anyone could possibly call this suit cheap."

Jack wasn't willing to let Grey get away with this. "Wouldn't that depend on your definition of what is considered cheap?"

Grey fingered a lapel. "I got this from Savile Row, I'll have you know."

Jack turned to the queen, who was getting impatient. "What would you call cheap?"

"Are we going to fight each other or . . ."

Jack tutted. "Please, we'll get around to the fighting in a minute. There's always plenty of time for fighting. We just have to establish if you just insulted all of us, some of us, or none of us. Now what would you consider cheap for a set of clothes?"

The queen's brow furrowed. "I don't know."

"Well, what did that suit of armor cost you?"

The queen shook her head. "What a ridiculous question. Human money couldn't buy this kind of garment. It is handmade by Atlantean craftsmen. The pearls on it alone would be worth tens of millions of pounds."

Jack turned back to Grey. "See, the queen wears clothes worth tens of millions of pounds. And that's a suit of armor. So that's technically what she spends on her *work clothes*. Imagine what she'd spend if she wanted to get all nicely dressed up."

"Okay, okay," Grey conceded. "In that case perhaps she would consider this a cheap suit."

Jack turned back to the queen. "So you haven't really insulted anyone."

A rapid hammering came from behind Jack. He turned to

see that Tim was tapping the ground with his legs. Jack was confused, but luckily Grey stepped in to help. "It's okay; I speak Morse code."[103]

Tim rapidly hammered while Grey nodded. Eventually Tim stopped and Grey spoke for him. "Well, what Tim here has pointed out is that she called him an insect and he isn't an insect. He then said something about thoraxes and stuff, which I didn't entirely catch—but the main part is that spiders and insects have completely different numbers of legs."

"Right, good, good," said Jack as he nodded. "So we've learned something there. And as it turns out that the queen did in fact insult one of us, we can fight now."

The queen narrowed her eyes. "You aren't taking this seriously, are you?"

Jack laughed. "Of course not. We outnumber you four to one. And even if that wasn't the case, we can use The Speed. Just because you've got fancy undersea armor and a mean-looking sword, do you think you can really beat us?"

"The sword? I'm not even going to need my sword to defeat you, you little fool."

Jack found the queen's absolute confidence more than a little unnerving.

---

[103] You might think that it's a great thing to be able to speak Morse code, but I really wouldn't advise it. It's a language that consists of bangs and rattles. At first it seems like fun, but the other day I got involved in the most unpleasant argument with a woodpecker who was using language that you wouldn't expect from a sailor.

SAVILE ROW SUITS
Buying Them on Credit

A lot of Ministry agents buy their suits from Savile Row. Many people wonder how they manage to afford such splendid and expensive clothing on a government salary. The truth is that, generally speaking, Ministry agents are in such a dangerous job that they have a tendency to buy almost everything on credit cards, assuming that they will have been flattened by a runaway octopus or roasted alive by a fire-breathing moose before the bill ever comes due.

It is interesting to note that if you ever come across someone who claims that the world is about to end, a good test of their sincerity is to ask to see their credit card bill. Anyone who claims the world is ending and still doesn't max out their credit card is almost certainly not to be trusted.

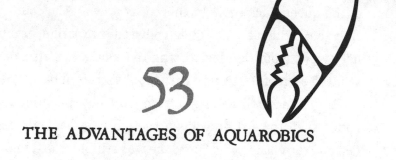

53

THE ADVANTAGES OF AQUAROBICS

The queen drew her sword from its scabbard and dropped it to the ground. That couldn't be a good sign, thought Jack. What was her secret? He began to wonder if instead of attacking they should . . .

Trudy launched herself at the queen using The Speed. Whatever Trudy had been thinking must have been the saddest thing ever. Her fists and feet blurred as she threw a thousand punches at the queen at once. Jack could barely count the punches as her fists lashed out. And yet the queen blocked each blow as if it were moving in slow motion. Finally the queen grabbed Trudy under the shoulder with an armlock, heaved her against her hip, and sent her flying across the deck of the drilling platform. Trudy came down with a heavy crash and skidded a dozen feet along the metal surface.

Grey had torn open one of the bags containing the bath bombs and, using The Speed, licked a dozen and threw them at the queen. Jack thought there was no way she could possibly avoid them all. The queen blurred into action, grabbing her sword from the deck. Using the blade, she effortlessly swatted each of the fizzing bath bombs straight back at Grey.

Grey's face fell as the fizzing, spitting, perfumed grenades sped toward him. Even though Grey was almost as fast as Trudy using The Speed, he was still not swift enough. He dodged three, then four, but the fifth bomb hit his rib cage and exploded. Grey was tossed backward like a rag doll. He hit the deck and lay limply. Jack's face froze. For the first time he began to contemplate the very real probability that he might be on the losing side. But the good guys never lost. . . . Did they?

"Now I don't seem to be quite so outnumbered, do I?" observed the queen smugly.

Only Jack and Tim were left. "Aren't you going to try?" Jack asked Tim.

Tim shrugged. You have never seen someone shrug until you have seen someone with four sets of shoulders shrugging. It's a very powerful shrug, which makes you understand that there really isn't anything to be done about the situation.

"Okay, you're right that it's a fairly hopeless situation," admitted Jack. "Still, it's a bit spineless."[104]

---

[104] It should be noted that spiders generally aren't very brave. But this is of course because they are invertebrates. They literally lack spines.

The queen expertly spun her sword around her hand. "Do you fancy your chances?"

"No," said Jack honestly. "But just before you cut me into two pieces[105] with that thing, I was wondering how come you're so strong and fast?" Even facing certain death Jack found that his curiosity prompted him to ask questions.

The queen smiled, happy to be flattered. "Easy—the original intention of the Atlanteans had been to wrinkle their brains further and make them smarter. But living underwater gave us another advantage. It's like your entire life is one long session of aquarobics and resistance training." The queen flexed an arm to show Jack her impressive muscle tone. Jack wondered whether, if he'd spent more time watching his mother's yoga tapes, he would possibly have been able to fight the queen more effectively.[106]

In the background Jack heard the enormous drill start whirring and crunching.

"Sounds like my warriors have gotten the drill working. So the only question is, should I kill you now or wait and let you drown?"

In the same way amoebas are generally gutless and bees have been known to have a yellow streak.

[105] Jack wasn't quite as frightened as he should have been at this stage. There was a small part of him that had seen magicians' assistants being cut in half for years and afterward they always seemed to be fine. A very small part of him believed that would be the case with him.

[106] He wouldn't, although it would have allowed the queen to bend him into a more interesting series of shapes.

Jack sighed. "I think you're probably going to kill me now because there's no way I'm letting this country sink."

Jack spun as quickly as he could and kicked all the bags of bath bombs off the side of the platform. They bobbed and floated around the nearest giant metal leg that reached deep down into the lough.

The queen screamed in anger. The sea began to bubble and fizz as the chemicals did their work. She turned to Jack. "You little fool, you'll pay for this!" She raised her sword above her head, ready to slice Jack in two.

Jack tensed his body for the blow and, thinking of magicians' assistants, shouted, "Wait a minute—shouldn't I be wearing something spangly?"

SAWING A WOMAN IN HALF
The Tragedy of the Great Monstro

It is generally agreed that one of the greatest magicians ever was the Great Monstro. He could perform the most wonderful magic tricks, and the cutting of a lady in half was the centerpiece of his act. However, one day he quarreled with his assistant, who was understandably upset that all her costumes consisted entirely of sequins and spangles, while Monstro wore a cloak and pretty purple turban.

His assistant stormed out of the room in a rage (which is pretty impressive in and of itself. It's hard to storm out of a room when wearing spangles—you generally just lack the gravitas).

However, when she slammed the stage door, the resultant vibrations caused a cabinet (used in Monstro's disappearing act) to fall from the theater rafters, striking Monstro on the head.

The blow from the cabinet caused Monstro a severe concussion. In point of fact he was only saved from certain death by the voluminousness of his purple turban.

When Monstro came around, he found himself on the empty stage of the theater with a wooden box that had been cut in half, a pile of sawdust, and a saw in his hand. Without anyone to tell him otherwise, the Great Monstro therefore assumed that he was a carpenter and wandered out of the theater to look for work.

Eventually the Great Monstro was offered work laying a floor in a local restaurant. Unfortunately, he didn't realize that the saw that he was using was a trick magic sword. Fifteen years later he is still trying to saw his first plank in two and the restaurant has yet to get a new wooden floor.

From this story we can learn two things. Firstly, sometimes being the person who saws someone in half can be as dangerous as being the person who gets sawed in half.

Secondly, although you may feel silly having your name sewn inside your underpants, when you get an amnesia-causing concussion, it can be a lifesaver.

54

BANG BANG

The queen's sword swung downward just as a mushroom cloud of water exploded out of the water. The force of it threw Jack, Tim, and the queen halfway across the platform.

Jack wiped the water from his eyes and peered across the platform. Tim was lying on his back, twitching. This was not turning out to be a good day for Ministry operatives. Still, twitching was a reasonably good sign. A better sign would have been if Tim had been up and tap dancing, but at least twitching was better than being absolutely motionless.

Jack struggled to his feet with difficulty. The bath bombs had done half their work and one leg of the huge platform had buckled, throwing the entire structure off balance— one edge of the platform was now dipped into the water. Jack found it difficult to balance on the platform's tilted, wet, and slippery surface.

The queen had also managed to regain her feet, but she looked quite different indeed. The sudden blast of water had restored her heavily wrinkled appearance. Jack realized this was why she had run from the sprinklers in the school. When she got wet, her real wrinkled appearance was revealed.

"You may want to reapply your moisturizer," observed Jack.

The queen let out a startling battle cry and leapt at Jack, swinging her sword arm. Which would have been the end of Jack if only her sword had not been knocked from her hand by the explosion.

Considering his options, Jack felt that the most appropriate action was to run and hide. However, he knew that trying to run on a wet, tilted metal surface in school shoes when you've been battered by an explosion is inadvisable. Jack felt as if it was all over. Trudy had been defeated, Grey had been defeated, Tim had been defeated. . . . Okay, maybe Jack himself hadn't been defeated, but he was fairly sure that was coming pretty soon. Therefore, he decided that he would leave life the way he had lived it—being sarcastic. "If you want that to be more dramatic, you might want to try that while holding a sword."

The queen paused and stared at Jack. "I don't need a sword to kill you; I can pull your head off with my bare hands." She threw a fist at Jack's head.

When Trudy and Grey asked Jack about this moment later on, he would claim that he had elegantly dodged the queen's blow by rolling his shoulders and bending his back like the perfect blend of ballet dancer and limbo expert. In reality he tried to duck and fell over, clanging onto the metal platform. The queen had put too much effort into her blow and tumbled over Jack. She slid down toward the edge of the platform and had to scrabble with her hands to avoid falling into the water.

For a moment Jack thought about throwing her a rope in case she fell off the platform entirely. Then he realized that falling into a lough probably wouldn't be desperately dangerous for someone who was the queen of Atlantis.

The queen hauled herself upright and, taking tiny baby steps, made her way across the treacherously slippy metal floor toward where Jack was sprawled. Jack decided to crawl rapidly away instead of trying to stand. It was the most preposterous slow-motion chase.[107]

Jack was saddened by the thought that if only Grey and Trudy were conscious now, they might be able to defeat the queen. With the tilted, slippery deck the queen's years of aquarobics practice would be less useful. Now it was all about balance.

And then Jack had an idea. He turned to face the queen, who was barely ten feet away from him. "This is a dramatic moment."

The queen ignored him. She was concentrating too hard on keeping her balance.

"And dramatic moments call for a drum roll." Jack used

---

[107] Interestingly enough, the second-most preposterous slow-motion chase was when Dr. Who was on crutches and was chased up a slight incline by a Dalek. Why did the Dalek have such difficulty with the incline, you may ask? Well, this was back in the 1960s before the Daleks had the optional extra of leather trim and a fourth gear.

his hands to beat out a drum roll on the metal platform. It echoed and rang loudly.

On the other side of the platform, Tim stopped twitching. The reverberations rattled through his head and brought him back to consciousness. Tim shook his head and sprang up, placing all eight legs on the platform.

"What use is the spider going to be? I already defeated your two strongest fighters."

Jack nodded from his crouched position. "You did. But that was before you could barely stand on a wet metal deck without slipping. Tim can balance easily—there are a few advantages to having eight legs."

Tim scampered across the deck to where Jack was sitting. He looked at Jack expectantly. Jack smiled. "I reckon she's going to be moving slowly enough for you to be able to web her."

Tim nodded enthusiastically. He shot one end of silk onto the deck and then set about capering around the queen like a medieval jester.

"What are you doing? You can't do this!" Within minutes the queen's legs were bound together and she fell to the ground. Tim took this opportunity to leap over her two or three times, pinning her to the ground.

And yet the queen still wasn't quite finished. "You think you've won, don't you?"

Even though this was only Jack's second week in the Ministry, he knew that gloating from an enemy was never to be considered a good thing. Enemies only ever felt the need to gloat if they had something hidden up their sleeves. Normally something sharp and deadly.

Jack responded cautiously. "Well, to be honest, I didn't think we were losing. But I get the feeling that I'll be reconsidering that soon, won't I?"

The queen jerked her head toward the shore of Lough Neagh. Three enormous objects were swimming toward the platform through the murky water.

"There was a reason I freed the hammerhead sharks, the octopuses, and the sawfish from your Ministry prison. They've been helping build my insurance policy."

Jack carefully stood up and gazed out over the lough. He could see what was coming for them and would have taken a step back in terror if that wouldn't have risked his falling over in terror. Tim had scampered over and was standing beside him.

"It's the remains of the Atlantean army in enormous crab machines," Jack said forlornly. "That isn't something that you see every day." The crab machines were made of shiny silver metal. Each had two glass pods in place of eyes. Groups of heavily armored Atlanteans sat in the pods, ready to do battle.

Tim nudged Jack's leg and pointed to Grey and Trudy, who were both beginning to recover. Jack had all but given up on trying to save the country from sinking. But perhaps at least he and his friends could escape somehow.

His heart sank when he looked over and saw that the buckled leg of the platform had tilted so far that the zip line was pulled taut and half underwater. That certainly wasn't going to be an escape route for them.

Jack looked back to see the crab machines clambering up the remaining unbuckled legs of the drilling platform. There was no way that Jack and Tim could possibly defeat an entire army, even if Grey and Trudy did regain consciousness. The warriors with their weapons and aquarobic training would make mincemeat out of them.

Jack despaired. He felt so lonely. What he needed was a creature of almost impossible size and strength. A creature capable of wanton destructive acts who hated all life and longed to destroy it wherever it could be sought. A creature who wanted to see the world burn. . . .

And then Jack had his best idea ever.

MINISTRY OF S.U.IT.S HANDBOOK

AQUAROBICS
THE FATAL FLAW

The natural resistance of water makes aquarobics a great exercise and can help you become fit incredibly quickly. The problem, however, is that spending all that time in water will make you all wrinkly.

Therefore the most you can hope for is that you'll end up looking like a really fit senior citizen. Which isn't the best of results.

55

THE CAVALRY HAS TENTACLES

The crab machines were standing on the far side of the platform. They were solid metal, Atlantean engineering. Each was filled with dozens of warriors. Occasionally one of the machines would snap its enormous metal claws in the air, sending out a dull ringing sound.

If only the sound had had a slightly more bass effect, it might have been exactly what Jack needed. But the noise he needed was a much deeper one. What Jack needed was the world's longest guitar string.

"Warriors!" called the queen of Atlantis from inside her spider's web cocoon. "Destroy this human filth and his pet insect." The crab machines started clanking directly toward Jack and Tim.

Tim poked Jack with a long leg. "He's an arachnid, not an insect," Jack corrected the queen. "And speaking of matters biological—those giant crab machines are walking forward, and that's cheating."

The queen glared at Jack. "You might think you're funny, but you'll be dead soon."

Jack nodded at her. "You might be more right than you think." Jack was fairly certain his plan would destroy the crab machines and the drilling platform. He just wasn't sure that it wouldn't also destroy him and his friends in the process.

He looked over to where Grey and Trudy were beginning to stir. Now was the time for all or nothing. Jack stood up and dived forward, sliding toward the edge of the platform. His aim was almost perfect, and he hit the water where the zip line was attached. Tim followed him.

"Right, help me with this." Jack was betting that the spider's web silk, strong as steel, would act like the world's largest, most bass guitar string. Jack braced his feet against the edge of the platform and pulled with both hands on the zip line. Although Tim wasn't really sure what was happening, he followed Jack's lead and helped him pull the zip line back. Atlantean warriors and enormous metal crabs were slowly stalking across the platform toward them.

Jack looked directly into Tim's eight eyes. "Now let go!"

Jack and Tim let go of the zip line, which vibrated, emitting an enormously deep humming note just as you would expect from a taut guitar string.

Two of the queen's warriors had just finished cutting her free from the spiderweb cocoon and had helped her upright. "What is this? Do you want music to accompany your doom?"

Jack ignored the queen and was looking out toward the middle of the lough. If the note had been bass enough . . . if his guess had been right . . . if he was correct about the Loch Ness Monster, then something pretty amazing was going to happen.

It did.

An enormous gray tentacle flung itself out of the water. The entire surface of the water was distorted as an ear-piercing screech made it ripple. The tentacle was topped with a tentacular club that was the size of a football field. Each of the suckers on it was the size of a house. The tentacle stretched a mile into the air.

Jack knew that he was probably facing almost certain death, and yet he smiled. Even if he died, Northern Ireland and the rest of the world would be safe. And that was good enough for Jack. The cherry on top of the ice cream was the look of sheer horror on the queen's face.

"Ohh, haven't you met my friend?" Jack asked innocently. "Queen of Atlantis, meet the Kraken. The Kraken, meet the queen of Atlantis."

The queen shook her head. "This is impossible. There was no Kraken here. My people dug out Lough Neagh. And they didn't leave a monster here. . . ."

Jack cocked his head to one side. "But you know that some-one changed the shape of Lough Neagh. Made it look more like a five-pointed star. And any creature who would do that was a creature of almost impossible power. After the lough was changed to a star shape, someone moved the Kraken into it. The star shape trapped the Kraken here."

Seven more tentacles shot up out of the lough, showering the platform in water. Jack held tight to the zip line to avoid being washed away. Tim scampered up the platform, away from the water. Each of the enormous tentacles was as deadly looking as the first.

"I think he's annoyed by the noise from this zip line. You already woke him up with your drilling and explosions— the Kraken's what caused the earthquake," said Jack. "It's got a squid head, you see. Almost totally jellylike. Bass noises vibrate through the head, causing enormous pain. I've got a friend called Cthulhu who hates this noise almost as much. Of course Cthulhu isn't the size of a small city, so he tends to run away from the noise. I don't think the Kraken is going to run, though." Jack paused and smiled. "So what do you think will happen if I pull this string again?"

The queen took a step forward. "I forbid it."

Her words made it so much sweeter when Jack tugged on the zip line for a final time and a deep bass note echoed through Lough Neagh.

Then the eight tentacles writhed in exquisite agony and then centered on the platform, coming down with the force of a meteor strike. Atlantean soldiers, crab machines, and metal were thrown through the air in a confetti of destruction. Jack was lucky that nothing hit him directly. But as his body was catapulted into the air he blacked out. His last thought was *Rats! I almost made it through an entire adventure without getting knocked unconscious for once.*

METEOR STRIKES
NUCLEAR MISSILES

You may have seen movies where enormous meteors are going to strike the planet Earth and kill everyone on it. Without exception the solution to these problems is presented as landing on the meteor and exploding a nuclear bomb on it.

This is a very bad idea, as it wouldn't actually help. In fact, it would just mean that we'd get killed by a meteor that was both enormous and radioactive.

56
EXPLANATIONS

Jack came back to consciousness inside a Atlantean crab machine. The only reason he didn't panic was that Trudy was above him, looking down and smiling.

"I don't know how you did it, Jack, but you saved Northern Ireland again."

Jack sat up painfully. Tim was at the controls of the crab machine. It normally took four Atlantean warriors to control one of the machines, but Tim with his eight limbs was driving it with ease.

Jack turned around and looked out of the domed bubble to see the Kraken's tentacles crushing the fracking platform into dust.

"We picked you up out of the water—but Tim really saved everyone—he dragged us all into this machine," Trudy admitted. Jack's face contorted; his head was ringing from the concussion, and it was annoying to learn that the minute he'd passed out an arachnid had stolen his hero status.

Grey walked into Jack's line of sight. "What I want to know is how you knew about the Kraken."

"Isn't it obvious?" Jack asked smugly, knowing that it wasn't. A look in Trudy's eyes said that Jack would have been the recipient of a severely bruised shoulder if he hadn't already been so badly hurt.

"Remember what the Misery said to Cthulhu about having to send someone away to 'boarding school'?"

Trudy nodded, remembering their training with the Misery.

"Well, that's it. I remembered that the drilling noise caused an earthquake. But why would drilling cause an earthquake? Walls don't start to shudder every time my dad puts up some shelves. There had to be something causing the earthquake. Something that responded with anger to deep bass drilling noises."

Trudy realized what Jack meant. "The way that Cthulhu ran when we played the Misery's MP3 player."

"Exactly!" Jack agreed. "And the Atlanteans said that when they left Lough Neagh it was a round lake. Something—a creature of immense power—then changed its shape to resemble a slightly out-of-shape star."

Grey thought about this for a moment. "It isn't a very well-shaped star."

"Well, no," admitted Jack, "but then again, although Cthulhu is a creature of evil and immense interdimensional powers, it doesn't mean that he has an enormous set of compasses and a huge protractor as well. So the shape's likely to be a little rough and ready."

Trudy shook her head. "I still don't get this. You're saying that Cthulhu changed the shape of Lough Neagh and trapped the Kraken in it? But why would he do that? Don't the legends about the Kraken say it destroyed boats and cities—wouldn't Cthulhu be pleased about that?"

"Well, he would—but what if he started getting worried that eventually people would start hunting the Kraken? Think about it. The Kraken is an enormous creature of evil power, who looks a bit squid-like and can be trapped in a star shape. Remind you of anyone?"

Trudy and Grey both looked shocked. Trudy was the first to speak. "Cthulhu and the Kraken! They're related."

Jack nodded. "Of course they are—and the one other thing that made me sure was that they both deal with their loneliness in the same way."

Trudy couldn't have been any more astonished and so she just asked the question. "And that is?"

Jack smiled. "Puppets. Hand puppets. When Cthulhu was looking at pictures of Loch Ness he wasn't looking at pictures of his relative. He was looking at pictures of his relative putting on a puppet show."

Grey took a deep breath. "You're saying that the Loch Ness Monster is a puppet?"

Jack laughed—he was enjoying explaining something to Grey for once. "Of course it is. Think about it. The names of both bodies of water are so similar—Loch Ness and Lough Neagh. I guessed that they've got similar names because there must be some kind of underwater caves that connect them—a secret passageway. Also, the Loch Ness Monster has to be a puppet. People have been looking for it for years. While it might be reasonable that they might miss a monster that was swimming about, you'd still expect them to find other evidence. A Loch Ness Monster footprint or Loch Ness Monster droppings. But they've never found that—and the reason is simple."

Grey beat Jack to the punch. "Puppets don't poo."

Jack wrinkled his nose. "Well, I might have put it slightly more elegantly than that—but fundamentally, yes."

"All this was a bit of a guess, Jack."

Jack smiled. "A bit, but it turned out to be right."

———

When they reached the shore, the Ministry operatives clambered out of the crab and found that Cthulhu was sitting and hugging one of the Kraken's enormous tentacles. He was weeping openly. Jack felt incredibly awkward and pretended to be looking elsewhere.

The other tentacles had corralled Atlantean warriors on the shore. One tentacle was holding the queen high in the air. The fight had gone from her and her body was as limp and wrinkled as a wet rag.

Grey walked over to Cthulhu and spoke to him in his strange gargling language. A few moments later he returned to speak to Jack, Trudy, and Tim.

"Jack was right. The Kraken is Cthulhu's child."

Trudy frowned. "Then why did he trap him in a star-shaped Lough Neagh?"

Grey sighed. "The Kraken is an enormous creature of evil and spent all its time destroying ships. Although that didn't really worry Cthulhu, he quickly realized that if it went on, the Ministry would have stepped in and imprisoned the Kraken. That was why, thousands of years ago, Cthulhu used his powers to reshape Lough Neagh—if the Kraken had to be imprisoned, he wanted it to be close to where he lived. It meant that Cthulhu could come every week to visit and refill the lough with eels. He also knew about the underground passages to Loch Ness—so he knew that the Kraken could amuse itself by putting on monster-puppet shows and scaring the Scottish locals."

"Sometimes parents have to discipline their children in order to protect them," Jack said.

Grey nodded. "And if the Kraken had stayed free, she was certain to be hunted by humans eventually. The last thing Cthulhu wanted was for his daughter to be attacked by a destroyer or a warship."

"His daughter?" Trudy was shocked. "That violent creature is a she?"

Jack looked at Trudy. He wasn't shocked at all.

THE KRAKEN
How It Got Its Name

Many people have wondered how the Kraken got her name. Interestingly enough, the Kraken isn't actually her real name at all. Her real name is Kirsten. The Kraken is just a nickname.

Essentially the Kraken is an enormous creature with hundreds of tentacles, which means that it is always getting up to mischief but still has a tentacle to spare to get a round of drinks in. In Ireland, anyone who can do this is said to be great "craic." Over the years people often said this about the Kraken—and with the Irish accent it changed from "Sure she always gets the craic in" to actually calling the great beast of submarine evil the Kraken.

EPILOGUE

Jack and Trudy were sitting on the banks of Lough Neagh with towels around their shoulders. Grey and Cthulhu walked over. Cthulhu made an obscene gargling noise and one of the Kraken's enormous tentacles lowered toward the shoreline, dropping the bedraggled queen of Atlantis in front of them.

Trudy stood up and looked her in the face. "Where's my mother?"

The queen of Atlantis shook her head. "I wouldn't tell you if I knew, but I don't know anyway. An accomplice of mine was supposed to bring her here. But with all this"—the queen indicated the devastation—"he'll have gone into hiding."

Trudy went to strike the queen with her hand but Grey stopped her. "That's not the way we do things, Trudy." Trudy fumed, but relented nevertheless.

"Anyway, she'll have a long time to think about how she can help us find your mother. She's going to prison."

Jack raised his head. "Have you repaired the Ministry prison already?"

"No," Grey admitted, "but I've sent for the king of the merpeople. He's agreed to take her away and imprison her until we get the party room up and running again."

Grey pointed to a river that ran out of Lough Neagh. The king of the merpeople had clearly just swum up it. The king was half man (human legs) with a fish head. He walked up the shore toward the heroes, looking very regal. He then began to suffocate in the air, and Jack and Tim had to roll him back into the river before he died. Jack wasn't altogether confident that he trusted the merpeople to be competent enough to stop the queen from escaping again.

Once the king was safe again Jack turned to Grey. "So how are you going to explain all the damage?"

Grey shrugged. "Easy enough—we'll just claim the fracking caused earthquakes. Everyone will believe that."

While Trudy and Jack waited for a car to take them home, they watched as Grey questioned the Atlantean soldiers. The whole plot was exactly as Jack had predicted; however, the one new thing they also learned was why the Atlanteans were selling sponges. It was relatively simple when you thought about it. The Atlanteans wanted to try and have all land with buildings covered in water. By taking sponges out of the sea and putting them on land, they made the sea level that little bit higher. If they harvested and sold enough sponges, eventually the entire world would be underwater.

When Jack finally got home that night, his mother and father were disappointed to reveal that they'd gotten a phone call from their lawyer. He had just received news that the company they were suing for providing a faulty bath bomb had gone out of business. In a strange turn of events the factory had exploded and its workforce had mysteriously disappeared. His parents' dreams of hot tubs and sports cars disappeared.

The next Monday morning Jack and Trudy found themselves sitting on the playground wall outside the school before they went in.

Jack yawned. "I don't think I've ever been this tired. Although that might just be the cumulative effect of all the concussions."

Trudy stretched her arm. She hadn't needed to put the sling back on, although it still ached a little when the weather was slightly rainy. Which meant that it ached almost continually.

"Well, you're going to need to start counting a lot of sheep, Jack. I need you well rested. We have to find my mother this week."

Jack nodded. "I've been thinking about this. And I'm sure we can figure it out. We just have to think about the clues we've gotten so far."

Trudy smiled at Jack. "You always figure these things out. I know you can do it again."

Jack was cheered by his friend's confidence. "I know I can too. I just need to focus, concentrate, and avoid getting distracted...."

David ran over to where they were sitting. "You want to

see this, guys. Edwyn has just had an allergic reaction to a peanut—and it's turned him into a monster!"

Jack felt like crying a little. "I never should have said that thing about not getting distracted," he grumbled as he followed David.

MINISTRY OF S.U.IT.S HANDBOOK

UNDERWATER CREATURES
THEIR EMOTIONS

Many people have called the shark a remorseless killing machine, although this is not entirely fair. For all we know the shark is absolutely devastated by the fact that it has to kill in order to survive. The thing about living underwater is that no one can tell when you are crying.[108]

It is for this reason that the Ministry had been unable to ascertain whether Regina Maris is remorseful for her crimes. The chance of her getting time off for good behavior is therefore slim.

---

[108] NOTE TO SELF: When they're making the poster for this film, suggest the tagline "Underwater: No one can see you cry." SECOND NOTE TO SELF: Check with lawyer to make sure Ridley Scott and Sigourney Weaver won't be able to sue.

ACKNOWLEDGMENTS

As always, thanks go to Holly and the team at Macmillan and Feiwel and Friends for helping to turn an idle daydream into something altogether more shipshape.

I'm glad I make mistakes when I'm writing because it means I get to work with you guys.